World War O

James Ward

COOL MILLENNIUM BOOKS

2

This is a work of fiction. All names, characters, and events are the product of the author's imagination, or used fictitiously. All resemblance to actual events, places, events or persons, living or dead, is entirely coincidental.

First published in KDP 2015.
This edition published 2021.

A CIP catalogue record for this book is available from the British Library.

ISBN: 978-1-913851-07-1

Cover shows London's Tower Bridge.

This novel was produced in the UK and uses British-English language conventions ('authorise' instead of 'authorize', 'The government are' instead of 'the government is', etc.)

To my wife

Chapter 1: Trouble at TB

Including the bride and groom, there were fifty people at Annabel's wedding, the exact capacity of London Tower Bridge's North Lounge, as advertised in the brochure. A solemn three-course meal followed a no-frills civil ceremony in front of the room's main gothic window. The bride's mother wasn't there because, despite the best efforts of a private detective, she couldn't be found; the bride's father was in prison, and hadn't been informed; the bride's boss, Ruby Parker, was at an official funeral. So most of the guests were from the groom's side: Mr and Mrs al-Banna, their three grown-up daughters, and twenty-seven extended family members. The remaining attendees comprised six of Annabel's work colleagues – not primarily friends: she didn't make those easily – and ten of Tariq's. Because both bride and groom worked in the same building, there was the occasional overlap: usually someone who knew and liked Tariq a little more than he or she did Annabel.

The rumour was that the bride had paid for everything. Not that the groom's side had been unwilling to chip in, but Annabel had forbidden it. Throughout the afternoon, she was the main focus of curiosity because hardly anyone – the groom included, some said – knew a thing about her. For this reason, and because the Master of Ceremonies had arranged the seating plan so that Annabel's guests were exiled amongst members of the al-Banna family, John Mordred spent almost the whole time fielding polite questions about her from obviously desperate-to-know-anything-at-all semi-strangers.

"My son doesn't tell us a whole lot about what he does in London," Mr al-Banna said. He and Mordred sat next to each other at a round table with six other guests, eating. He was small with black rings beneath his eyes, and a thin head of grey hair. "But they don't give job descriptions in a lot of places any more. Apparently, it makes it easier to fire or demote you."

"We know he's doing quite well," the woman sitting next to al-Banna chimed in, putting half a green bean in her mouth. She hadn't introduced herself: she was about forty, with a bob. "He works in the City, apparently. Something to do with IT."

"You're a friend of the bride, I assume," al-Banna asked Mordred.

"From university," he replied.

"What does she actually do for a living, if you don't mind my asking?" the woman asked. "She must be pretty wealthy to afford all this. Tower Bridge, mid-afternoon, fifty guests, fine food."

"I believe she works in the City too," Mordred said. "I haven't seen her for a few years. Not in the flesh. She's on Facebook."

"*I* couldn't find her," Mr al-Banna said. "Mind you, I'm not really *au fait* with social networking. I tried."

"People always talk about 'the City'," the woman went on, "as if it means something. Whereas actually, it's just a pretentious way of saying someone works in London. I could say *I* work in the City if I wanted. The city of Bradford."

"London isn't the City," al-Banna told her gently. "Only a part of London is. The so-called 'Square Mile'."

She looked at him as if he was mad. "Whatever you say, Ali."

"It's sometimes difficult to find out precisely what someone does when they work in the City," al-Banna went on dejectedly, ignoring her. "A lot of it's pretty murky stuff, from what I hear. Libor fixing, bankers' bonuses, hedge funds, that sort of thing. Things that make you rich rather than good."

"Maybe," Mordred said.

"My guess is she's with an investment bank, or something like that," the woman said.

"I must ask her," Mordred said. "We haven't really had time to catch up yet." He couldn't stand much more of this. He caught sight of his reflection in the silver vase at the table's centre: a tormented curly-haired blond guy of thirty-one. He felt more like shrivelled, bald and ninety. To the vase's credit, though, 'tormented' was accurate. He stood up. "Excuse me a moment. Bathroom."

It was a silly name for it. There was never a bath in there, but most people didn't quibble if you employed an Americanism. The alternatives - 'loo' versus 'toilet' – were just more landmines in the Great UK Class War. He couldn't step on a landmine right now. It would be the perfect end to a perfect day.

When he reached the bathroom/toilet/loo, he found Alec leaning against the row of washbasins, next to the drier. Tall, with receding hair, but looking haggard for a change. "I can't take any more of this," he told Mordred. "It's hell."

You always felt better when someone you liked was suffering alongside you for exactly the same reasons. "Who is this 'Annabel'?" Mordred said, trying, and failing, to imitate the woman next to Mr al-Banna. "Where does she come from? What does she do for a living?"

"What did you tell them?" Alec asked.

"Something in the City. You?"

"A vet."

"A *vet*? What – like a veterinary surgeon? Where did you get that from?"

"She told me that's what I had to say. She's got Phyllis telling everyone she's a high-flying architect, apparently. I didn't find that out till a few moments ago. I'm actually shit-scared to go back out there."

"I wonder what Edna's telling them."

"She'll have been given a completely different story. Mind you, knowing Edna, she's probably having a whale of a time. She's young enough to think complete anarchy's cool."

Suddenly, the door flew open and banged against the wall. Annabel in her wedding dress. What the hell? Both men froze. This was the gents', so ... She looked at them as if she was having the same breakdown they were, only worse. For a moment, none of them spoke. Annabel faced the two men. They faced her.

"Sorry," she said quietly. "I thought this was the Ladies'." She did an about-turn and left.

Mordred and Alec looked at each other. They were about to vocalise their consternation when the door banged open a second time. Annabel again, but this time they didn't get chance to take her in. She ran across the floor and threw herself at Mordred's feet and grabbed his shirt in what seemed like a single gesture.

"You've got to save me, John!" she exclaimed. *"This is my last chance! For God's sake, drop everything and come downstairs with me, and let's go! We don't have to work at Thames House any more, we can do anything! Anything you like! I'll do whatever you want! Please, John, I'm begging you, PLEASE!"*

Er - ? Sudden light-headedness, almost like the prelude to a blackout. Her words were lost on him for a moment: all he saw was her frenzy.

Then the thoughts began. How it didn't make sense, this was her wedding day. He could just about understand *The Graduate*, everyone could – someone being torn from the altar by a plea from the heart – but this wasn't that. She must have had countless opportunities to voice something like this. Why wait until *now* of all times? He opened his mouth to speak – he had to, didn't he? – but nothing emerged.

She stood up and wiped her eyes. "Sorry, I …" she said. She turned round and left at exactly the speed she'd entered.

Five whole seconds elapsed. Alec let out a long stream of air. He laughed, but not in a humorous way: more like someone in psychiatric shock. "Penny for your thoughts," he said at last.

"I haven't any," Mordred snapped.

"You're not thinking of going after her, are you? Because that would be - "

"Of course I'm not thinking of going after her! This is her bloody wedding day! Where did it come from, that's all I want to know. What's going on?"

Alec put a hand on his shoulder. "Steady on. Bloody weird, I know. *Bloody* weird. We'll talk about it later. People will be starting to ask where we are."

The door opened again, but this time it was Tariq. Thirty, slim and well-built, slicked back hair and a goatee, he wore his morning suit as unaffectedly as if been born in it. "I know what you're up to," he said. His expression made it clear he'd come in here expressly to find them, but he didn't look angry. Mordred felt sick.

"We're strategizing," Alec said weakly.

"Understood," Tariq replied. "I wasn't aware she'd given you all different tales to tell. I've just been talking to Phyllis. I didn't realise my wife was one of the designers of Bishopsgate Tower."

"I've been telling everyone she's a vet," Alec said with a little too much relief in his voice. "I don't mean this to sound rude, but I never realised she had a sense of humour."

"Now you do," Tariq said tetchily. "Listen, I've come to help. A piece of advice. You must have seen everyone looking surreptitiously at their mobiles? Well, just talk about that. It's what's on just about everyone's minds, after all. No one's thinking about Annabel and I."

"You mean …?" Mordred said. He didn't know what Tariq meant. His mind was still blank, but he had to say something, just to look normal.

"Come on, John," Alec said. "All those refugees in boats off the Italian coast, all those Hollywood stars snuck in there with them, it's the only thing that's been on the news for about a week now. It's all *anyone's* talking about, let alone here."

"Yes, I remember," Mordred said.

Tariq smiled. "Just talk about that."

They nodded obediently as if it was an instruction rather than a piece of advice.

"Incidentally, have either of you seen Annabel?" Tariq asked. "I couldn't find her a moment ago."

Mordred and Alec looked at each other.

"She came in here by mistake," Alec said, "but she headed straight out again when she saw us."

Tariq didn't smile. He looked like he thought something might be up, but he stood aside to let them out.

When they reached the lounge, she was standing over Tariq's father, talking to him as if nothing had happened. When Mordred resumed his seat, she didn't even acknowledge him. She was speaking about architecture.

"I don't think she was joking," Alec said, two hours later. They sat on a bench on the Thames embankment, watching a barge plough upstream. Around them, tourists ate and took photos and looked at the skyline. A small fairground with a roundabout and a coconut shy piped canned organ music. The sun shone hard, low and bright, a perfect evening in late July.

"If she was, it wasn't very funny," Mordred replied.

"That wouldn't necessarily be relevant. She never used to have a sense of humour at all. It's only since she met you that she's changed in that regard. Nowadays, she's trying hard to produce the impression that she knows what a laugh is. I'm not saying she loves you but you've definitely had a lasting influence on her."

"Bloody hell, I don't want to think about it. I had a narrow escape there. Imagine if Tariq had come in a few seconds earlier."

"You honestly didn't foresee it? She did tell you she was in love with you, about a year ago, when we were on the ISIS case. I was there."

"Er, how could *that* have made me foresee *that*?"

Alec shrugged. "Point taken."

"Anyway, afterwards she practically ordered me to forget it. And she was going out with Tariq at the time, remember? Her future husband."

"You should have pursued her. Maybe."

"Exactly the opposite of your advice at the time. 'Run a mile' was what you said."

"Yes, well … was I right, or was I right?"

Mordred sighed. He shook his head. "On her wedding day! I mean, if she'd come to me last night, even."

"What? You'd have run off with her?"

"Probably not, but it'd have been comprehensible. I could have got my head round it. Cold feet, but in a conventional way."

"Just 'probably' not?"

"I like her. And as you keep reminding me, she's very attractive."

"And of course, you feel sorry for her because she was 'badly abused as a child'. We've only got her word for that, remember. And we do have evidence that she's a fantasist."

Mordred looked at him. "And yet we both believe her, don't we? We know it rings all too true."

Alec thought for a moment. "It makes sense of everything else, yes. She's probably not going to make Tariq a very good wife, I'm sorry to say."

"She took me aside about three weeks ago and told me he'd proposed and she'd accepted."

"Nice of her. Why do you think she did that? I mean, to you specifically?"

"She said it was because she'd once told me she loved me and meant it, but that was all in the past now. 'Life isn't like *Grey's Anatomy*. We don't have soul mates. I was in love with you for a while. Now I'm not. I'm in love with Tariq'."

"Must have affected you quite deeply to remember her actual words."

"I suppose so."

"I think you're actually in love with her, John. Don't get me wrong, I'm not suggesting you should do anything about it. That boat's sailed now, thank God. But I do think you've got a more general problem. You're in love with everyone. It used to be Daoming Chou, then it was Gina Fairburn, now it's Annabel Gould. It's anyone that sets their cap at you."

"The so-called 'curse of Mordred'."

"I really fear for Phyllis and Edna."

Mordred laughed. "I can't see either of them 'setting their cap at me'."

"Why not? You're a good listener, kind to animals, slightly wet, all your own hair, four functioning limbs, thirty-two inch waist, clean shaven. Women love all that."

"Women are just people. They're all different."

"Just for the sake of argument, let's say Phyllis or Edna, or both, took a fancy to you, what would you do?"

"What do you mean, 'do'? Obviously, if I knew one or the other was keen on me, I'd probably ask her out and we'd see how it went."

"You're quite big on the probablies. Most men would jump at the chance."

"Is that what I'm supposed to say? I'd jump? It makes me sound a little desperate."

"And aren't you?"

"I haven't got a girlfriend. I wouldn't say I'm 'desperate' for one. I hardly lack for female company. I've got four sisters and three female colleagues, four if you count Ruby Parker."

"You never cease to amaze me."

"Meaning what?"

"You're thirty-one. Pretty soon you're going to be 'on the shelf', as they used to say."

Mordred looked at the river but didn't see it. He was back in the gents' on Tower Bridge. *Please, John, I'm begging you, PLEASE!* And instead of going into shock, he grabbed her by the arm, and they made for the exit. Yes, it was wrong, he could see that, and he had no idea what was going to happen next, but –

"Would you like a candy floss?" Alec asked. "From that booth, over there? I'm having one."

"A candy floss?"

"I know it's a bit infantile, but I just feel like one."

"Thank you. Yes, I will."

Alec got up, leaving Mordred alone with the temporal bifurcation. Somewhere, in a parallel universe, he and Annabel were at Heathrow now. What was that like for them? Where would it lead? Would the universe somehow restore the balance someday, making both couples end up in the same place and state, or were they forever separated? Her *Please, John!* was still fresh in his mind. Other-Mordred and Other-Annabel. Like the originals but somehow subtly different … and becoming more so all the time. They only existed as a couple now, not as two separate individuals. And in two dimensions. And on the other side of the galaxy.

"I got cinnamon," Alec said, coming up behind him and handing him his candy floss on a stick. "I thought they only did it in strawberry. Shows how old I am."

"Thank you."

"I've never asked you this before," he said, as he sat down, "but it's not a trivial question. I'm genuinely interested. Who's your ideal woman?"

"How do you mean? Looks-wise? I've never thought about it."

"Rubbish. You must have."

"I know what an attractive woman is. I don't rank them. That would be pointless."

"Okay, put it another way. If you could go out with *any woman* in the whole world, who would it be? And don't tell me you haven't thought about it this time. Think about it now."

"Probably Naomi Klein."

"Who?"

"Naomi Klein."

"Singer, model or actress?"

"She writes books."

Alec clicked his tongue. "Bloody typical of you. Is she attractive?"

"To me, yes."

"How old?"

"Late thirties, probably. I don't know for certain."

"She's famous, yes? She's not just some spinster from down the road who writes Thomas the Tank Engine sequels for Kindle and Kobo?"

"You've got a phone. Look her up."

"Damn right I will." He scrolled through his smartphone for a few moments. "Yeah, not bad for a writer," he said at last. "Bone structure and teeth, I mean. I'm assuming she's actually a hardened leftie underneath?"

"Of course, otherwise we wouldn't be getting married. There'd be no future."

Alec turned to look at him. "What the - "

"I've been waiting for the right opportunity to tell you. We met at a climate change conference last January. Naomi Klein-Mordred she's going to be called, once we've tied the knot."

"You're joking. She's on the internet. I mean, on there big time. Wait a minute, though, *of course* you wouldn't have as your ideal woman someone you didn't already know. That's so typically you. Why didn't I - "

"Sadly, yes, I am joking."

They sat in silence for a few moments. Eventually, Alec nodded. "Another brilliant joke, John. Well done."

"Thank you for the candy floss."

"Good God, I've just thought of something."

"What?"

"Everyone was saying, Annabel's paid for all this. All the wedding stuff: venue hire, hotels, the honeymoon, etcetera. She didn't let the groom or his family pay for anything. Not even the taxis or the clothes they arrived in."

"So?"

"Well, don't you see? She must have known something like what happened was going to happen. She took care in advance to limit the blowback."

"Only you can't pay upfront for people's emotional investment."

"But you can isolate it. And she's not exactly *compos mentis*."

"Let's just forget it, shall we? Listen, can I ask you a favour? Please don't mention the gents' episode to anyone else. I mean anyone."

"As far as I'm concerned, it's forgotten. Or put it another way: I'm going to *try* and forget it. It was disturbing enough to ruin my day, actually. And I say that without the prior advantage of being a complete drip. God knows how it must have affected you."

"Don't mention it to Phyllis or Edna."

"I do understand what 'anyone else' means, John. I may not know who Naomi Klein is, but I'm not stupid."

"Just being cautious."

"Paranoid." Alec's phone beeped. He took it out and looked at it. "Good God."

"What is it?"

"I'm on e-mail alerts about the Mediterranean."

"Not you as well. Funny, nobody seemed to care before all the celebs started getting involved."

"That's the whole point, isn't it? Anyway, a boat's capsized. Fifty refugees plus Jennifer Hallowell."

"Are they okay?"

"Not sure. Imagine that. An A-lister. *Funny November*'s up for an Oscar. And everyone knows *The Veil of Green Sand*."

"Even me."

"Jennifer Hallowell-Mordred, how does that sound? You're both bleeding hearts. You should get on like a house on fire."

"Assuming she survives today."

"Yes, we shouldn't joke," Alec said. "She's already lucky not to have been kidnapped by ISIS. They're active in Libya. And a person's only got so much luck. You've got to admit she's got guts."

"And of course there are the other forty-nine non-celebrities on board."

"What are you saying? She's just doing it for the publicity? Because that doesn't ring true. She's got two Baftas and a *Palme d'Or*, for crying out loud."

"Sorry, you're right, I'm not thinking. I'm still in the gents' with Annabel. God, what a day. I hope she's okay."

"Who?" Alec asked. "Annabel or Jennifer?"

"Both, obviously. I might stop by at a church on the way home."

"I like that about you. The way you're religious and yet not religious. Wishy-washy, but not necessarily in a negative sense."

"Will you get an e-mail when she's okay?" Mordred asked.

"*If*, not when. I'll get a message if she drowns, so either way at least I'll know."

"That's nice."

"Don't get me wrong, I'm rooting for her. Be fair, John. There's not much else I can do, sitting here on the Thames embankment with a half-eaten candy floss."

"Guess not. Doesn't it make you want to join in?"

Alec chuckled. "With what? The Great Hollywood Migrant Protest? I'd be no good. I'd just be taking up someone's place. One less refugee in the safety of Italy or Malta."

"Or lying waterlogged at the bottom of the Med."

"True, but I'd be giving my life for theirs. One for one. Who's to say their life's worth more than mine? I'm not saying it's worth less, obviously, but in the absence of further evidence I think a good case can be made for rough equivalence."

"I suppose."

"What *would* be immoral," Alec said, "would be betting on the outcome. Will Jennifer drown or will she make it?"

"That would be obscene," Mordred said.

"The unacceptable face of capitalism, yes. And not remotely legal."

"You're not trying to tell me it actually happens? Are you?"

"You'd be surprised."

"Who? Where?"

"Commercial and investment bankers, financial advisers, non-doms, hedge-fund administrators, stockbrokers – mostly people not so very far from where we're sitting now."

Mordred smiled. "Did you know they've taken the word 'gullible' out of the Oxford English Dictionary?"

"I'm not saying I've encountered it first-hand but - "

"It's an urban myth. It must be. Come on, people hate those guys, so they make things up about them, and everyone's all too ready to believe it. You'll be telling me they sacrifice children and poison wells next."

Alec laughed. "I thought you were some kind of liberal."

"So I've got to be full of the toxic freethinking hatred, right? Look, I'm not saying Goldman Sachs and Pricewaterhouse-Coopers are good for the world, but every single person working there's a human being. I can't believe they'd bet on a possible fatality. It doesn't ring true."

"Of human nature, you mean."

"What's wrong with that?"

"Ever been to the Central African Republic?" Alec asked. "Ever heard of ISIS?"

"Oh, don't let's go through that again."

Alec seemed to realise enough was enough. He smiled. "How about another candy floss?"

"If it helps bring about world peace, yes."

"Any preference as to the flavour?"

"How about vodka?"

"I can only ask the lady in the kiosk."

"Or we could repair to a pub."

"Bloody hell, you must be depressed to be suggesting alcohol. A John Mordred first, I'd say. Normally, you have to be dragged."

"First Annabel, now Jennifer. And us just sitting here discussing bare-faced lies about our world-class financial services industry."

"We might get to see action on the shores of Africa sooner than you think."

"Oh?" Mordred said.

"There's a little rumour going round the office. The CIA want young, good-looking Brits *in situ* to dissuade their Jennifer

Hallowells from making complete arses of themselves on European TV. I'm not joking."

"Bloody hell. Sounds like one hell of a gig … if you weren't making it up."

"I'm not, I swear. Brits have more authority, apparently. Something to do with the accent and that, in Tinseltown, we're always baddies. People respect baddies. They're the people who make things happen. Goodies are always on the defensive."

"What's wrong with the world in a single sentence."

"If we can only persuade Jen that you're a baddie, we're onto a winner. We can pull off the otherwise improbable Hallowell-Mordred union of two ancient houses. Mind you, we've got our work cut out. On the plus side, we've got your accent. After that, it's all downhill. Come on, there's a bar just round the corner. I'll buy you a drink."

"Where's Annabel going on her honeymoon? Do you know?"

"I shouldn't think anyone does," Alec said. "She's Annabel. Probably North Korea."

His phone beeped again. He took it out and looked at it. In the same instant, Mordred's gave a single ring. *Ruby Parker.*

"Don't bother reading it," Alec said. "We're wanted urgently back at Thames House. What did I tell you? Pack your bucket and spade and your AK-47. We're going to Libya."

Chapter 2: Welcome to TV Hell

When they arrived at Thames house, the two men went straight to Basement One and knocked on Ruby Parker's door. No reply.

"Knock again," Mordred said.

Alec tapped and put his ear closer. "Nothing," he said, after a few seconds.

"Maybe we should ask at reception."

They double-backed and looked in the offices on their way out. All empty.

"Where the hell is everyone?" Alec asked. Usually there were at least ten people on this floor. It was like the fire bell had gone off, only it couldn't be that because they'd have heard it. And there was no sign that anyone had left in a rush.

They got in the lift and went back to reception. Colin Bale stood behind his desk, a bald, stout man with a vigilant expression.

"We were called back here to see Ruby Parker," Alec told him. "And yet we can't find her."

"She's been at a funeral," Bale replied. "She's not back yet and won't be for some time."

"Any particular reason you know of?" Alec asked.

"Traffic on the A214, but as well as that, she's making a detour. I believe the foreign secretary wants a word with her."

"Where's everyone else?" Mordred said.

"I take it you haven't been watching the news," Bale replied.

"Alec's got e-mail alerts on his phone."

Bale smiled in a 'how quaint' way. "About what?"

"Jennifer Hallowell in the Med. Is she okay?"

"This isn't about that, although I must say, you're not the only person in this building who's rooting for her. Go Jennifer. No, she's old news. If I was you, I'd make my way to the second floor, the television suite. They're all on, all the TVs. The BBC will explain what's happening better than I ever can. Also, look at a news site on your phone on your way up there. It'll help prepare you."

Mordred smiled. "Thanks, Colin." Their relationship had been a little better of late. Nowadays, Bale seldom treated him with complete contempt, and was occasionally even cooperative.

They took the stairs to Floor 2, and Alec looked at his phone, as advised. "Well, I never," he said. "There's some kind of hippy sit-in on Jersey. That's the headline. That's the actual headline. Like it's news."

"It's not something I can recall happening before," Mordred said.

"That's not the chief criteria for newsworthiness," Alec replied. "You've also got to consider impact. Like 'will anyone care'?"

The second floor was full of people sitting gazing at televisions showing news programmes. About a hundred souls stood or sat by about fifty desks discussing and pointing. This also wasn't something Mordred could recall before either. The conversational noise was such that some people had to shout, which made it worse. He guessed it was what 9/11 must have been like up here. Although it surely couldn't be anything of that magnitude, could it?

Edna Watson came over. Two inches taller than Mordred and three than Alec, thin and black with a 1960s beehive, she was still wearing the beige skirt-suit and heels she'd had on at the wedding. "Welcome to TV hell," she said.

"Exactly what's going on?" Alec said.

"How much do you already know?" she replied.

"Next to nothing," Mordred said. "Alec discovered there's a sit-in on Jersey."

She smiled wryly. "Let's go down to the basement then. I've already got a headache and it'll be quiet down there."

"Like a ghost town," Alec said.

They walked into the corridor and called the lift.

"What did you think of the wedding?" Mordred asked her, when they got in.

"I've never been inside Tower Bridge before," she replied. "The food was good, but I'm not keen on eating with strangers, especially the type that keep asking questions. Still, it gave me an excuse to buy a new suit."

They'd reached the basement now. They went into an office and sat down at a desk topped with a teddy bear, a tubular stationery holder and a monitor.

"I take it that whatever's happening, it's pretty momentous?" Alec began. "I mean, judging by the chaos upstairs?"

"The world's major tax havens have been invaded by protesters," she replied. "Bern, Zürich, Luxembourg, the City of London, Jersey, Guernsey, Wilmington and Dover in Delaware, Singapore, the Cook Islands, the Caymans, Hong Kong, Mauritius, Bermuda, Turks and Caicos … Shall I go on? Thousands of protesters in each one, some of them right here in the capital, today. It's amazing we didn't trip over them on the way back from Tower Bridge. Well, I didn't. You might have."

"What sort of 'protesters'?" Alec said. "My newsfeed mentioned a 'sit-in'. I guess that must mean they're white and middle class?"

She smiled. "It's a bit more complex than that, sir. We're looking at a global phenomenon."

"Exactly like the white middle-classes," Alec replied.

"Alec's an unreconstructed rightie," Mordred told her. "He hates the white middle-classes."

"And no one saw it coming?" Alec went on, ignoring him. "How is that even possible?"

"I don't know," she said. "I'm only a junior agent. They're calling it 'World War Offshore'. Or rather, that's what they're chanting."

"How many protesters in all?" Mordred asked.

"No one knows," she replied. "Tens, possibly even hundreds of thousands. It's still happening as we speak."

"When did it begin?" Mordred asked.

"Sometime while we were at the wedding," she said. "Obviously, it must have been coordinated, but no one can work out how. Neither GCHQ nor the NSA picked up on it. It's a significant mystery."

"Have they a common list of demands?" Mordred asked.

"As I say, sir, it's still unfolding. It's probably best watched on TV. Just not on the second floor, because no one can actually hear the commentary."

A phone began to ring in another office, somewhere down the corridor.

"I'll get it," Mordred said, rising to his feet. He looked in two rooms before he found it. Whoever it was, he or she was persistent. Twenty-two rings. Any normal caller hung up after five or six.

"Is this Mr Mordred?" the caller asked. Ian. 'Young Ian' as opposed to 'Previous Ian' whom no one was still allowed to speak of because he'd gone to Syria to help the Kurds fight ISIS.

"Speaking," Mordred said.

"We're going to the projection room to watch BBC News 24. Ruby Parker's just called reception. She says you and Mr Cunningham are to report there and keep watching until she gets back."

"We'll be up pronto. Thanks."

He put the phone down. There was a lot of overlap between Young Ian and Previous Ian: they both dressed like relics from the 1950s, for a start. He and Edna were roughly the same age –early twenties – but you wouldn't know it of either of them. Phyllis had been giving Edna style instructions – it didn't quite capture their spirit to call them 'tips' – but Ian had no excuse. Both looked like they were *Mad Men* fans.

Mordred went back to Alec and Edna. "We're expected in the projection room."

"You two go ahead," Edna said. "I might get a glass of water. The wedding was quite a stressful experience."

"I didn't like to ask," Mordred said, when he and Alec were in the lift again. "How could that wedding be a 'stressful experience' I mean, given that Edna's not me, and that she is training to be a spy?"

"Having to 'reveal' to everyone that Annabel's an escort."

"Bloody hell, those were her actual instructions?"

"Apparently so."

"What the hell was Annabel thinking, giving everyone a different story to tell? She must have worked out it's precisely the sort of thing that'll make people dig deeper. Does she *want* them to find out she's a spy?"

"I wonder whether we should let Ruby Parker know," Alec said. "She's behaving like someone who's on the edge."

"Probably. I don't know. Hasn't she always been like that?"

"No, I believe she's got worse. Think of the gents'."

They went straight to the projection room – a forty-seat theatre with a four metre screen - and sat down at the back. People were beginning to leave, presumably to go to briefings or to catch up with their work, but it was clear that quite recently there had been standing room only in here.

The screen showed a middle-aged female presenter with a microphone, in the midst of a large moving crowd, above which could be seen a row of ornate buildings, the HSBC logo, and a tiny strip of blue sky. At the bottom of the screen: 'Saint Helier Town Centre, Jersey'. Beneath that, a tickertape with breaking news elsewhere in the world. As far as Mordred could tell, all the places mentioned were tax havens, 'secrecy jurisdictions' as MI7 tended to refer to them.

"I don't know whether you can hear that in the studio, Aidan," she said, holding the microphone out, as if it was a talent show. "'No more offshore'," she added, just in case he couldn't and because, like a lot of live TV reporters, she apparently felt under a contractual obligation to keep talking, no matter what.

"What's the exact scale of the protest in Saint Helier?" Aidan asked.

"According to my own estimates, here in the capital, we're looking at about ten thousand people. So far the protests have been entirely peaceful, but it could pose a problem for the Jersey police if that changes. There are only two hundred and forty officers on the island. They've been told, I hear, to take a low-key approach."

"Thank you, Jennifer. Now we're just going to have a look at what's been happening in the Cayman Islands, because we've just received some footage from a protester on the island. It's now just gone midday there. It looks like this."

The screen switched to show marching protesters – men and women of all ages, most of them noticeably less European-looking – chanting 'no more offshore, no más fraude fiscal' – with their fists held up. Apart from a palm tree in the background, it could have been anywhere. Most of them didn't look like they were having a good time. They looked vaguely worried.

"I've been told the police have just arrived in Wilmington, Delaware, to monitor the protest," Aidan said. "They're not looking to disperse it yet, although the State Governor, Chandler Brydon, has pointed out that it is not a legal gathering, and called on demonstrators to go home. There: you can see the police … lining the streets. We'll keep you fully updated on that while we go now to Hong Kong, where it's one o'clock in the morning."

More protesters. Then Aidan showed some protesters in Singapore, then Panama, then Zürich, then Luxembourg, before finally coming to rest outside St Paul's Cathedral in the City of London. All the footage was similar, and after you'd seen four or five clips, it began to get a bit boring. Even Aidan seemed to be losing interest. Luckily, someone had dug up a university analyst to talk about how tax havens worked, what companies used them, why, and what the protesters might hope to gain in terms of tighter regulation.

Alec leaned over to Mordred. "What this really needs is some kind of alternative point of view. Disgusted from Tunbridge

Wells, maybe, to rail against any kind of dissent. Seriously, where the hell are the politicians?"

Mordred chuckled. "Probably hiding, hoping it'll go away."

The analyst started to talk about how the British government had actually made tax avoidance easier in recent years, but 'only for big companies'. And how the US had felt compelled to follow suit. And how the Bank of England bore a large portion of the blame.

"That ought to smoke them out," Alec said.

"It's vaguely surreal," Mordred said.

"Really? You don't say. If only every day at the office could be like this. Us two guys sitting on comfy chairs, watching the TV. Maybe we should order some pizza in."

Mordred laughed. "Imagine Colin Bale. Guy in a Dominos uniform: 'Mordred and Cunningham live here? Three cheeses and a pepperoni'."

"'Oh my, what's MI7 coming to?'" Alec said in an Edinburgh accent. "'Oh, my, my.'"

Mordred laughed. "Keep my seat. I'm going to the toilet."

"Yeah, okay. If I'm gone, it means Ruby Parker's come back."

In the toilet/loo/bathroom, Mordred met Young Ian. He wondered how long it would be before he stopped thinking of him that way and he just became Ian. They went to urinals at opposite ends of the row, even though there was no one else in there.

"How are you getting on?" Mordred asked.

"Very well, thank you, sir. I'm enjoying it."

"What do you think of the protests?"

Young Ian looked as if he'd been caught off guard, but to his credit, he didn't urinate on the wall. "The protests? How do you mean?"

"Do you agree with them? Do you wish you were there?"

"That depends."

"On what?"

"Whether they're threatening the realm."

Mordred got it now. Young Ian thought it was a test. *How loyal are you to Queen and Country?* He was less than ten years younger than Mordred, but Mordred suddenly felt like his dad. "Well, do *you* think they are?" he continued. "Threatening the realm?"

"Er, it's not for me to say."

"Listen, Ian, this isn't the army. We're spies. We're expected to work things out for ourselves. And we're allowed our own opinions. Take me, for example. I'm a communist."

Ian urinated on the wall. To his credit, he washed his hands then blew-dry them. *Always stay calm when you're defending the realm.* He left without speaking or making eye-contact.

Mordred sighed. Another Christmas card he wouldn't be getting. When he came out of the toilet, he noticed something subtly different. It took him a moment to realise: everyone was looking at him. Only one or two directly; most people were following him out of the corners of their eyes. As far as he could tell, there was nothing hostile in their expressions, rather a mixture of pity and amusement. Bloody hell, you couldn't even have a joke in here. What had Young Ian said? It must have been pretty drastic to get *everyone* on board. Perhaps he'd run out of the building, screaming.

But what could you possibly do or say that would clear up such a misunderstanding? He felt self-conscious now. He was probably blushing a bit. Maybe he should just keep walking till he reached the Chinese embassy. *I'm a communist. I'm here to claim political asylum.* But not that kind, no. Not the genocidal kind that writes little red books and has great leaps forward.

When he returned to his seat in the projection room, Ian was sitting six rows away next to Edna in the front row. Crisis averted … probably. Alec was eating an apple. "You're about to be world-famous," he told Mordred.

"What do you mean? Where did you get that apple, by the way?"

"I pinched it from the wedding. No one eats fruit at a wedding."

"How am I going to be 'world-famous'?"

"They've set up a Youtube channel. The protesters. Keep watching."

"What am I looking for?"

"If I tell you, it'll spoil the surprise."

Even in here, everyone was slyly looking at him. A few people changed seats, from the front to the back and wide, obviously so they could get a better look at him. It was starting to feel oppressive, the sort of thing that turns a man into a paranoid wreck. Focus. There was something behind it, obviously. All he had to do, if Alec was right, was keep watching.

Lots more shots of protesters in various parts of the world. He hadn't noticed before, but the chant wasn't the only thing all the groups had in common. They were all sporting Jolly Rogers, but not the white-on-black variety, rather, any on any colour. Here, yellow on tie-dye blue, there, multi-coloured on orange, farther afield, purple on pink and white polka dots, and so on. Obviously someone had sat down and made these: there was nothing ad-hoc about them.

He suddenly felt depressed. Something momentous in the history of the world, something good for a change, and what was he doing? Sitting in a projection room with an apple thief and a man who'd just urinated on a wall.

"Meanwhile, in the last few minutes, some of the protesters have set up a Youtube channel," Aidan the newscaster said. "The movement's spokesperson in Jersey, music executive Hannah Lexingwood, used that channel to make what she described as an 'announcement to the world' a few moments ago."

From there, the screen cut straight to a head and shoulders shot of his older sister - Lexingwood *née* Mordred - in Saint Helier. She was addressing a crowd of protesters beneath candy-coloured Jolly Rogers and the red flags of Real Alternative.

He didn't hear what she said. He was too busy having an out-of-body experience.

Chapter 3: Ladies and Gentlemen, Introducing the Remembrancer!

Hannah said something about how she was middle-class and cheesed off. The crowd in Saint Helier obviously loved her, and after a minute, even Mordred had to admit she was quite good. A real demagogue. How the hell had she got into this? He remembered she'd been quite enthusiastic about Chapman Hill when he'd been around. So now she was a politico. What were their mum and dad thinking now, probably sitting at home in Northumbria watching the TV? Knowing them, they'd probably be proud. But of course, petrified, because in the end, protesters always tended to get trampled by men with truncheons. And what would the neighbours say?

Oh, God. And there was Soraya from Fully Magic Coal Tar Lounge. All Mordred's old crowd. He could see what was coming already. Ruby Parker: *John, we're going to put you in there as a mole.*

"Enjoying the show?" Alec asked.

Bloody moles. He wished they'd never been invented.

" … and they come to places like this," Hannah was saying, "so they don't have to pay for the upkeep of the NHS or our schools or any of our public services. They only want the benefits. They don't want to contribute."

"I've never noticed before," Alec said, "but she's actually quite attractive. Especially when she gets going. She doesn't look anything like you either."

"We're not twins. She's four years older than me."

"And let's not pretend the British government's powerless to do anything about it," she continued. "They're fully complicit. And the opposition are no better. The revolving door between Westminster and industry …"

"Why does four years make any difference?" Alec asked. "You've still got the same mother and father, haven't you? Or have you?"

"She's my full sister, yes," Mordred said. "I don't know. I guess egg and sperm production changes as you get older."

"And the newspapers are mostly owned by non-doms, so we don't expect to get a good press there!"

"You mean," Alec continued, "if she'd only been one year older, she'd have looked a lot more like you? That doesn't sound right to me."

"I'm just hypothesising," Mordred said. "My feeling is, the more time goes on, the more likely it is two siblings will look different."

"Offshore means sucking wealth and resources from those countries who can least afford it," Hannah said. "According to Global Financial Integrity in Washington, re-invoicing *alone* drains *one hundred billion dollars a year* from the developing world."

"Your so-called 'hypothesis' smacks of Lamarckism," Alec said. "Your body changes so your DNA does, that's your argument. It can't work like that. If you lost an arm, you probably wouldn't give birth to a one-armed baby."

"I'm not saying the *parents'* appearance is preserved," Mordred said. "At least not their present appearance. That would be ridiculous."

"And given how bad a lot of these companies are for the environment," Hannah went on, "the world urgently needs full financial transparency everywhere. We need to reverse de-regulation."

"So what *are* you saying?" Alec said.

"I'd like to ask you the same question," Mordred replied. "Are you saying my mother had an affair four years after she gave birth to my sister?"

Hannah cut a piece of red tape with some scissors. "I hereby declare World War O open!"

Everyone in Jersey cheered. A middle-aged woman leaned slightly over Mordred. "Ruby Parker would like to see you both, downstairs in her office."

"It's not for me to say whether your mother had an affair," Alec said.

"I beg your pardon?" the middle-aged woman replied.

"All I'm saying is, your theory of why you and your sister look different doesn't hold water. It's pseudo-science."

"Oh … yes, right," she said, looking scared.

They knocked on Ruby Parker's door and put their ears close. This time they heard it – 'enter!' - so they went in. She was putting her coat on a peg on the far side of her tiny office, a small middle-aged black woman in a black skirt-suit, black veiled hat, black shoes. "Sit down," she said, removing the hat.

Three chairs had been put out in a row. The office consisted of a small desk with a computer, a framed picture of the Queen, a large tropical fish tank and several potted plants at different heights.

Ruby Parker sat down and turned to Mordred. "First things first. John, Ian's just been to see me. He claims you approached him in the gents' toilet and told him you were a communist."

Alec chuckled. "Probably the worst chat-up line in the history of homosexuality."

"I tried to explain," she went on, "that it's one of the main reasons we keep you on the payroll. But I did say I'd issue you with a warning. Don't go scaring the staff."

"Understood," Mordred said.

"How was the wedding?" she asked. Strangely, she didn't seem particularly bothered about World War O.

"I think I speak for both of us," Alec said, "when I say that, much as we love and respect Annabel, we're bloody glad it's over. How was the funeral?"

"Emotional. Ronald Chewton was quite a bit older than me, but hardly elderly. The truth is, he never got over losing his wife and son."

"I didn't know his wife had died," Mordred said. "Poor man."

"An overdose. Her, I mean, not him. She'd been mentally ill for some time. Sebastian's death pushed her over the edge. Afterwards, according to what I've been told, Sir Ronald just abandoned the will to live."

They listened to the fish tank bubble for a few moments.

"Well, I suppose we'd better get down to business," she said. "Of course, you know what's going on, I assume you've been watching the news as per instructions. However, my request that you wait for me in the projector room may well have misled you. 'World War O', as they charmingly call it, only concerns us very indirectly, if at all. My strong feeling is that it'll dissipate, or be broken up, in week at the outside. These things don't usually last, and they're always a matter for the police, not the security services."

"Have you seen John's sister?" Alec asked.

"I think everyone has," she replied shortly.

"Is that why you've asked to see us?" Mordred asked. "To tell us we're going to do nothing? I mean, I'm not complaining. I just want to be clear."

"Perhaps I should have come to the point earlier," she replied. "The funeral. Then I had a meeting at the Foreign and Commonwealth Office. All in all, it's been a busy day." There was a knock at the door. "Come in," she said.

Phyllis entered. Tall with long light brown hair, expert make up, immaculate red skirt-suit and matching heels, she looked like she always did: a cross between high glamour and Amazonian warfare.

"Please sit down," Ruby Parker told her.

"She's there," Phyllis said, without explaining who 'she' or 'there' were. "She checked in an hour ago, no problems. The airport's still open, but I believe it's bringing in a lot of protesters too. The Lieutenant Governor and the Chief Minister of Jersey are currently meeting to decide whether to close it till further notice."

"Where did you hear that?" Ruby Parker asked.

"Sky News."

"There will be hell to pay if they do," Ruby Parker said. "It's the height of the tourist season. Mind you, they won't care. That's not how most of them make a living."

"Since John and I are actually in the room," Alec said, "do you mind me asking who you're talking about? Who 'checked in an hour ago'?"

"Annabel Gould-al-Banna," Ruby Parker said. "By an incredible stroke of luck, she and Tariq are honeymooning in Jersey. She owns a cottage there."

"She must be even more loaded than I thought she was," Alec said.

"It means that, in the unlikely event we need someone on the ground, she's our woman," Phyllis put in. "Not that we've told her yet. No point in ruining her honeymoon."

"No," Alec said, "we'll let John's sister do that."

Phyllis laughed. "Yes, sorry about that, John. How come you're always at the centre of these maelstroms of leftiness? Pardon me, but you don't seem political enough."

Best not to rise to the bait. You couldn't win against Phyllis, not in one of her whimsical-ironic moods. He still didn't know why this meeting had been called, and it had been going on for nearly ten minutes now.

"Now that we're all here," Ruby Parker said, "I think it's time to begin. Can any of you tell me who 'the Remembrancer' is?"

"Excuse me for sounding frivolous," Phyllis said after a long enough pause to suggest no other answer was coming, "but it sounds like a character from a JRR Tolkien novel."

"I was thinking more Batman," Alec replied. "The Joker, the Riddler and the Remembrancer."

"If only there were as many pages in Wikipedia devoted to him as there are to those characters," Ruby Parker. "It's a role within the City of London Corporation. It dates back to 1571. Since 2004, it's been occupied by a former Barclays Bank accountant named Norman Pruett. Yesterday, sometime after 5pm, Mr Pruett disappeared."

"It might help if we knew what a 'Remembrancer' does," Mordred said. "I mean what's his job description?"

"He sits in the Commons chamber facing the Speaker's Chair, and his job is to protect the interests of the City of London. In the words of the City's own website" – she picked up a piece of paper from her desk and read – "'day to day examination of Parliamentary business including examination of and briefing on proposed legislation and amendments to it, regular liaison with the Select Committees of both Houses and contact with officials in Government departments dealing with Parliamentary Bills'."

Phyllis scoffed. "You mean we've got someone sitting in the House of Commons who none of us have ever voted for, and he's got all those powers?"

"And he's disappeared," Ruby Parker said. "I'm always a little surprised when people are shocked by how little democracy there is in this country. It ought to be obvious if you only think about it."

"With respect," Phyllis replied, "I can't see how anyone could discover the existence of a post such as the Remembrancer through introspection."

Ruby Parker smiled. Obviously, she'd also discerned that Phyllis was in a whimsical-ironic mood. "In any case," she said, "we can't rule out the possibility that his disappearance is linked to so-called World War O. The Home Office thinks it's a matter of national security, apparently. I'm assigning you and Alec to it. Find him, or find out what happened to him. I've deputed Ian and Edna to assist you."

"And what about me?" Mordred said.

"You're going to the Caribbean," she replied.

He smiled. Might have known it'd be something like that. That was how she thought. *John and Hannah are related. To avoid John getting into trouble, I have to get him as far away from his sister as I possibly can.*

"The Cayman Islands, I assume?" he said.

"No."

"Then …"

"It must have occurred to you that one of the things that *should* interest the security services about the protesters – perhaps the only thing - is, how did they manage to achieve such a high degree of organisation and go completely undetected? Of course, it now looks as if Jennifer Hallowell and her fellow activists were acting in concert to create a smokescreen. Which only makes the problem more acute. With all the millions of pounds of resources GCHQ and the NSA possess between them, *how did we pick up precisely nothing?*"

"And the answer's in the Caribbean."

"I've just spent an hour at the Foreign and Commonwealth office and the consensus is, yes, maybe. At least it's an avenue worth investigating. I'm not going to say any more. Go home now, get a good rest, and report to briefing room five tomorrow afternoon at 1pm sharp. Brian's putting together a Powerpoint. He'll tell you everything you need to know and more. Afterwards, Kevin will drive you to the airport. Your plane leaves at six."

Chapter 4: Brian, Lord of Powerpoint

12.55pm. Mordred left his suitcase with Colin Bale at reception, switched off his phone and climbed the stairs to the first floor of Thames House. He wore a grey blazer, open-neck shirt, smart trousers and brogues, and carried a *Guardian* and a large coffee in a paper cup. He passed seven people on his way to briefing room five and they all looked at him for longer than was strictly necessary then averted their gazes. He heard someone whisper 'Hannah Lexingwood's brother' - or that's what it sounded like. Maybe he was just becoming paranoid. If so, coffee wasn't necessarily a good idea. But then, he had to stay awake and Brian was famed for his monotonous voice.

Overnight, things in the world's tax havens had stayed more or less the same, except perhaps that the number of protesters had grown. Some places were trying to set up 'exclusion zones' – geographical perimeters beyond which outsiders were forbidden to proceed – but unfortunately, they made the possibility of these public before considering the practicalities, and most of their police forces weren't fit for purpose. A few places – Jersey, Guernsey and the Caymans – had formally appealed to London for help. While Westminster dragged its feet, Wapping and Fleet Street went into full polemical overdrive. The protesters were socialist troublemakers, most of whom had never seen a bar of soap, and they were living in the past.

Briefing room five. He didn't knock because, as far as he knew, it was just him and Brian Penford. Brian – a bearded, bespectacled fifty-two year old in a worn tweed jacket and trousers, who looked as if he only needed a pair of turned down wellies to complete his look - was already standing by his interactive whiteboard. The room was big enough for about ten people. Its windows would normally give a view of the river Thames, but the blinds were lowered and the lights on. Mordred offered a handshake and sat down.

"Ready?" Brian said.

Mordred took a sip his coffee and nodded. "Didn't sleep much last night," he said, suddenly aware that taking a huge caffeine shot might look discourteous. "Worried about my sister."

"Every family's got an eccentric," Brian said. "I'm sure she'll be okay. As will you."

"Fire away."

Brian switched the lights off. The screen showed a picture of a man of about seventy in a sports jacket and brogues, photographed, probably clandestinely, from some distance away. He was exiting a car somewhere sunny with a young woman of about Mordred's age, quite slim, in a pinafore dress.

"Peter Decristoforo," Brian said, "and his Mexican grand-daughter-in-law, now – as of 2011 - adopted *daughter*, Fenella Decristoforo-Salvaterra. These days, they share a house. 'Share' partly on the basis of mutual grief. Peter's wife, Jill, daughter, Madeleine, and grandson, Arnold – also Fenella's husband - died in a car crash in Honduras in 2001. Peter was on the back seat, but survived; Fenella was in the holiday apartment they'd hired, waiting for them all to get back."

"Rotten break," Mordred said.

"He adopted her as his daughter a year later. Presumably, it simplified matters for the will. But it was also intended as a strong signal to outsiders that their continued cohabitation was purely platonic. If you meet her, by the way – which you will - she's his *daughter*, not his 'grand-daughter-in-law'. The latter tends to put their hackles up. She's from Coahuila, originally, near the US border. Her own family – mother, father, sister, even one aunt - are all deceased. Again, if you meet her, she may talk about the Salvaterra family 'curse'. Bullshit, but no need to get into an argument about it."

"I wouldn't dream of it. But does it seem odd that people around these two keep dying? Or am I just misreading the story? Do we suspect foul play?"

"According to what we've been able to discover, they're just very unlucky. Besides, you'd have to be a bit crazed to bump off your mum and dad."

Mordred folded his hands. "You'd be surprised how many crazed people I run into in this job."

"Let's focus on Peter. He was born in 1940 in Norfolk. Right now, he's one of Tax Justice Network's biggest supporters, which is partly why we're so interested in him. Last year, he made an undisclosed donation to the organisation's campaign work, believed to be in the region of two hundred thousand pounds. Not much in proportion to his personal fortune, but hugely significant for the organisation."

Another still of Decristoforo. This time, he sat at a table outside a café, again with Fenella. They wore different clothes, but it was still sunny.

"I'm only showing you this one," Brian said, "so you can get a sense of what he looks like today. He's not keen on being photographed."

"He supports TJN, but he doesn't live here," Mordred said. "Is he a UK taxpayer?"

"Yes, from the income he makes in this country. He's also a United States taxpayer, a Canadian taxpayer and a French taxpayer. Among others. That's not double taxation, of course. He just pays on what he owns there."

"Clean hands."

"As far as we know. Of course, he may have secret income. Or non-taxable. He owns the Caribbean island he lives on. He isn't obliged to report what he does there. And of course tax avoidance isn't the only way of being a bad person."

"Do we think he's up to something dubious?"

Brian smiled. "Obviously some of us do, otherwise why would you be flying out to see him?"

"Point taken."

"Maybe save your questions till the end."

He changed slides. A black and white picture of a very young-looking Peter Decristoforo in a lab coat. "In the early sixties, he was part of the IBM team that helped effect the transition from punched card computers to electronics."

Another slide of the protagonist, in colour now and standing over a reel-to-reel tape-recorder. "Once he'd taken his team as far as it could go, he moved on. In the 1970s, he worked part-time as a researcher at the Xerox Palo Alto Research Centre. He was highly spoken of for his innovative solutions to long-running technical conundrums."

"'Part time'?"

"The mid-sixties being when he came into possession of his island. A wedding present from his late father-in-law, a Texan oil magnate. Intended as somewhere for him to do his own, personal scientific research. We'll come back to that in a moment."

Next slide. Decristoforo standing outside a warehouse, hands in pockets, smiling. "In the 80s, he set up his own software business, 'Massive Micro' – that was its actual name, I kid you not - in nearby Turks and Caicos. Bought out in 1993 by the American giant, Verdinelli-Clair, for thirteen million dollars. Obviously, they immediately changed its moniker to something non-naff."

Next slide. Decristoforo in an open necked shirt with rather less hair on his head, still smiling, possibly for the benefit of the stock exchange. "Set up a new firm, Decristoforo Software Solutions in 2000, much better name, much more diversified. Still lives on Saint Martha's Rock, roughly sixty kilometres southwest of the Caymans, where the DSSol factory is. Yes, that's right, John, *the factory's on the island.*"

Mordred sat up. "What's the significance of that?"

"Doesn't it strike you as a bit James Bond-y? I mean, here's this guy, top scientist, lives on *his own island with a secret factory?* Just about everyone on the island's an employee of his, or a tenant of some kind, probably sworn to secrecy."

"I see what you mean. Is there an extinct volcano on the island, by any chance?"

"As a matter of fact, yes. That's actually what the island is. I don't know whether it's got a fully-functioning space-rocket inside, but we can only hope and pray. Anyway, you're going there on your own. We're not sending you with backup or anything … Not that it's my decision, obviously. I'm just Mr Powerpoint."

"Yes, thanks for cheering me up. That's right, I'll be all alone in the middle of the Caribbean with Blofeld. Why is everyone in this building obsessed with James Bond?"

"Oh, I don't know. Maybe because he's the reason we all came to work here. Then, when we arrived, we found out it was all about filing cabinets and Post-it notes. *I have known the inexorable sadness of pencils neat in their boxes.* By that time, we couldn't escape because we all had mortgages and families to support. Don't knock it, John. You're living the dream."

A new slide appeared on the screen. A young woman in a bikini, sunning herself on a beach.

"Fenella Decristoforo-Salvaterra again, I presume," Mordred said.

"You bet," Brian replied. "As I said earlier, she lives with the old man on the island. I only put her in there to show you it's got *all* the ingredients. So much so, it's spooky. She's actually got an *hourglass figure*, for God's sake."

"Would *you* like to go?"

Brian chuckled. "Not a chance. Not at my time of life; not with my leg. Not when there's a possibility you might get shot dead."

"Yes, I suppose being murdered's much easier when you're younger."

"Well, you haven't got as many people depending on you."

The way Brian was talking, it half-sounded like there might be some sort of plot within MI7 to get rid of him, like they were sending him to Saint Martha's Rock for specifically that reason. *He's the brother of Hannah Lexingwood, the chief conspirator. We'll have to think of some way of disposing of him, but make it look like an accident.* He took a deep breath. He'd known from the start that coffee would only make him more paranoid, but he hadn't reckoned with Mr Powerpoint. (Hang on: the Riddler, the Joker, the Remembrancer, *Mr Powerpoint?*) Brian – let's call him that, maybe, yes. Brian was a one-man paranoia-inducing machine.

"How big is Saint Martha's Rock?" he asked.

"Forty-six square miles."

"Does it admit tourists?"

"The northern half of the island, yes. The southern half, where Decristoforo's factory and house are, no. They're subtly off-limits."

"By 'subtly'," Mordred said, "what do you mean?"

"Cut off by thick undergrowth and wild animals rather than perimeter fences and guards. To give it a natural feel."

"But I could go out to sea and swim around it."

"You could. No one does. It costs a packet to stay there. You don't want to get on the wrong side of the owner, otherwise you may not be allowed back. He's not exactly in charge of the guest list, but he does have the power to exclude undesirables."

"How am I supposed to approach him? You must have a plan. And what am I looking for when I get there?"

"You're Detective Inspector Jonas Eagleton of the Royal Cayman Islands Police Service. You're making a neighbourly visit to reassure yourself that Mr Decristoforo and his *daughter* are safe. But you've been told by your opposite number in London that GCHQ didn't anticipate the invasions, so you're also looking to discover whether Peter might know of any technology that might block the sort of electronic surveillance Government Communications employs."

"The 'invasions'? That's actually what we're calling them?"

"The newspapers are. Obviously not that one," he said, noting Mordred's *Guardian*. "Anyway, you're going Heathrow to Owen Roberts International Airport in the Cayman Islands, arriving midnight our time. There'll be someone there waiting for you. Get a sense of what's happening on the ground, and pick up the documentation. He or she will field any questions you might want to ask and drive you to your connecting boat. You should arrive at St Martha's at about 3am our time, 9am local time. A taxi will be waiting at the harbour. A reservation's been made for you at the Sunshine Suite Hotel fronting Saint Martha's Bay. Obviously, you can't afford to look jetlagged because, from Peter Decristoforo's point of view, you've only come from the Caymans, so try to get some sleep on the plane."

"How do I get off the island if things go wrong?"

"We don't anticipate they will, but it is possible. You'll have a direct line to the Royal Cayman Islands Police Service. Encrypted, of course. Failing that, if we haven't heard from you in twenty-four hours of your arrival, we'll send in the big guns. It's not in Decristoforo's interests to harm you, *especially* if he's involved in this, which he probably is."

"'Probably'. Is that just your assessment, or is it official?"

"Nothing's official in this building, John. You should know that by now. But I'd say pretty much everyone that matters thinks that way. And by that, I mean Ruby Parker."

"Do I have an appointment with Decristoforo, or am I expected to wangle my own introduction?"

"The Cayman Police will ring ahead to set that up after you've arrived at Owen Roberts Airport, and after you've left Grand Cayman *en route* to Saint Martha's." He passed a document wallet across the table. "Some reading for the flight, plus plane tickets, etcetera. Pick up a pistol from Amber. Kevin will be ready to take you to the airport in about an hour. He'll buzz you. I assume you've packed yourself a suitcase."

"Er, hang on. Did you say a pistol?"

"Yep. Who does that remind you of? Beginning with a J and a B?"

"I'm not taking a gun."

"What?"

"They're a waste of space."

"I don't see how you work that out. They're supposed to make you feel special. You've been chosen. How many other people in this country can say they've got a gun and the police can't touch them?"

"I don't know."

"What if someone tries to shoot you?" Brian persisted.

"I'll duck. Look, I'm not a particularly good shot, and if I'm confronted with someone hostile, I'll only shoot them if I'm absolutely certain there's no other alternative."

"Yes, that's the general idea. So?"

"So how can I ever be that certain? What'll happen is I *won't* shoot them and we'll have a fight for the gun, and there's a good chance I'll get killed. So no, I won't take one if that's okay."

Brian shrugged. "Fine. I gave you the choice. You'll have to explain to Amber, though."

"Amber doesn't want me to get killed with something she gave me. She'd never forgive herself."

"If your argument's correct, it'd be happening all the time, in which case, she'd have had a breakdown by now. The alternative is that you're not as good with a gun as you ought to be, in which case you probably need more practice. Refusal to carry isn't a long-term solution. You can always shoot someone in the foot if you're worried about them overpowering you. Nobody says you have to aim for the heart every time."

Mordred sighed. "Yes, okay, that's a good argument. I'll think about it. Next time."

"Suit yourself then."

"It's nothing personal."

He could see Brian wanted him to carry a gun. Maybe he was writing a novel. That's what people did sometimes. They came to work here for two or three years – or sometimes, only for a couple of months – so they could pen a spy thriller and sell themselves to a literary agent as 'someone who once worked at MI5', 'an insider'. The problem with that theory was, Brian had been here since 1905. Still, it was never too late.

He stood up and they shook hands. As he picked up the document wallet with the tickets in, he happened to catch sight of

Brian's briefing papers. Sticking out from amongst them was one with the heading *A Very Bad Time to be in Berlin*, with 'Chapter One' underneath. He must have paused for a split second because, when he looked up again, Brian was blushing. They didn't say anything.

He'd go and see Amber before switching his phone back on and facing the inevitable 'two million missed calls' notice from his sisters and parents. He walked along four corridors and went through a fire-door with a glass panel. Inside, a little waiting area with a bench, and a long counter with what looked like a cloakroom behind. Amber - a solid middle-aged woman with scarlet-framed glasses – was sitting at a PC, typing. It was too distant for detail, but at the top, he could just make out an emboldened, 'Chapter 14: Caravan From Odessa'. Bloody hell, her as well. She hastily minimised the window when she saw him.

"I've been through your suitcase," she said. "Everything's fine. It's back at reception."

"Could I please not have a gun?"

"Any particular reason?" She looked disappointed.

"I always think it might go off by accident."

"You don't really know much about them, do you? Okay, I'll call the Caymans and tell them to put it back in storage. But you really need to get a grip on this phobia of yours, John. Speak to Phyllis. She's a world-class marksperson. She's won prizes."

"True, but I always think it's different in the heat of the moment."

"Too right. That's why you need training. Keep a level head."

He felt he was being given a series of telling-offs. First Brian, now Amber. Hopefully, he wouldn't bump into Ruby Parker on his way out. *John, it's about time you overcame your foolish reluctance to carry a gun. Here's my advice …*

"I've put some extra-strong condoms in for you," Amber said.

"Thanks, but I - "

"You never know when you may need to use sex to create an opening. It's not pleasure, it's business. Although in this case, they'll probably overlap. Depending on the beneficiary, of course."

"How's the novel coming along?" It was the only way he could think of to change the subject.

"Oh." She actually took a step backwards. "I, er - "

"My sister's a novelist, that's all. I'm interested."

"Don't tell anyone, will you? I write it at home, mostly. It's just, I'm on a particularly difficult bit."

"I probably won't be having sex, incidentally. Nowadays, it never carries an entitlement to view a woman's secret missile base."

She laughed. "I'd better scrap chapter twelve then."

They joked a bit more about other things and he made his excuses. Only another half hour till Kevin – the man who never spoke – brought the car round. He went up to the canteen. There were three people in there in total, all sitting alone with laptops. He bought a cup of tea and a scone from the counter, slid in at the nearest empty table, and switched his phone on. Six missed calls, divided between three of his four sisters. One from Julia, one from Mabel, four from Charlotte. None from Hannah.

He rang Julia first, and asked her how it was in Norway. "Could you ring home?" she said. By 'home' she meant their parents in Hexham. "Where have you been?"

"Getting ready for a trip abroad."

"Bloody hell, not you too. It's not Jersey, is it?"

"No. And before you go through a list, it's not *any* tax-haven."

"They're worried and they expect you to call. Ring them now."

"Okay."

He didn't. He rang Mabel. "Hi, John," she said. Probably because she was eight years his junior and thus part of a completely different socio-biological bracket, she always treated him like a rarely-glimpsed uncle. "Could you ring mum and dad, please? They're worried, and they need someone to talk to who isn't me. I'm in Italy right now and I've got my hands full."

"Doing what?"

"*Médecins Sans Frontières*? Remember? The people I work for? Refugees?" All this was said so nicely that he couldn't possibly think she was being sarcastic. "Could you ring mum and dad right away?" she asked again.

"Will do."

He didn't. He rang Charlotte. "Where the bloody hell have you been?" she asked. "I've been ringing and ringing and all I got was your stupid voicemail. Have you actually *seen* the news, John? Did it not *occur* to you to think that this is what counts as a family emergency? Didn't you think we'd be *frantic* to get in touch? What the hell were you thinking, switching your phone off at a time like this?"

"Nice to speak to you," he said. "How's Marcus?"

"He's fine. And before you ask, little Seth's fine too. Don't try to change the subject. You need to get on the phone to mum and reassure her."

"Why can't you do that? I mean, just out of interest."

"You just don't get it, do you? If your phone's switched off, it makes her think you're in Jersey too. You're not, are you?"

"No."

"Where are you?"

"London."

"Typical bloody Gemini. Ruling planet: Mercury. You'd better not be lying. You'd better not be in Jersey."

"Or what?"

"Or ..." – he'd obviously called her bluff – "I don't know. It's not nice to lie to someone. I'm your sister."

"Well, anyway, it's been great touching base. I suppose I'd better ring mum now."

"I love you. I'm sorry for shouting. I'm just worried about mum and dad, that's all."

"Yes, well I - "

"Get on the phone to them *now*. Good bye." She hung up.

It seemed odd that Hannah hadn't rung anyone. Maybe she expected to be told to stop making an exhibition of herself and come on home. Difficult to say that to a thirty-five year old, but Charlotte would probably find a way. He rang her, expecting it to be switched off, but it wasn't. It rang three times and Tim, her paediatrician husband, picked up. "Hi, John. Thank God."

"Is Hannah there?"

"She's in Jersey. Haven't you seen the news?"

"I just thought you might be with her, that's all. This is her phone."

He scoffed. "She left it here deliberately. Unfortunately, I couldn't get the time off work. I had no idea it would be this big. I thought it was just a normal protest. You know: like people sitting outside *Topshop* or *Starbuck's*, giving out leaflets and maybe singing *We Shall Not Be Moved*. I didn't expect it to last more than a few hours. I certainly didn't expect this."

"Well, it'll probably peter out in a few days."

"Not in Jersey, it won't. Haven't you heard? Bloody Soraya's announced she's going to be playing an illegal concert somewhere on the island at the end of next month. That's near four weeks away, so they're obviously planning to stay put at least that long. Don't come round here, by the way. The house is surrounded by journalists. I've been given the day off work, though I'll probably have to go in tomorrow, whatever."

"I'm leaving the country."

"Bit drastic, isn't it? Where are you going? Please don't say Jersey."

"America. On business. Scheduled a month ago. I've no choice."

"I'd count my lucky stars if I was you."

"So we've actually no way of contacting her?"

"I've tried Soraya's phone but it's switched off. All I can do is keep watching TV. She forbade me to fly out there, and I'm not so much of a macho man that I don't tend to do exactly what I'm told 100% of the time."

"Understood. Give me a call if you want someone to talk to."

"I've got the cat for company, so I'll survive. She's pregnant, by the way. We were going to tell you - "

"What? The cat?"

"Hannah."

It took a split second to sink in. "Wow, congratulations. When did you find out?"

"Four days ago."

"Yet she still went to bloody Jersey to lead a revolution."

"Start as you mean to go on, that's Hannah's motto."

"Why didn't you say anything?"

"We wanted to announce it when all the family's together. Your mum and dad are coming to London to see *Wicked* at the Apollo Victoria, beginning of next month."

"Sounds like Soraya may have put a spoke in that."

"Will you tell them? Your mum and dad?"

"Don't *you* want to do it?"

"I don't feel much like the bearer of good news right now. My wife and possible child may be in mortal danger."

"Listen, Hannah may not be very streetwise, but Soraya knows a few tricks. They'll be okay."

"I hope so. You'd better get off the phone. Give your parents my love."

He hung up. Time for the big one. But suddenly, Kevin was standing by his table. As per custom, he didn't say anything. Mordred pretended not to have seen him for a moment. He casually put his phone away and finished his tea and scone.

But he couldn't keep it up. He could hardly ask Kevin what he wanted, or why he was standing there. Driving was all he did. "Have you got my suitcase?" he asked.

Kevin nodded and turned round and exited.

Mordred followed him. As he left the canteen, he caught sight of the screens of two of the three laptops. Novels, both getting written at breakneck speed.

Chapter 5: Into Grand Cayman

Once he got in the car and Kevin took them out onto the main road, Mordred realised he'd had a lucky escape. Had he been left alone, he'd have rung his parents and told them Hannah was pregnant. He wouldn't even have thought about it. A moment's reflection persuaded him the situation was more complex than that. His parents were probably already worried about her. Adding a foetus into the mix might well make things worse.

On the other hand, with Tim now relying on him, how could he not tell them?

Easy. Get back to Tim, tell him he'd had second thoughts.

He rang his phone. Switched off. He tried Hannah's. Switched off. He rang Tim's again and left a message explaining his change of heart. He ended, "Probably best for you to do it when they come and see *Wicked*." His head was reeling now. He was supposed to be concentrating on Decristoforo and Saint Martha's Rock, not this. He rang his parents.

"John!" his mum exclaimed, when she picked up the phone. "Listen, I can't talk now, I've a reporter here from *The Northern Echo*."

"I'm leaving the country."

"Where are you going? Not J - "

"America. On business."

"Oh, that's good. Well, have a lovely time. I'd better get going, I'm afraid. I've got a few other newspapers to speak to, and there are one or two TV stations."

"Do you think that's wise? Talking to the press?"

"I've spoken about it to your dad. We think if we talk to all of them, they're all likely to feel they've got a bit of a stake in us, and if one of them then goes making things up, the others won't take kindly to it, and the general public will have enough context to realise it's a fabrication. Plus, we're treating them all to tea and biscuits."

"You realise a lot of our national newspapers are actually owned by tax avoiders?"

"Oh, yes, but the *reporters* aren't necessarily bad. Some of them are very nice."

"I'm sure they are."

"Come on, John. If you flood the market with something – in this case, information – it finds its own level. If you restrict it, people fight over it, and it gets distorted. Anyway, it's better than staying in here while the reporters lay siege."

"Is it that bad?"

"It would be. This is World War O, John, haven't you heard? And I don't want people thinking I'm ashamed of my own daughter."

"Is there anything I can get you? Do you want anything?"

"Only for you to have a good time in America."

He was going to tell her – *Hannah's pregnant* - but the words caught in his throat.

"John, are you still there?" she said.

"I'd better let you go now."

"Don't forget to eat properly."

"I should be back in a few days or so. I'll call you." They exchanged a Keep Well, two Bye Thens and one See You Soon, and he hung up.

"What time do you think we'll arrive at Heathrow?" he asked Kevin.

More silence. The car sped up.

He boarded British Airways flight LHRGCM at 3pm. It was first class so he could watch TV and access the internet if he needed to. The protests were beginning to turn ugly in one or two places. Mauritius was the first to resume normal service because there was no distinction between the police force and the army there, and there were twelve thousand trained personnel to call on. As always, barricades had been erected and tear gas was thrown. In Delaware, the National Guard had taken control of the capital's streets after a series of skirmishes in which one boy was left critically injured. Outside Saint Paul's in London, police were resolutely arresting Occupiers. Elsewhere, so the press persistently reported, manpower and resources were being discreetly airlifted into isolated places – islands, mostly - whose police forces were too small and ill-equipped to respond effectively to the crisis alone. The protestors' Youtube channel was awash with amateur footage of heavy-handed law enforcement. The broad media consensus was that the protests in all places would fall on a version of the domino principle. Once one authority had rid itself of its demonstrations, others would see it as a matter of pride to do the same. Fatalities were inevitable, but the important thing was to restore business as usual, and there was no such thing, any more, as a government that wasn't, in some way, firmly in the pocket of the big corporations. There could be just one outcome. The only question was, how long would it take?

Then there was Hannah. Why was he going in the wrong direction? Sod Ruby Parker and her touching desire to stop him making an arse of himself, this was his sister, and she might be about to get beaten to death. You always took out the leaders first, that had been received military wisdom since at least the time of the Romans. She was in real danger. Nowadays, Jersey was full of tax avoiders and tax avoiders' friends. Most of them weren't good people. Probably not above hurting someone, or even bumping them off, if she made enough trouble for them.

He should be sleeping, really. *Obviously, you can't look jetlagged because, from Peter Decristoforo's point of view, you've only come from the Caymans, so try and get some sleep on the plane.* Failing a snooze, he ought to be reading Brian's documents. But he couldn't, not while he was worried about his bloody sister.

She could take care of herself, though, couldn't she? Of course she could. They'd been here before. Although no: it was Julia he usually worried about. As a rule, Hannah worried about him, but he didn't worry about her; he worried about Julia, but she didn't worry about him, and so, skipping anyone to worry about Charlotte, because she was so obviously capable, that left Julia and Charlotte to worry about Mabel. Which made him worrying about Hannah even odder. Against the established order of things.

After a few seconds, he knew what it was. He had the vaguest of vague memories of once hearing something unpleasant about Jersey. He couldn't even remember the outlines, just the disagreeable feeling of being unsettled. It was a democracy, wasn't it? He took out his smartphone.

Wikipedia, always a good place to start. 'Politics of Jersey'.

Well, it definitely looked democratic, although they'd recently reformed the electoral system, and cut the number of representatives. Following "widespread criticisms", an independent electoral commission had been brought in to look at the new system.

Fishy? Not necessarily. But there were lots of questions the article left unanswered. Most organisations vetted their Wikipedia pages anyway. You wouldn't necessarily find the whole truth here.

Try Google. 'Corruption in Jersey'. Top result: 'Ian Evans Against Jersey Corruption And Police Brutality'.

"I am a carpet fitter who came to Jersey in 1988. I have been persecuted incessantly by the police and judiciary since my arrival, reason being I am big, ugly, speak my mind and my face does not fit as I will not be controlled by anyone. It is hard to imagine a place like this outside of Zimbabwe, but here we are, the good old Channel Islands."

Okay, he'd got the gist. Quite a lot of detail about the subject. Too long to read it all now. Try another. Here: 'Trevor Pitman's Blog: The Bald Truth'.

"Just when will the UK Justice Ministry finally step in and demand that Jersey's laws are applied fairly and to all - rather than being manipulated by our so-called 'justice' system as a tool of oppression to hound and abuse any who are deemed as critics of the local Establishment - or as we are now even seeing against individuals who simply have the misfortune to be family members or friends of such critics?"

Well, every society had its discontents. Maybe these were just two.

Next up, *The Financial Secrecy Index narrative report on Jersey 2013*: " ... many of the problems of contemporary Britain: conflicts of interest and corruption are rife and the elite have made their own interests synonymous with the interests of the entire population. In the near-absence of opposition politics and independent media this is a recipe for stifling dissent – especially when it challenges the dominant offshore financial sector."

Didn't sound good. But this was the Tax Justice Network, maybe they ... he didn't know. 'Rife' sounded a bit vague for an official report.

Hang on, *the text of an affidavit signed by the former Deputy Chief of the States Police.* Bit more like it. Out of the pressure-groups and into the establishment.

"I went to Jersey in 2002 full of expectation of the challenge that lay ahead. I soon learnt that it was like nowhere else in the British Isles. I was puzzled at first by the hostile reaction from politicians to our efforts to stop the few bullies in the force from making the lives of their colleagues miserable. This turned to anger at the complete obstruction to all our efforts to regulate the possession of high velocity weapons on the island."

Bloody hell. Okay, this was serious. He had to get back home and on a plane to Jersey – if they'd let him. No, they wouldn't. They'd put him straight on the boat to Saint Martha's, as per instructions. Good God.

In the absence of an alternative, he needed to get some perspective. Remember the danger of the internet? How you read a few headlines on a few pages and suddenly you thought you were an expert? Lesson number one: no one online is who they seem. Lesson two: don't get carried away. It could all be nonsense, like Alec's tale about City traders betting on Jennifer Hallowell's death. People liked those sorts of stories. They liked to think the world was crooked. It made them feel better about themselves.

Okay, but he had to get on and off Saint Martha's Rock as quickly as possible. No loitering. And for now, he needed to get some sleep so he could think clearly.

He awoke when the stewardess gave him a gentle shake and asked if he'd like his lunch. He sat up and nodded, and she brought him the aubergine and chickpea curry he'd requested on boarding. He looked at his watch. Midday exactly. He wound it on three hours, and finished his meal. He ate a dessert and then got down to the serious business of reading the documents Brian had prepared for him. Mostly news clippings about Peter Decristoforo, plus a few maps of the island, and his identity documents. Good old DI Jonas Eagleton.

The plane arrived at 6am, and he exited with ten grim business-looking types in suits with briefcases. Too early for tourists, even though this was the height of the season. There were presumably lots to be found somewhere on the island, even with the protests.

He was suddenly struck, as he always was when he got off a plane in a hot place, by the blasting heat and white and the sheer difference to rainy London. No matter how many times he disembarked in tropical locations, he always got the sense of a magical world just behind the appearance and somehow present in it. These trees, this runway, this dense purple sky with the sun still low on the horizon, this smell of pines and clear ocean - they were always here, no matter what he was doing, irrespective even of whether he was even alive, and it seemed momentarily astonishing. Then he forgot about it as the stewardess thanked him for flying with BA and he boarded the bus to the terminal.

The ride was short and took them past perfectly clipped lawns and evenly spaced palms. As far as he could tell from the horizon, the island was perfectly flat. The lounge was a high-ceilinged, prestigious-looking affair with shiny metallic pillars and marmoreal floors. It was noticeably cooler and lighter in here. A young black woman in a white shirt and black trousers with red stripes down the sides held up a notice saying 'Jonas Eagleton'. She clasped her peaked cap under her elbow.

Mordred strode over. He didn't know whether she knew his real name, or the rough purpose of his visit, but he'd better err on the side of caution. He offered a handshake. "Thank you for coming to meet me."

"Good to make your acquaintance, sir," she replied gravely. "Your suitcase is already in the car. I'm your driver. PC Bedford, sir."

"DI Jonas Eagleton. But, of course, you knew that. Nice to meet you."

He wasn't keen on the sir-ing. It reminded him of Edna and Young Ian, and made him realise, for the first time, why he always felt slightly uncomfortable in their company. He must remember to tell them to cut it out when he got home. Even if it meant reinforcing Ian's conviction that he was a real communist, not just a pretend one.

"I'm to give you our documentation in exchange for yours," Bedford said, as they walked to the car. "I understand you're going undercover."

"Yes. Saint Martha's Rock. To meet Mr Decristoforo."

"I've got everything in the car, sir." She ran ahead slightly and opened the glass exit door for him, as if he was royalty.

"I hear you've been experiencing a few protests," Mordred said, as she held the car door open for him too. She didn't answer immediately. She ran round the front and got into the driver's seat.

"George Town, mostly, sir," she said. She started the engine. "We've got them contained now, but we've got a lot of angry people out there."

"It's not for me to express an opinion on whether big companies should pay their fair share of tax."

She smiled. "I didn't mean the protestors, sir. I meant the financiers."

"Are we going through George Town, by any chance?"

"I'm taking you to meet the Superintendent, sir. It'll only take a few minutes. He feels it would be impolite not to introduce himself to you on your way through."

"I would imagine he's fairly busy at the moment."

"Yes, but he knows you're here to help, sir."

They didn't say any more. The streets were filled with locals and early-bird tourists. High-rise hotels vied with large creole-style townhouses whose sloping roofs were painted blue or purple or green, construction sites, endless telegraph wires and the odd Union Jack. After about ten minutes, they arrived at the police station. Bedford stopped the car and got out and opened Mordred's door so quickly she might have been attempting to prevent an explosion.

"Thank you," he said.

"Please leave your suitcase in the car, sir. Bring your documents."

She proceeded to open every door for him until they reached the Super's office. She knocked and then opened that door as well. Mordred entered. She followed him, retired to a position against the wall, and stood to attention. Her eyes went to standby.

The Superintendent was a thin man with flat, grey, side-swept hair and large hands. His face was lined and his eyes jocular. He looked like he was already having a bad day. An air-conditioner fan blew gently from the ceiling. Beneath it, there were six filing cabinets and an untidy desk. The wall was hung with group photographs of official occasions, each starring the superintendent.

"Steve Perkins," he said, coming forward with another handshake. "Good to have you on the island. Only sorry it can't be longer."

"That's very kind of you," Mordred replied.

"We'll look after your passport for you. And we'll look after your real documents and give you …" he picked up a sheaf from the desk "… these."

Mordred gave him the document wallet and accepted the papers.

"Anything more I can do for you," the superintendent said, "just ask."

"I'm sure you're busy enough with the protests."

"It's rather early in the day. I don't expect they'll revive till everyone's breakfasted."

"Yes, I quite forgot the time-difference."

"My officers have got them hemmed in. They won't be going anywhere. It's mainly a question of getting them off the island before they start having a wider effect. We've got quite a lot of feral youths roundabout, so you know how it is. Remember the London riots of 2011? It's like that. It may start off with ideology but it'll spread through the imitation of supposed bravado. If we let it."

"Well, I don't know much about the Caymans - "

"One half heaven, one half hell. I'm never sure which is which. You know, these protests are completely out of date. We've got the US Foreign Account Tax Compliance Act nowadays, and the UK one. Everything's transparent. It has to be. Five years ago, I'd have understood it, but today?"

"Crossed wires," Mordred said.

"I've tried speaking to them, a few of them, but of course, I'm in a Catch-22 situation. I'm the police, so naturally I *would* say that. After you've been to Saint Martha's, do you think you could do a bit of undercover here? I mean, I could ask London."

"You mean, infiltrate the protestors in George Town?"

"You could work with Bedford here. You'd need local knowledge, obviously. She's got it in buckets."

Mordred smiled. "It's out of the question, I'm afraid, though I'm flattered to be asked. I have personal reasons for needing to get home as soon as possible."

"I'm sorry to hear that." He obviously didn't believe him. "Well, it doesn't matter. I'm sure we'll have the whole mess tidied away soon anyway. And our fabulous financiers can rest easy in their beds."

"Do I detect a note of disapproval?"

"Let's just say I'm not keen on the way a lot of them seen to think they own the Royal Cayman Islands Police Service. And I'm not keen on their cowardice. They're leaving the island in numbers at the moment. They'll be back when we've cleaned up their mess. Sorry, *the* mess." He looked at his watch. "You'd better get going, Detective Inspector. Your boat's due to leave any minute. Don't worry, the captain has instructions to wait till you've boarded. Good luck."

They shook hands again. Bedford held the door open.

The boat was a green double-ended ferry with a wide hull and plenty of deck space on which a variety of folding chairs had been put out. It cast off as soon as Mordred lugged his suitcase aboard. Bedford stood on the quay for sixty seconds exactly and waved twice. He couldn't read her expression. He didn't feel attracted to her but, since there was nothing to do once they were out to sea but sit and think, his mind wandered. What would their lives be like if they were married? He'd have to come and live on the Caymans, probably. Did her family live there? Probably. Perkins had spoken approvingly of her local knowledge.

But maybe she was already married. Or wanted to stay single.

What was he thinking? He knew nothing whatsoever about her. She probably hated him. *He didn't even* try *to open the bloody door for me!* He was having a mental discussion with her now, trying to justify himself. *You're just like all the financiers,* she said. *They all expect me to open doors for them too!* In a way, he liked it that she was angry, it made her more human. *I only didn't open any of the doors because I'd have had to run,* he told her. *It would have ended in a competition, and you'd have thought I was making fun of you.* Later on, they'd walk barefoot along the beach together, and maybe call in at a restaurant for a meal. He was utterly devoted to her, even her friends and his potential rivals admitted it. Now she was nine months pregnant with his baby and –

"Do you mind if I take this chair?" a voice from one side said.

He felt himself jump and say 'no, that's fine". He'd fallen asleep briefly – hadn't he? An elderly man in shorts, sandals and long socks, who took the chair and plodded off with it.

The sun rose slowly over the ocean. It was going to be a beautiful day. Thoughts of PC Bedford segued into thoughts of Annabel and the incident in the gents'. He didn't want to think about that, but he was trapped alone with himself now. He didn't know whether he loved her, or whether it was even important to ask that question, or whether his love was actually worth anything given that he could even fall head over heels with a police constable whose only relation to him was that she'd opened a lot of doors, and that only in the literal sense. God, he was a weirdo! Luckily, he was young. Young weirdos were forgivable. It was only when you hit forty that the public censure began in earnest. Hopefully, he'd have changed by then. Become normal. Stopped telling junior colleagues he was a communist.

Being married might help. Maybe ask PC Bedford for a date on the way back.

No, he had to get back for Hannah. Besides, it wasn't professional.

He emptied his mind of everything unpleasant and forced himself to think about the sea and the sky, and to exist wholly in the moment. A great feeling of peace stole over him like a breeze, and he knew he was all right. Nothing bad could ever happen to him. He was part of the great universal language. It spoke to him, and he to it.

Chapter 6: Conversation With Satan

An hour later, a dot appeared on the horizon. It grew to the recognisable outline of a mountain, then loomed larger until it was the only thing in that direction. As usual, arriving seemed to take a lot longer than it should, even after the shore seemed within hailing distance. The first frisson that ran through the passengers slowly dissipated in the apparent eternity.

When they finally disembarked, Mordred felt stiff, hungry and in need of a shower. Luckily, his taxi was waiting. At the end of the wooden jetty stood a 1957 Chevrolet whose driver – a thin man of about thirty in a black T-shirt and shades - held up a 'Jonas Eagleton' sign.

Saint Martha's was very different to the Caymans. The volcano completely dominated the skyline, yet left a long low-lying mantle round its base. There were even, supposedly, some good beaches here, albeit of dark grey rather than white sand. 'Myrrhbearers Point', where everyone went ashore, was a hamlet of bars, restaurants, stores in magnolia colours and boats for hire.

The taxi was about a hundred yards up the jetty. Mordred put his suitcase down, extended its handle and wheeled it, waiting for the right moment to greet the driver. Not that it should be necessary. As far as he could tell, he was the only passenger here under retirement age.

The driver put his notice away, removed his sunglasses and nodded to Mordred. Not in a friendly way, but then this wasn't a pleasure trip. He was here to issue a warning about protesters. Maybe some of the islanders had heard a human storm was on the way, and were feeling grim about it. That was usually how it worked: people just across the horizon listened to the news, got talking, and blew it up out of all proportion. Then just stood there, looking grim.

He was about to offer the customary handshake and introduction when he noticed an old woman sitting against one of the wooden posts either side of the jetty entrance. She had a piece of card in her lap onto which people had tossed coins. She didn't look at Mordred. She was ragged and emaciated, almost stereotypical.

Anyone who travelled a lot got used to this sort of thing. *You can't take the problems of the world on yourself* was so obvious nowadays it didn't even merit a mention in the guidebooks. At best, you'd give her a few coins and move on, telling yourself that if everyone did the same as you she'd eat properly for the rest of her life. Unless she was being pimped as a beggar, or wasn't the genuine article, or… the permutations were infinite. Mordred parked his suitcase and was about to get his wallet when it struck him. *Look around you.*

There wasn't another beggar in sight. And this wasn't that sort of location. He knew from his reading that there was full employment and something like a welfare system on Saint Martha's. Maybe she was the local eccentric. Maybe she was lost.

He'd stopped long enough to make not giving her something awkward. He knelt down and asked her name. She didn't reply.

It would probably be best to take her to the police station, ask about her there. But what counted as such a thing round here? There had been nothing about it in Brian's files. Strange, because where you had tourists and a workforce, you needed laws, and where there were laws, you needed law enforcement and a judiciary.

But then he remembered. *You don't want to get on the wrong side of the owner, otherwise you may not be allowed back.*

Of course. It made sense now. Saint Martha's was a monarchy with Decristoforo as sovereign, judge and jury. To the extent that there was a police force, it was probably a private army. In such setups, difference was usually incomprehensible and outsiders were either despatched or ostracised. Suddenly, he felt very alone. Probably not as much as her, though. Assuming she hadn't passed that point years ago.

"Let me buy you something to eat," he told her. "There's a restaurant across the road."

She raised her head and looked at him blankly. The taxi driver came over, looking amused. He took the suitcase and put it in the boot.

Mordred took her hand. "Where do you live? Do you have relatives on the island? Would you like me to give you a lift home?"

No response. He tried saying the same things again in Spanish, then Portuguese, but her expression didn't change. He obviously had her attention though. She was looking into him somehow, as if she'd lost something and his eyes contained the key to finding it.

Then she pulled out a gun and stood up as deftly as an eighteen year-old. She took a pace backwards to stop him making a lunge.

"Get in the car," she said.

It took him a moment to realise what had happened; how completely he'd been caught off guard. He didn't know whether to put his hands up or not. It was all so surreal he had to suppress a laugh. The taxi driver was holding the door for him. He accepted the gun and Mordred got on the back seat with him.

The old woman got into the driving seat and pulled out quickly into the road.

Best thing in these sorts of situations was always to talk. Calmly. About neutral topics. Show them you were a human being. Sometimes people found it more difficult to kill a human being. If you kept schtum, you were just a bit of meat, and they could imbue you with all sorts of undesirable traits. You were the guy next door who'd once slighted them; you were the unreasonable official; you were their boss. Mute, you were anybody.

"I was actually asked if I wanted to bring a gun with me," he began, hardly knowing what he was saying until he actually heard the words come out of his mouth, "and I told them I didn't want one. I thought everyone here would be friendly. I mean, we are neighbours, Saint Martha's and the Caymans. Yes, okay, you've a whopping great volcano on your island, and we haven't, and I can understand that making you a bit jealous, but actually pulling a revolver on me is an over-reaction. I only came here to help."

The man with the gun smiled. "Look, we know who you are," he said in a Lancashire accent, "so cut the crap. You're John Mordred, British spy, not Jonas Eagleton, Cayman Islands policeman."

How the hell did they find that out? Irrelevant. He had to think quickly. "True, but I still came in peace."

"Oh, sure."

"Do you mind me asking how you discovered my real identity?"

"You're not in much of a position to ask anything, pal."

"There's no harm in my trying," Mordred said. "In any case, you might as *well* tell me. It's not like I'm going to escape or anything."

"No you're bloody well not. We're going to kill you."

"Do you believe in Hell?"

"What?"

"Just a question. I mean, I don't actually myself, but there *might* be such a place, no one really knows. I'm sure Saint Martha accepted it. All I'm saying is, if you kill me, it'll make it much more likely you'll go there. *If* it exists, that is. Your skin peeling off, flames all over the place, red hot pokers on every part of your body, and, dear me, it'll never ever end." He chuckled. "Don't get me wrong, though, it probably doesn't exist. You should be all right. Probably."

"Is there something wrong with you?"

"Before I die, five words. Good luck in the afterlife, I'll be waiting. Sorry, eight. That is, counting 'I'll' as one word, not two as in, 'I will'."

He could see the old woman looking at him in the rear view.

"*You'll* probably be all right," he told her. "You're just the driver. Still adds up to quite a long time in Purgatory, but you'll get out in the end. Mind you, two hundred years *is* a long time, isn't it? Not that I would imagine there's the slightest truth in it. No, death's the end, that's what I think. But I don't know for certain. I don't suppose anyone *can*. I've always erred on the side of caution personally, for that very reason." He chuckled again. "Mind you, who am I to talk? I'm just the local dead guy. "

He grabbed the gun, twisting it into the upholstery. He head-butted the man holding it then punched him twice in the face and head-butted him again, harder this time. Best to use every last ounce height and bulk offered in a situation like this. The old woman started screaming. The car was going all over the road now and braking in jerks. Suddenly, Mordred had the gun. He opened the door and thrust the driver out, then put the barrel to the old woman's head. Highly uncharacteristic behaviour, all of it, but nice to know he still had it in him when the chips were down. She brought the car under control again and slowed down.

"The Sunshine Suite Hotel, please," he said. "And while you're driving, think of the number of years I've just saved you in purgatory."

He caught her eyes in the rear view again. Terror. He felt almost sorry for her now, but then she had just collaborated in a plot to murder him. No time to give in to sentiment.

They arrived at the hotel four minutes later. He ordered her out of the car, and took the keys off her. Then the shock hit him and he lost his temper.

"Aren't you ashamed of yourself?" he said. "I actually tried to help you back there. I offered you a meal at a restaurant or a lift home!" He sounded ridiculous, even to himself, but he couldn't stop. "When people like you do things like that, it makes people like me more wary. Sooner or later we'll all end up in a world where no one ever helps anyone. Is that what you want?"

God, he was actually shouting. He sounded like Mr Suburbia, chairman of the neighbourhood watch. To complete the idiocy, he should really repeat it in Spanish and Portuguese. He rolled his eyes and almost laughed at himself.

"And yes, I may be a spy," he said, "but that doesn't mean I deserve to die. I can still be a nice guy, someone who tries to help old ladies down on their luck!"

She began to cry, probably because she was scared. Maybe she thought he was yelling as a prelude to shooting her. Maybe it was her version of trying to look human. A few people had stopped to look at them from afar.

Time to get a grip. Best keep the gun. Looked like Brian might be right about that, after all. He got in the car, slammed the door and drove off.

He had no idea where he was going. Okay, so he was a known quantity. Probably the best thing to do now was get off the island. Slow down, too.

He tried ringing police HQ in George Town, but there was no signal. There had to have been one sometime, otherwise Brian wouldn't have told him he had a direct line. He'd also said that if they hadn't heard from him in twenty-four hours, they'd know something was wrong. And that it wasn't in Decristoforo's interests to harm him.

Some hope.

What if this whole thing was a setup, with Brian behind it? He remembered the odd feeling he'd had in Thames House that maybe someone in the building was trying to get rid of him.

No, it couldn't be that.

Could it?

If so, it was probably best to put it out of his mind. That way madness lay. Moles coming at you from all directions, waving their trowels and leaving little mud hills in your back garden.

Likely, he wasn't welcome because the owner didn't want him here. Decristoforo did run the island, by all accounts. Something like an abduction and a murder probably couldn't happen without his authorisation. And he had – supposedly - been informed in advance of Mordred's arrival.

It all added up, which meant there was no chance of taking the next boat out. That possibility would already have been foreclosed.

Hey-ho. Attack was the best form of defence, so attack he must. He took the nearest road up the mountain and when he reached the expected dead-end, pulled off into the undergrowth. Might as well leave his suitcase where it was. He wouldn't be needing it anytime soon and as things were, carrying it was impossible. He tore five leafy branches from the surrounding trees, combined them with two armfuls of dead foliage, and concealed the car. Maybe he could come back for everything later, but if not, so be it.

He took one of the maps of Saint Martha's Rock from the inside pocket of his jacket. With almost half the landmass spread out in a spectacular vista beneath him, it was fairly easy to work out where he was.

And where Peter Decristoforo was. Where he needed to go. He knelt down against the car and said The Lord's Prayer and asked God to help his parents cope if he was killed. He wished he'd found something out about Saint Martha before he'd come here, but no use crying over spilt milk. He asked her to protect him anyway. He said thanks for his life so far.

Next up, the gun. Once they discovered where he was, it was unlikely he'd be able to shoot his way out. In which case, attempting to do so seemed pointless. Also, what if he lost his temper, like he had with the old woman? He might end up murdering someone. Even once he got to Decristoforo Mansion, it'd probably come down to either talking his way in or not getting in at all. Decristoforo almost certainly had soldiers to spare. The gift of the gab had saved him once today. He shouldn't despise it. No, he should probably leave the gun in the car, or better still, bury it.

Wait a minute. Who was he kidding? The truth was, it was the same old handicap. Cowardice, maybe, or some sort of idealistic sickness – he'd never found the correct name for it. Suddenly, he could see Saint Martha and Satan, just in front of him.

"The trouble is," Satan said, "he's got this saint-complex. Put it like this: if his parents were here, they'd say 'take the gun'; his sisters, ditto; Brian, Alec, his other colleagues, Ruby Parker, ditto. I could go on. But no: he's got to be a saint."

"The rewards are so great, though," Saint Martha said.

"For who? Not for his parents. They'll be devastated."

"How many years has this planet been around? They'll be distraught for, like, fifteen, twenty years. That's nothing. Anyway, they know as well as he does that it's better to suffer wrong than do wrong."

Satan shrugged. "It's not like he's never killed anyone before. He has. Which makes him a hypocrite in my books."

"There's a difference between killing someone you know will go on to kill others and just killing someone because he or she happens to be threatening you."

"He doesn't even know there *is* an afterlife. What's he doing it for? Because *he can't do any other*, that's the truth. He's the victim of your ideology."

"Not all 'ideologies' are false."

"Is yours?"

She smiled. "I don't know. He doesn't think so."

They dissolved. Bloody hell, another consideration: who knew what wild animals were lurking out there? Rich people liked large and varied menageries, that was common knowledge. Lion, tigers, cheetahs, bears, whatever Decristoforo thought would amuse his guests and deter trespassers. There could be anything.

If he met a Grisly in the woods, however, he wouldn't necessarily have to kill it. Firing in the air would make it retreat. The flip side was he'd give his position away. Providing he kept moving, that needn't be a problem. The key was to make a bee-line for the boss. No detours.

He hadn't actually seen the gun used yet – even during the struggle, it hadn't gone off - which raised the question, how many wild animals could he meet before he ran out of bullets? He needed to ration them. He pulled some of the branches away from the car and retrieved the gun from the front seat.

As soon as he picked it up he knew something was wrong. Very wrong. Or maybe right … He suddenly felt light-headed enough not to know which.

This wasn't a real gun. It was a replica.

Which meant … what? That the taxi driver had brought the wrong revolver along?

That didn't seem very likely.

More probably, they'd only meant to scare him. But then, why not scare him with a real gun?

One thing was sure: the moment he met a lion now, he was a goner.

Hang on, he'd just asked Saint Martha for her help, and now this! Okay, the sun was getting to him. He sat down on the driver's seat with his feet on the forest floor, and tried to weigh up the implications.

There was nothing else for it. He had to get this car out of the forest and back on the road as soon as possible. He had a room with an *en suite* waiting for him at the Sunshine Suite Hotel.

His mind stopped reeling and the truth dawned like an epiphany. *Lord, if I must die, let it be no more than fifteen minutes after I've been in the shower.*

Chapter 7: Your Satisfaction is Our Credit

It took him five minutes to retrieve the car from the foliage. It wasn't bad-looking at all, and not obviously a taxi, but of course it was a '57 Chevy and therefore recognisable - even here, where a lot of the cars seemed to be vintage. He drove slowly back to the hotel and found a space in the car-park. He guessed there would be people waiting for him somewhere inside, but he preferred not to think about that right now. One step at a time and anticipate the next half-hour, no more.

The hotel was cuboid modernist – as high and long as it was deep, and only six floors high – whose balconies all had wavy wrought-iron railings, but which was otherwise pure concrete. In its defence, it looked clean. It was surrounded by freshly cut lawns with sprinklers and tall, well-spaced palm trees. A broad pavement surrounded it, converging on the entrance path. Mordred took his suitcase into a carpeted reception area with a long white counter manned by two women in what looked like red airline hostess uniforms.

"Detective Inspector Jonas Eagleton," he said in a voice cynical enough to suggest he didn't care who knew it wasn't true. He presented his papers.

The receptionist looked at them for a moment, then got on the phone and turned her back to him in a single gesture. All he heard her say was his name. She didn't speak at all after that.

When she turned back to him, she was all smiles. Or rather, all teeth. There was nothing really friendly in her manner. But then, that was one of the privileges of her job.

"Pedro will be along in a moment," she said. "He'll take your bag and show you to your room."

Mordred sat down. Time passed. Pedro arrived after ten minutes, a short middle-aged black man in a bell-boy uniform. "Please follow me, sir," he said.

"Where have you been?" Mordred asked.

"Sorry, I was delayed."

"What were you doing?"

"I, er … can't say. One of the guests had an accident. Not the fault of the hotel, but we at the Sunshine Suite love to make your stay as enjoyable as possible. Nothing's too much or too little. Anything you want, we'll get it. Your satisfaction is our credit."

Mordred nodded. "Okay, then."

The receptionist gave Pedro a key and a room number. As per the manual, the first thing Mordred had to do was ask for a change of room. Save doing a sweep for listening devices.

They ascended four floors in the lift. Pedro wheeled the suitcase along a long corridor and opened the door onto a big carpeted room with a double bed, lots of space and a landscape window overlooking the sea.

"I don't like it," Mordred said. "I want to change."

Pedro did a double-take. "What? The room?"

"That's right. It's unsuitable. I want another."

"I'm just the concierge, sir. I can't authorise such things."

"Well, get me the manager then."

Pedro's eyes swept about like they were trying to escape. "I'm not sure - "

"Remember: anything you want, we'll get it."

"I fully accept that, sir, but - "

"Your satisfaction is our credit. You said."

"I think we may be full up."

"I checked the vacancies while the receptionist was on the phone. You're not."

It clearly didn't take much to get in Pedro's bad books. "I'll have to get the manager then, sir," he said in a 'die, punk, die' voice. "Just wait here."

Mordred took his suitcase inside and sat down on the bed. He had the feeling of a camera focussed on him, so he remained motionless.

Twenty minutes later – they'd obviously decided to wage a campaign of attrition, but only in so far as it didn't affect his satisfaction being their credit – Pedro returned alongside a stout man of about fifty with a bald head, a beige suit, and a built-up shoe. "I'm David, your manager," he said. He held an unexplained sealed envelope. Mordred could already tell from his body-language that he wanted to hand it over, but didn't quite know how. Maybe an anonymous death-threat, left at reception? "What can I do for you, sir?"

"I'd like another room."

"What's wrong with this one, if you don't mind me asking?"

"I don't like the view. I get seasick."

The manager laughed. "Anything you want then, sir. Anything at all! Have you any preferences?"

"I'd like a room on the top floor on the opposite side."

"We've four available. Would you like to choose one?"

"Thank you, yes."

He'd seen this sort of thing before. You immediately demanded a change of room; they were murderously annoyed, because they'd spent so long planting devices, but it was obvious you were suspicious, and the best way of allaying that was to appear super-cooperative. The last thing they wanted was for you to leave the premises. It usually took them about twenty minutes to overcome their frustration, hence the long wait. They'd smile and apologise and occasionally, bow – he'd actually had that once. Then they'd look for another way to get you.

Or maybe he was just paranoid.

The manager gave Pedro a master-key and instructed him to take the detective inspector to the top floor and show him everything available. Then he shook hands with Mordred. "Anything you want, we'll get it," he said. "Your satisfaction is our credit."

"Where's the nearest supermarket?" Mordred asked.

"Just round the corner. You'll find a map of the local area in every magazine rack. Failing that, I'll call you a taxi and have the driver show you."

"Great."

"I've, er … got a letter for you. At least, I assume that's what it is."

"Already? I've only just arrived. Who knows I'm here?"

The manager looked frightened. "It was handed in by a man at reception, a few moments ago. He didn't stay, or give his name."

"Did you recognise him? This is a small island."

"I've … seen him. Maybe best read the letter, sir. I was told to give you an oral message in person, but only after you've read the … whatever it is."

"Don't move."

He tore it open. It was an invitation on a single piece of gilt-edged card. 'Fenella Decristofo-Salvaterra requests the company of Mr John Mordred for dinner this evening at eight.'

"So what's your part of the message?" he asked the manager.

"'A car will arrive at 7.30 to pick you up' and, er, 'you may now use your phone'."

Okay, so things were looking up. He'd planned to eat out of the supermarket – who knew if the hotel would drug his food? – but this put a different spin on things. There was no RSVP included: she obviously took it for granted that he would comply. But then, that was why he was here.

On the other hand, it was addressed to John Mordred, not DI Eagleton, so not everything was according to the play script.

But then that's why he'd decided to become a spy rather than go to RADA, spend three years in repertory and join the Royal Shakespeare Company. He didn't like play scripts.

He wondered if she knew he was a vegetarian.

Lunch was a nut cutlet with new potatoes and green beans. Afterwards, he went out for a walk. He noticed the Chevy had gone from the car park.

The town was a short bus ride away, and consisted entirely of a beachfront of shops and food and drink outlets each separated by several hundred yards of scrubland with defunct fishing boats or skeletons of cars. Outside a café, two men played a card game that, as far as Mordred knew was only popular in Thailand. One of them announced an intention to Ziggedy, added 'north', and then folded with a look of manic exasperation. The bars were mostly empty. The supermarkets – there were two, half a mile apart – stocked mainly household cleaning products, frozen foods and locally-made spirits at colossal prices.

He thought he'd better take a present round this evening: bunch of flowers, box of chocolates or bottle of wine. But there weren't any of those in either shop. In the second – 'Big Shop Experience' - he decided to ask some advice. The woman at the till was about his age, thin, with long curly hair and wearing an apron. She sat on a revolving chair reading a copy of *Veintitantos*, oblivious to the possibility anyone might be shoplifting.

"I want to buy a present for a young lady," he said in Spanish. "Could you recommend anything?"

She looked up. "What sort of a young lady?"

"Quite a rich one."

"What about jewellery? We haven't any here, but I know someone who makes it."

"It may be a bit early in the relationship for that. I've never met her before."

"Is she your girlfriend?"

"No. More like a business associate."

She furrowed her brow. "I don't think we've really got anything suitable. It's mainly hardware and cleaning supplies for the locals and drink for the tourists."

"Is there any particular drink you think would appeal?"

"No, most of it's get-wasted stuff."

"I see."

"How about a shrub?" she said. "Or a parrot? There's a shop a bit further on called 'Exciting Trees and Exotic Birds'."

"I can't really give her a parrot. It's too much of a responsibility."

"It's not like that. You buy the bird, then you and your associate let it go together. It's quite nice, but I suppose if she's a businesswoman, she might see that as a bit like jewellery. You know, too overfriendly. It's not a bad gig for the parrot, though. The owner's trained them all to come back to him. Shit, don't tell anyone I said that. He treats them well, honestly. Lots of nuts."

"A shrub might work, if it's small."

"*I* know what you might get!" she said, making him jump. "Something from the gift shop! *I completely forgot about the gift shop!*"

The gift shop was a small church-like building made out of granite. It sold paraphernalia relating to Saint Martha. She was the patron saint of servants and cooks, so there were two recipe books and three devotional manuals on the theme of service. You could buy Saint Martha medallions and pendants and plastic figurines. Then there were pictures of Saint Martha appearing in visions to the earliest colonists, including one of the miracle in which, by calling on the saint's name, Anselmo de Poveda de la Sierra (1501-1566) had diverted a river of molten lava and saved the island's earliest settlement. Not really the kinds of things to present to the hostess of a dinner date, any of them.

Maybe he should ask the manager of the Sunshine Suite: David, that's right. He would probably know. The correct question would be, *do you think you could procure me a bottle of wine, a box of chocolates or a bunch of flowers for this evening.* Be specific, don't leave it open, otherwise you might end up arriving at the Decristoforos' with a homing-parrot and *The Collected Encyclicals of John Paul II.*

The car arrived at 7.30 sharp. Mordred wore his evening suit, which he'd packed at the last minute for just such an occasion, and David had found a bunch of roses at short notice – God knows how.

He was picked up by the Chevy and by the driver he'd headbutted and thrown from the car. His face was badly bruised and he had a black eye. "Sorry for what I did," was his opening remark. "The name's Rory, by the way."

"I didn't realise it wasn't a real gun," Mordred said.

"You weren't meant to."

The exchanged handshakes. "Apology accepted," Mordred said. "Are you okay to drive with that eye? It looks pretty bad. I could take the wheel if you like."

The driver laughed. "Leave me some pride."

Mordred got into the front seat so they could converse. "What was the idea?"

"Ms DS. She found out you were a spy and she didn't like it. She likes people to be who they say they are. Can't blame her for that."

"Fair enough. Just because I'm a spy, though, it doesn't mean I'm coming to spy on her or anyone on this island. It's just, people open up a little bit more if they think you're local. If you tell them you've come from the other side of the world, they're suspicious."

"Hey, save that for her. Where did you get the flowers from?"

"The hotel manager got them for me," Mordred replied.

"David?"

"I believe that's his name."

The driver hooted. "And where do you think David got them?"

"I've no idea. I looked in both supermarkets - "

"Ms D's greenhouse, that's where."

"Bloody hell. Do you think she knows?"

"Should think so. She might be surprised to see them again. My guess is, you asked David for some flowers, David's been given instructions to keep you happy."

"Anything you want," Mordred said, "we'll get it."

"Your satisfaction is our credit. David daren't tell you no. So he rings Fenella's place. They get the message: you like flowers. They don't ask why; they just cut you some. And now you're going to return them to point of origin."

"Do you think she'll recognise them?"

"She's the only person on this island who grows them."

Mordred let out a long breath. "Okay, I'm in trouble. I need you to do something now."

"Your satisfaction is my credit."

"I believe there's a shop in town called 'Exciting Trees and Exotic Birds'. I need to call in."

"We've got time. If you're quick."

Chapter 8: Wishing on Kiki

Decristoforo Mansion – it didn't have any other name that he could see – was like a castle out of an Edgar Allan Poe story, completely at odds with its tropical setting. Huge and almost black with sloping roofs at odd angles to each other, it had three high towers topped with spires that seemed to sit on them like witches' hats. The steep road up to it was lined with firs. The door was twice the size of a man. Standing in the porch you got a view of the whole of this side of the island, but at such an altitude that almost all you could see was the ocean in which the landmass sat. You seemed to be much, much closer to the sun up here.

Mordred got out of the car, clutching the bunch of roses in one hand and holding a caged parrot in the other. Rory knocked.

The old woman answered the door – the same one who'd driven the car. "I'm very sorry for deceiving you," she said emotionally. "You were kind and I abused that. You were quite right to chastise me."

"Sorry I lost my temper."

"Come through."

Fenella was waiting to greet him. She wore a plain black dress with long sleeves and matching heels. Her hair was dark; her face was well-defined, lean and severe. She was about Mordred's age, but gave off a consuming gravitas that made her seem at least a decade older. Suddenly, a bunch of roses and a parrot seemed wholly inappropriate.

She smiled and came over. "My roses."

"I realised they were yours after I bought them. There didn't seem to be any wine on the island or chocolates and when I realised the flowers were a failure – 'failure' because they're already yours, not because they're not attractive – I went into 'Exciting Trees and Exotic Birds'."

She eyed the parrot through the cage bars. "That's Kiki, isn't it?"

"I don't know. As far as the owner's concerned, I'm a tourist, so he's got an unlimited supply of birds specially imported from the Amazon whose release he's promoting to encourage biodiversity."

"Whereas the reality is, he's got exactly three." She took the cage and examined the bird's markings. "This is Kiki, definitely."

"Will she be getting anxious?"

"She's a cool customer. We'll release her in a moment." She led him through into a much larger room, very Victorian with dark furniture, expensive wallpaper and huge portraits of 19th century men looking miserable. "I'm Fenella Decristoforo-Salvaterra. I understand you're John Mordred, British spy."

"I tried to explain to Rory on the way over that I didn't come here with any hostile intent."

"When I heard about you, I thought you must be on your way to kill Peter. That's partly why I sent a scare-squad."

"Why would you think that?"

"Because of the secrecy, and because he's the only person on the island in which MI6 could conceivably have an interest."

"Unfortunately, in my job, wherever you go, you've got to pretend you're someone else. You can't enter a location on the understanding that you've no harmful intentions so it's okay to let everyone know what you actually do for a living."

"In any case, you were nice to Maria. Even before you knew who she was. That impressed me a lot. I realised then you probably weren't a killer. You could and would have killed her if you'd been our enemy. To stop her reporting back."

"Okay, well, now we know I'm not the Terminator, let's call it quits."

"Agreed. Dinner will be ready in about ten minutes. Sit down, and tell me what you want. Although I think I can guess."

"Is your grandfather-in-law available? This concerns him too."

"He's in England. At least, that's what he told me. He doesn't share everything with me. We're not blood relatives, but we're each the nearest to family the other now has. That makes us very close. We're not lovers, before you ask. That would be wrong, and distasteful. I know women my age sometimes go for men his age, especially when they have money and there might be a big inheritance in the offing, but it's not that. I love – *loved* – my husband. Peter's son, Arnold. So did he. We're both looking forward to seeing him again in the afterlife. That gives us a stronger bond than you might imagine."

"I understand."

"My own side of the family's cursed, Mr Mordred, believe it or not. I won't divulge the details, you'd probably think I had a screw loose. But I have no close blood relatives left, and I was selfish enough to hitch my fate to Arnold's family. I thought they could save me, you see, and I was in love with him. In fact, I doomed them. Sorry, I'm rambling." She pressed her fingertips to her temples. "What was it you wanted to ask?"

"You said you could guess. That's not me playing games. I'm interested to see if you're right."

She smiled. "Admit that the waters around you have grown and accept it that soon you'll be drenched to the bone. I'm talking – we both are – about World War O."

"You've even heard the phrase here."

"We do have one of the world's greatest computer scientists on the island. Most of the time, not right now. That means we know more about the world than some governments. You haven't asked me yet how I knew you were a spy."

"I prefer conversing with people to interrogating them, even where the latter's a possibility, which it isn't here."

"Why isn't it?" she asked.

"Because as far as I know, you haven't done anything wrong."

"So if the entire evening was to pass without me mentioning it, you wouldn't ask?"

"Asking isn't interrogating," he replied. "You might choose not to tell me, in which case, I'd drop the subject."

"It's your job to find out, surely?"

"Except I already know. As you say, you have one of the world's greatest computer scientists on the island. Most of the time."

She gave a wide smile. "I like you, Mr Mordred. This may sound strange, given that we've only just met, but I already feel I can trust you."

Maria came in to announce that dinner was served. They got up and went across the corridor into a small room with a polished walnut table. There was a fireplace, three armchairs, a picture of Christ showing his heart, and a TV. They sat down facing each other at the table and Maria brought two bowls of tortilla soup.

"I know you're a vegetarian," she said. "I asked the Sunshine Suite to wire me your lunch choices. Only a vegetarian would order their nut cutlet for the first meal of his first day on the island."

"Don't you get lonely here?" he asked. "Excuse me if that's too personal a question."

"Not at all. I used to. I haven't left this house in years, unless you count going into the garden. I love it here."

"It's an unusual design."

"Entirely my own. Peter gave me *carte blanche*, no expenses spared. Probably to keep me from brooding. We used to live in a typical pastel coloured town house fronting the bay. We moved up here after Arnold, Madeleine and Jill died, for grief's sake – we had to get away from the mementoes or go insane. I designed it to be the flat opposite of what we'd left behind. We came specifically here because this is where Peter's laboratory is. Underground"

"I heard."

She raised her eyebrows. "Really? You heard about his laboratory?"

"They told me back at base. They love it. They love anything that reminds them of the big J and B."

She put her head quizzically on one side. "The … whisky?"

"The secret agent."

She laughed. "Oh, I see, yes."

"Sorry, I forgot about your two supermarkets. All those expensive spirits and not a bottle of wine in sight."

"You won't find J&B here, Mr Mordred. We only do moonshine."

"Can I ask you about Peter again?"

"Anything you like."

"I'm here because the British and US intelligence services were caught unawares by so-called World War O. It must have been organised via the internet, but we picked nothing up. The theory is that we were prevented from seeing it by some unknown electronic means. That would require an advance beyond our existing technology. Peter is known for his support for the Tax Justice Network. He's also - "

"You want to know if he's responsible for the black hole in your surveillance."

"Yes."

"I honestly don't know. But it's plausible. And admirable, I think. Bankers, hedge-fund managers, stockbrokers and the like don't contribute anything to society. Parasites are part of nature – any given system can tolerate them up to a point – but when they rule the world, you've got problems. Peter's a goodie, Mr Mordred."

"World War O is probably a passing fad. It'll have blown over in a week or two - "

"I sincerely hope not."

"However, you must be able to appreciate what this kind of technology could do in the wrong hands. Say a country wants to launch a nuclear strike."

"What are you suggesting? That we hand the science over to you?" She laughed. "That would be stupid."

"I'm suggesting you destroy it."

"That would also mean killing the person in whose brain it exists. Otherwise, he might be abducted and menaced into divulging it. Are you sure you didn't come here to murder him?"

"Absolutely not."

"Because his would-be assassin might think he's acting for the sake of global security. That would be perfectly consistent with kindness to old ladies."

He sighed. "Look, I'll be honest with you. If he is behind it, then theoretically perhaps it would be better if he died. What if someone *does* kidnap and torture him?"

"He wouldn't crack. Maybe you should leave, Mr Mordred."

"If I wanted to kill him, all I'd have to do is kidnap you. He might not crack when *he's* being tortured, but you're a different matter. If I really had his death in mind, I'd have killed Rory and Maria and marched you out of here with a gun."

They finished their soup and sat looking at each other for a long time. She seemed to have forgotten her suggestion that he should leave.

"Maybe we should release the parrot now," he said.

"If your plan is to make me fall in love with you, forget it. That's never going to happen. No insult intended."

He could see he was losing her trust quickly. He had to do something. "There were lots of spies you could have been talking to now. I was sent to see you for a specific reason."

She smiled bitterly. "And that reason: it wasn't, by any chance, because you're conventionally good-looking, a bit of a smoothie and about my age?"

"To get me as far away from Jersey as possible."

She looked at him as if he was mad. "Sorry, I don't understand."

"Have you been following World War O?"

"There's very little else on the television at the moment," she replied. "Not that I watch TV a lot, but Peter likes me to keep up to date. How is it relevant?"

"Then I suppose you've heard of Hannah Lexingwood?"

"Jersey's a long way away from here," she said. "I've been following the local protests more closely. The Caymans, Turks and Caicos, the British Virgin Islands, Barbados, Panama. But yes. It's an unusual name, so it stayed with me. Why?"

"Because she's my older sister."

She put her spoon down. "I don't believe you."

He took his phone out - *Christmas photos* – and passed it over.

She scrolled through them. Her mood switched and she laughed. Something in her seemed to relax completely. Maria brought in two plates of sweet potato burritos and set them down on the table. Fenella gave no indication of noticing. She passed the phone back.

"I suppose it must have been a bit of a shock when you turned on the TV and saw her at the front of a ten-thousand strong crowd," she said, "berating Saint Helier financiers. Or did you know in advance?"

"I had no idea."

She started to eat. "What's your view of the matter?"

"I love my sister and I don't necessarily disagree with her politics."

"But?"

"I don't know enough about the subject. When I was in the Caymans the other day, the superintendent of police told me it's all happening too late. He says there are already measures in place to make tax evasion virtually impossible."

"And you fell for that?"

"He's a policeman. He may be mistaken, but I doubt he was trying to deceive me. He'd have nothing to gain."

"That's your criterion of truth, is it? The moral status of the messenger?"

"One of them, yes."

"In any case, not all financial immorality is tax evasion. The world's corporations haven't zeroed in on 102 square miles of otherwise insignificant land in the middle of the Caribbean just because they like being together."

"We're getting off the point. I'm not here to kill Peter or kidnap you. If you want me to leave, I will."

"I don't want you to leave. I'm very sorry I suggested it. I should have trusted my earlier instincts."

"So we're friends again?"

"It may strike you as hypocritical, me railing against 'parasites'. What do *I* do, after all? I'm a kept woman, and not even the kind who dispenses sex, or cooks, or cleans. The truth is, if it hadn't been for Peter, I'd have curled up and died. I'm keeping him alive, that's my purpose, and he does good. When he dies, I probably will."

"I hope not."

"It's not a question of my getting over Arnold's death. As I've already told you, I'm cursed. That makes all the difference."

He remembered Brian's words: *don't get into an argument about it.* "You say you think Peter's in England?" he asked. "I don't want to scare you, but are you sure he's okay?"

"It hadn't occurred to me until now, but no."

"You do realise that I've been sent here to ask about the science of surveillance-blocking. Once I've gone, it's only a matter of time before the military arrives. By 'time', I mean days, possibly even hours. They'll go through Peter's laboratory and take you away for questioning. Somewhere in the world, he'll be apprehended. I'm not sure what will happen to you then. Either of you."

She stopped eating. "This – what you're saying ... This is inevitable, isn't it?"

"I'm not trying to scare you, if that's what you mean."

"I need to talk to Peter and destroy everything of value in his laboratory."

"And then you need to come with me. We need to get you off the island."

"And go where?"

"Wherever Peter is. We can separate once I know you're safe."

"I don't want a life on the run. I don't want to leave this house."

"You've got to."

She stood up and opened the door. "Come on," she said.

He followed her up a wide, winding staircase. They passed two floors and emerged into a dimly lit corridor. They turned right, and she opened a pair of French windows. Suddenly, they were on a balcony, overlooking the island. In the distance, the sun had just gone down, leaving a smear of orange beneath the purple. The sky sparkled with stars. Beneath them, only darkness. On a table to one side stood a caged parrot. She opened its door, coaxed it onto her finger and brought it out.

"We can't let her go now," Mordred said. "She probably can't navigate in the dark."

Fenella smiled. "She's well trained, and she's got good night vision. She'll find a branch somewhere and wait till morning." She took Mordred's hand. "Make a wish."

"Right now, I wish you'd come with me."

"A secret wish."

She kissed the bird and let it go. They watched it for a while before it disappeared into the darkness.

She turned to him, suddenly practical. "I'd like you to leave now, Mr Mordred. I have lots to do."

Her voice cracked on the last sentence, but he could already see there was no point in arguing with her. She'd made up her mind. Even he could appreciate she didn't have many options, and those she did have were all unpleasant.

"Thank you for a lovely evening," he said. It sounded woeful, but he couldn't think of anything beyond the conventional.

She waked to the edge of the balcony as if he'd already gone. Rory arrived and escorted him downstairs and to the car. Mordred got onto the back seat this time; he no more felt like speaking than the other man apparently did. But in Rory's case, it was probably mere tiredness.

As they drove along the fir-lined road away from the house, Mordred wound down the window, He half-expected to hear the crack of a gun. That was obviously what she'd been thinking.

But it never came. On the highest turret of the house, he could just make out a multi-coloured pirate flag, waving in the breeze. Overhead, he heard the low rumble of a troop-carrying plane.

Chapter 9: The 'Other' Bob Wellington

He stayed overnight in the Sunshine Suite, hoping she might change her mind. But when the Caymans ferry arrived the following morning, and he'd still heard nothing, he decided he had to leave. He disembarked at Heathrow at midnight and took a taxi first to Thames House to file his report, then home to sleep. The following morning, he returned to work feeling shattered and hardly knowing what to expect.

"Ruby Parker's upstairs with the Lord Mayor of London," Colin Bale told him at reception. "B14. She wants you to report straight there."

He'd been hoping for a few moments alone with his colleagues, but he'd listened to the radio as he got ready for work and read a newspaper on his way in, so he guessed he was about as prepared as he'd ever be. Bob Wellington was known to be a colourful figure, given to publicity stunts. Mordred hadn't voted for him, but he didn't dislike him in principle. Maybe he'd make for a fun meeting, but it seemed unlikely. However congenial a politician seemed in the media, when he or she came to Thames House it was always to administer a bollocking.

When he walked into B14, however, there was no Bob Wellington. Instead, Ruby Parker sat at the head of the table with a small, bald, choleric looking man of about sixty with an invisible neck, and his hands folded in front of him. Also present were Phyllis, Edna, Alec, Young Ian and, sitting slightly apart, a middle-aged woman with a pencil and notepad, possibly the minute-taker, although they didn't usually have one. None of them looked happy. None of them acknowledged Mordred's entry. He sat down.

Ruby Parker stood up languidly. "Now that we're all here," she said, "This is Sir Ashley Cavendish, the Lord Mayor of London. He's here to observe our meeting. Karen" – she indicated the woman with the notepad – "is here to take the minutes."

There was something she wasn't telling them. Her body language was all wrong. What was going on?

"Why does Sir Ashley want to observe our meeting?" Mordred asked.

"What do you mean?" she replied. She didn't sound overly surprised or annoyed by the interruption, which was equally odd.

"Can I talk directly to him?" he asked.

"No," she said.

Triply odd. "What's he hoping to learn?"

"I have to admit," she said, "it wasn't my idea, and – with respect, sir, but you already know this - I'm not in favour of it, but it turns out I have no choice. Although Thames House lies outside the boundaries of the City of London, *within* those boundaries this gentleman has almost absolute authority, and we need his full cooperation if we're to make progress with our investigation."

No one spoke. The Lord Mayor remained as unresponsive as a frog in the shade. Nothing so far seemed to have made the slightest impression on him. Apart from the fact that his eyes were open and he sat upright, he displayed every visible sign of being dead.

"Let's begin," she said. "John, I've read your report. Things have moved on since your return. I'm obliged to ask you a number of questions."

"Sounds grim. Am I under suspicion of anything?"

She ignored him. "Last night, a landing party from the HMS Bridlington, including representatives from the Caymans Police Force, assumed provisional control of Saint Martha's Rock. We've managed to confirm that Peter Decristoforo arrived at Heathrow three days ago, but we still don't know his whereabouts. Do you know where his adopted daughter is?"

"Not unless she's at home in the Caribbean."

"She isn't," the Lord Mayor said, suddenly coming alive. "And she's destroyed a lot of what we were looking for. So here's my theory, boy. You told her who you were, what you were after, and what she'd have to do to escape. You went there to seduce her, and she ended up turning the tables. You're a gullible idiot."

"Well, what a lovely theory," Mordred replied.

"Is it true, John?" Ruby Parker asked quietly. "For the minutes."

"She's a beautiful woman," the Lord Mayor said. "You don't get the opportunity to sleep with her sort every day."

"Let him answer the question, Sir Ashley. And may I remind you you're here solely to observe."

"Before I left," Mordred said, "Brian jokingly mooted the idea of sex for statements. I told him that wasn't on the cards. Even if I was temperamentally disposed to one-night stands, which I'm not, it's a very ineffective way of gaining information. So no, it isn't true. And of course, check my file. I'm actually forbidden to employ sex as a means of acquiring intelligence."

"Why?" the Lord Mayor said, apparently genuinely interested. "Isn't that one of the main perks?"

"When I entered MI7, I was given a psychological evaluation. The results showed I wouldn't be very good at it."

"What? Sex?"

"Using sex as a means to an end."

"Because you'd get emotionally involved, I assume," the Lord Mayor said.

Mordred paused long enough to make his annoyance clear. "Yes. Besides, she's in mourning. According to what she told me, she has no intention of sleeping with anyone again. So even if I'd - "

"So what did she invite you up to her house for?" the Lord Mayor persisted.

"Dinner."

"*Sex*. You had *sex*. Admit it! Long, glorious *fornication*, and - "

Phyllis ejected a laugh.

Everyone turned to look at her. She opened her mouth to apologise, but obviously couldn't. She waved her hand before her face.

The Lord Mayor had stood up. *"What the hell's so funny about that, woman? This is serious!"*

"Enough," Ruby Parker said. "Karen, let the minutes record that at thirteen minutes exactly, I instructed Sir Ashley Cavendish to leave the meeting."

The Lord Mayor didn't argue. He pulled his shirt cuffs down. "I don't think I need stay any longer. I suspected you were pathetic, but I needed to confirm it in person. You're doing *nothing*. The bloody Remembrancer's disappeared, and what are these 'Occupy' goons asking for? That the 'post of Remembrancer be abolished'."

"Amongst other things," Phyllis said.

He laughed incredulously. "And you can't see the *connection?* This needs to end now. The City of London is the last thing this *crummy country's* got going for it, and if you think *I'm* going to be the Lord Mayor who presides over its dissolution into 'Greater' London, you've another think coming! Let me tell you something, 'Ruby Parker' – assuming that's even your real name: yesterday the City of London Corporation acquired two private security firms: your old enemy Horvath, and your old friend Chewton Black. From now on, we'll do things our own way, in our own time. Which means, *double-quick!*"

He tried to slam the door as he left, but it had a slide-track arm which took a full four seconds to run down. Everyone listened to his footsteps recede along the corridor. They watched the door until it closed with a loud clunk. Then they let out loud sighs of relief.

"Where the hell's Bob bloody Wellington?" Alec asked.

Ruby Parker sighed. "Bob Wellington's the Mayor of London, Alec. Sir Ashley Cavendish is the lord Mayor of the *City* of London. They have virtually nothing to do with each other."

"By 'City of London'," Alec said, "you mean, the Square Mile? I thought that was just an abstraction, like old town-new town."

"I'm afraid it's anything but."

"So how many people live there? In this one measly square mile?"

"About nine thousand."

Alec hooted. "As against – what? – nearly two million in Greater London? What's its point?"

"It's slightly more complex than that."

"Really? I don't see how it can be."

"The votes in a City mayoral election – just shy of thirty thousand – mostly come from big corporations, many not even British. Goldman Sachs, Moscow Narodny Bank, the Bank of China, and so on. It's not even as democratic as my use of the words 'nine' and 'thousand' may have led you to suppose."

"I see," Alec replied, apparently chastened. "Sorry, I thought you were going to defend the indefensible."

"No wonder he's running scared," Mordred said. "That's not something you'd want to publicise. 'The capital city of your country's being run by powerful overseas interests'. No wonder the economy's up the spout."

"Factor in the City's notoriously lax regulation," Ruby Parker said, "and you'll understand why some people think it's the greatest recipe for global corruption ever invented. And why the protesters want it abolished. I can't say I don't sympathise. Especially after what we've just witnessed."

"He seemed like a man who likes to get things done," Phyllis commented.

Ruby Parker took a deep breath. "Had the Home Secretary not insisted, I'd never have allowed him in, but you'd be surprised who the Lord Mayor of London City has in his pocket. Be careful. He's a dangerous man to have as an enemy."

Phyllis smiled. "With respect, I think that ship's already sailed. Sorry I laughed, by the way. It was as much John's fault as his."

"*Mine?*" Mordred said.

"Your face," she replied. "You long, glorious fornicator, you." She laughed and again, couldn't control it. "Sorry, sorry. Just give me a few seconds."

"Are you getting this down?" Alec asked Karen. She ignored him.

"Shall we get back to business?" Ruby Parker asked.

"I've no idea where Fenella Decristoforo-Salvaterra is," Mordred said. "The last time I saw her, she was at home. When I arrived on the island, there was no mobile signal, and the taxi driver threatened me with a gun, which I later discovered to be a replica. All of which was her doing. She knew who I was because her father had told her. I don't know how he found out, except for the obvious fact that that it was something to do with computers."

"What about the supposed surveillance blind spot that allowed the protesters to organise?" Alec asked. "Did she say anything about that?"

"That she wouldn't be surprised if Peter was behind it, but she wasn't sure. She made no secret of their shared sympathy for the demonstrators."

"If you'd thought to keep an eye on her, John," Phyllis said, "she might have led us to her father."

"I followed my brief," Mordred said.

"Sometimes, you're expected to go off-brief," Alec chimed in. "That's the nature of the job."

"Given that she knew I was a spy, don't you think she'd have tried to lose me? She wouldn't have found it difficult. She's probably familiar with the entire Caribbean coastline. I'm not. Had I tried to follow her, I'd have forfeited her trust."

"Whereas this way," Phyllis said, "you've simply forfeited her, period."

"Better just one than both," he replied. "Anyway, she's got the entire US and UK law enforcement and security agencies looking for her. I'm sure she won't get far. When they do eventually pick her up, they'll need someone to talk to her."

"And that'll be you, will it?" Alec said. "With respect, John, you're dreaming. What we're all after is her father's technology. If she is caught, she's bait, that's all. We won't need anyone to join her for a cream tea and a tête-à-tête."

"Well, I'm pleased not to be a part of that," Mordred said.

Alec chuckled. "Oh, for the luxury of an unsullied conscience."

"Item two on the agenda," Ruby Parker said, "Alec, perhaps you'd like to tell us how much progress you've made tracking down Norman Pruett, the Remembrancer."

"We've got virtually nowhere," he replied. "We've spoken to his former wife, Jean, in Northampton. She doesn't know where he is, hasn't seen him in years. Two children, both living in Australia, not seen him since secondary school. We spent a day searching his flat, nothing. We need higher level clearance. We need to start speaking to some of the people who knew him at work: either members of the City of London Corporation, or some MPs."

"Would we need the Mayor's permission for the former?" Edna asked.

"It would be polite to ask him," Ruby Parker replied, "but luckily, it's not strictly necessary. Given his announcement a moment ago, he's probably instructed his colleagues not to talk to anyone, especially us."

"We may be able to steal a march on that particular instruction," Ian said.

"What do you mean?" Phyllis asked.

"Up till a moment ago," Ian went on, "we had instructions from the Lord Mayor to find out what happened to Norman Pruett, and not involve the police. Since hardly anyone in this country knows who the Remembrancer is, or that he exists, that would mean he must have expected us to speak to Pruett's colleagues in the City of London Corporation. If that's true, he probably told them to cooperate with us. He may have changed his mind a moment ago, but it takes time to countermand an order. My guess is that if we act quickly, we may be able to sneak a deal of information out from under his nose."

"The only problem with that," Edna said, "is there's a reason we haven't spoken to his colleagues that goes beyond clearance."

"Oh?" Ruby Parker said.

"He has no family and no friends that we can discover," Edna said. "Therefore his disappearance could well be something to do with work. If that's true, in an organisation as secretive as this, it may well be that his work colleagues have collaborated to peddle us a story. They may be waiting for us to come and speak to them. Of course, that doesn't mean we shouldn't, it just explains why we put it on the back burner."

"It's a pretty bold working assumption," Ruby Parker said, "and, as far as I know, completely unfounded. If you're not careful, it could warp the entire investigation."

"Sorry, Edna's right," Alec said. "The Lord Mayor instigated this inquiry. He reported the Remembrancer missing and he stipulated: no police. He must have known that Pruett's family would be a dead-end, but he didn't see fit to inform us. He must have known we'd be forced to fall back on his and Pruett's City colleagues, but he didn't explicitly offer them up. I don't think it's wholly unreasonable to imagine there's something he hopes we won't discover, and that he's primed his Corporation buddies as far as is consistent with their need to know, but that, from his point of view, that may not be enough, and he's therefore not wholly confident we won't discover the truth."

"Which puts a whole new spin on his behaviour today," Phyllis said. "Arguably – I'm just saying arguably - he doesn't even want us to talk to his colleagues, and he was looking for a pretext to exclude us. Exclude everybody. He can't completely hide Pruett's disappearance, so he wants the fact that he reported it to the appropriate authorities recorded somewhere, as a kind of insurance. Then he wants it forgotten."

"Why don't we get Pruett's wife or children to report his disappearance to the police?" Mordred asked.

"It wouldn't do any good," Ruby Parker said. "The police would fill in a missing persons report and the Home Secretary would tell them hands off, it's a security service matter. That's as far as it would get. Because, apart from anything else, there's no reason to suspect foul play ... yet, at least."

"More interesting then," Ian said, "would be to discover whether the Lord Mayor *does* actually prevent us gaining access to his colleagues. Depending on how hard he's worked to lead the investigation astray, he may be reluctant to close the door in our faces, regardless of what he said a few moments ago."

"You're saying he might actually *encourage* us to investigate," Phyllis said. "Despite his outburst?"

"If our suspicions are correct, yes," Ian said. "If he's somehow implicated, he may not know his own mind. Typically, guilty suspects tend to alternate between different and conflicting strategies for diverting attention."

"Maybe we should try and get in early anyway," Alec said. "Cover all bases."

"You'd better get moving," Ruby Parker said. "Karen, you can stop now. Close the minutes at the point where I expelled the Lord Mayor and provide me with an extra copy of the published version FAO Her Majesty's Principal Secretary of State for the Home Department. John, you stay here."

Everyone except Mordred and Ruby Parker got up and left.

Chapter 10: Er, Deceived By an Egg?

The door took forever to shut again, and Mordred folded his hands in front of him. He knew what Ruby Parker was going to say. *Find Peter Decristoforo.* And he knew what he was going to reply: four people to locate the Remembrancer against one for the Inventor wasn't a rational allocation of manpower.

She sat down. He liked the way she sometimes seemed to relax a little in his presence. One day, she'd say something unguarded and he'd suddenly find out everything there was to know about her from cradle to grave. But probably not today.

"I won't beat about the bush, John," she said. "This is getting serious. In itself, it may not seem like more than a big prank, but people are getting hurt and there were ten fatalities last night alone. This is how terrorist movements sometimes start: heavy-handedness by the authorities gives rise to a perceived sense of gross injustice plus cynicism about peaceful democratic means. It's a potent brew."

"Meanwhile, no one feels threatened by an egg. They don't think about it hatching."

"We need to do something to defuse the situation now. London's one thing. Our powers are limited here for reasons to do with Sir Ashley Cavendish. The good thing is, he wants to preserve the Corporation from too-close public scrutiny, and the best way of doing that is simply to wait things out. Violence is the last thing he needs. Jersey's another matter. If people get killed there – and they might - it'll be a completely different kettle of fish."

"You're sending me to Jersey? What about finding Peter Decristoforo?"

"It must have occurred to you that that's where he might be. Hiding in plain sight, as the expression goes."

"But that's not the only reason I'm going, right?"

"One major way in which all this might escalate is that other people try to get involved. And I'm afraid it's a process that's already happening."

"What do you mean, 'other people'?"

"You've probably heard that there's been some violence in Zurich and Luxembourg. What you may *not* have heard, because the authorities have been trying to play it down, is that groups of French and German youths – from both ends of the political spectrum, incidentally - have been crossing into those countries to bolster resistance to the establishment. Understandably, the Swiss government and media have dubbed it an offensive. Something similar is happening in Jersey, except there, the invasion's mainly French youths, and by sea. Meanwhile, there's a large demonstration decamped outside the French embassy on Knightsbridge Road with a signed petition 'from the people of the United Kingdom' to 'the people of France', asking them to 'resume' control of the Channel Islands. The *ambassadeur*'s denying them an opportunity to hand it over, but the French media are loving every minute. Understandably, Jersey's Lieutenant Governor is getting jumpy."

Mordred grinned. "Eat your heart out, Wat Tyler."

"I rather like Jersey. I don't like what it's become, but it would be wrong to sell out the ordinary islander for the sake of the corrupt establishment."

"It's another publicity stunt, that's all. And a complete castle in the air. Like setting up a petition to dismantle the Tower of London and rebuild it in Greenland, or ban smartphones in Madame Tussauds."

"It's part of a more general attempt to re-align perceptions. Which may or may not be a good thing, because once you've succeeded, you might find people noticing things you didn't anticipate. Before long, everyone's in the midst of an entirely new set of problems. Things that never entered anyone's head at the outset."

"I take it you've a particular worst-case scenario in mind."

"Obviously I can only foresee so much. Causes have effects which become causes and so on."

"Granted, and so ..."

"Yesterday afternoon, we received a report from the *Police nationale* that a large contingent of asylum-seekers is on its way out of Calais. Walking westwards, with Saint-Germain-sur-Ay as its goal. A little town on the coast directly facing Jersey."

"How far away?"

"Roughly nineteen miles across a stretch of unpredictable sea. But many of them have already made the crossing from Libya to Italy, compared to which, nineteen miles probably sounds like nothing. And of course, the French themselves are blazing a trail, some of them."

"Why would asylum-seekers want to go to Jersey? It's four times farther away from Britain than Calais."

"Or maybe it *is* Britain. Depending on how you look at it. Forget the rationality of it, just look at what it might do to the future. Detention centres, increased coastal surveillance, possible political instability, the odd disaster at sea just like we're seeing in the Med right now."

"It'll chase the financiers away, though. They tend not to like that sort of thing."

"Which raises the possibility that some of the protesters may be encouraging it."

"And you're sending me to Jersey to find out?"

"I'm afraid your brief's rather bigger than that, John. Annabel's made herself known as a member of MI5 to the States' Chief Minister, Jeremy Pownall. She's having a miserable honeymoon, as you might expect."

"In fairness, it's probably not what she expected to be doing."

"He's the belligerent type, and not terribly bright. He's all for teaching the protesters 'a lesson they'll never forget'. The substantial deployment of shock and awe."

"Can he do that?"

"As the head of a Crown Dependency government, he has a certain amount of leeway to do as he pleases. We don't know how much. His powers have never been tested in a court of law, so it's a constitutional grey area."

"But he's a bit of a bulldozer."

"The point is, if Pownall gets his way, there could be a bloodbath. Even if he's only out to scare them, which I think he probably is. These things escalate, especially on an island, where, in this particular case, the potential for running away is limited to forty-five square miles."

"I hate to say this, but is there a possibility he could be right?"

"Pragmatically, you mean?"

"If he's looked into the future and foreseen what you have – detention camps, political instability, all the rest of it – he may have decided a bit of carnage now is a price worth paying. After all, he wouldn't be the first, even as a Crown Dependency. You must have seen the news this morning: policemen on the other side of the world beating people half senseless as they herd them to the ports."

"I don't think it'll quite come to that."

"I wouldn't bet on it, but that's not my point. In ten years' time the people of Jersey might look around at the prison camp their country's become and wonder why Jeremy Pownall wasn't a tad more brutal when the chips were down. If you want to steer history rather than be steered by it, you've usually got to take your gloves off."

"I accept that."

"I'm only trying to see things from his point of view. I'm not saying I approve. What's my brief?"

"You've got a point of entry to the heart of the protesters. Your sister."

He chuckled. "If you're asking me to betray my own flesh and blood, you've got the wrong guy. Queen and Country can take a long walk off a short pier."

"We've been working together for quite some time, John. Does family treachery really strike you as something I might request?"

"Okay, no. Sorry. Go on."

"If I wanted someone to betray your sister, I'd choose one of the others. In *that highly unlikely event.*"

"Yes, point taken."

"We need someone to act as a go-between; to defuse tensions as far as possible between both sides. Annabel's temperamentally unsuited. For all her distaste for him personally, she's inclined to sympathise with Jeremy Pownall, which doesn't really help matters. Finally, she's got no currency whatsoever with the protesters."

"And of course, she's supposed to be on her honeymoon."

"There is that consideration too. Look, John, I think if you can just keep a lid on this for a few weeks, the whole thing will peter out of its own accord. There will be no need for the Jersey States to tarnish their image by taking a horsewhip to a group of peaceful demonstrators, and no reason to fear the kinds of consequences of which I spoke earlier. A lot of the protesters are middle-class. Once the summer's over, they've got jobs to go to, houses to live in, bills to pay. They'll decamp. Sheepishly, maybe, but surely. This is just the latest craze. "

"They won't all go. They hardly ever do. There are always the die-hards."

"True, but you can learn to live with them."

"*I* can, but can Jeremy Pownall?"

"That's where the Lieutenant-Governor comes in, the Queen's representative on the islands. He'll make it politely but firmly clear to Mr Pownall that yes, he can. And will."

"Sounds neat in theory. Let's hope it works in practice."

"It's a plan, and it's better than nothing."

"So what exactly am I doing?"

"Your sister thinks you're a salesman for a subcontracting machine, fabrication and welding company called BMN Technologies. Following a survey of the island's Second World

War tunnels, your company was one of five invited to bid for the contract to repair and maintain them. You're there to make a presentation, but you also believe your girlfriend may be on the island. You met her in France a year ago."

"Brian's going to love this. Who is my girlfriend?"

"Edna."

"Isn't she working with Alec and Phyllis?"

"Alec and Phyllis already know about this. I instructed them to maintain their poker faces while you were around."

"So what's Edna going to do?"

"She'll be a permanent fixture in the protesters' camp. Annabel will fulfil the same role with the Chief Minister. If you're a shuttle, you can't always be there to achieve pacification on the ground. We have to deploy permanent fixtures to do that."

"So Annabel's honeymoon from hell continues. How's Tariq holding up?"

"I can well imagine. On the other hand, he does know what she does for a living, so he can't complain too much."

"Oh, I don't know. When your wife's permanently holed up with the Chief Minister of the local government, and that's your honeymoon, I think you can complain a lot, whatever your wife does for a living."

"Possibly. I'll make it up to them."

Mordred smiled. "Knowing Tariq, he probably blames me."

"You're due for another meeting with Brian in an hour. He'll tell you all about your sister, all about Edna, all about the BMN Technologies background, everything. He's putting together a file as we speak. You'll need time to learn it, so as soon as he's finished with you, I want you to go home and get stuck in. Your plane leaves for Jersey tomorrow afternoon. All commercial trips to the island – air and sea – have been indefinitely suspended, so you'll be travelling in a four-seater private plane from Henley to a small airfield in the northwest of the island. As usual, a car will be waiting to pick you up. Good luck."

"Thank you."

"And John?"

"Yes?"

"I know I hardly need say this, but keep an eye out for Peter Decristoforo."

Chapter 11: Look at Altamont, Sixty-Nine ...

As Mordred's Cessna 172 took off from Henley, he suppressed a yawn. Yawning was supposed to wake you up – at least that's what they used to say. He'd read lately that it was about keeping your brain at the right temperature. Either way, trying to suppress one was pointless. The value of a good upbringing. Zilch.

Brian: *Edna's new name is Gabrielle Duchamp. You met just over eighteen months ago during a conference in Paris. At that time, she was studying design at the* Ecole Superieuredes Arts et Techniques de la Mode – ESMOD, *for short. Now she's working for a charity,* Aider L'Impuissance. *We've built it a website, just in case. She'll find you, by the way. You don't have to find her.*

As the plane took to the air, the ground stopped being real. Fields and buildings became toy versions. That was what stopped you having vertigo, probably. Your mind couldn't really take it in.

You're staying at the Hotel Alfonso in Saint Helier, near the Saint Clements Golf and Sports Centre. Do you play golf? Pity. Jeremy Pownall does. Bond did. Remember Goldfinger?

A few moments later they hit a bank of cloud and things got wobbly, then they ascended and it was like hovering over a duvet. Even less real. When, a short time later, the clouds parted a little, all he could see beneath was grey. It took him a moment to realise he was looking at the sea.

Jersey's Chief Minister, Jeremy Pownall, Eton, blah, blah, Oxford, then the City. The continual drone of the plane's engine. Another yawn, as his brain overheated again.

He didn't really want to work with Annabel. Not till a long time had elapsed since the incident in the gents. Of course, he knew how she'd be now: oblivious. She could do off-the-wall things and act like they'd never happened. In his universe, though, once something had happened, that was it: it had. And it usually led to awkwardness.

Perhaps if he put it out of his mind. Think of something more important. *Keep an eye out for Peter Decristoforo*, that should do it.

But that thought was instantly shoved out by his cover story. He imagined himself in the dining room of the Alfonso, sitting at a table on his own, everyone looking at him. *Yes, they all thought, he's the sales rep, probably lives out of a suitcase, poor man.* Meanwhile, a million miles below him, on the dinner table itself, ten croutons were soaking up his asparagus soup. To avert an expansionary disaster, he had to shovel them into his mouth pronto. Then Fenella Decristoforo-Salvaterra arrived and –

No, that was another thing not to think about. The plane was descending now, thank God. He needed to get away from his own head. Was that why people in his profession took to drink? So they wouldn't think about Fenella?

Bloody hell, he was pathetic. In any decent spy novel, she'd be the one that was enthralled, not him. But it was always the same with him. He always ended up pining like a lovelorn adolescent. Even when he wasn't even in love, because the truth was, he only thought about women like Fenella – particular women he'd met, never women in general - because he had too much time on his hands, and probably because it was expected of a man his age. Deep down, he probably felt nothing at all, unless boredom was a feeling.

When he stopped and thought about it, he was probably bored most of the time. Let's see, he'd got out of bed this morning. Probably *bored* while he was getting ready to go to work. Okay, yes, there'd been parts of the news where he wasn't bored, but then the analyst started going round in circles and he'd lost interest. *Bored* for most of the journey in. *Not-bored* during the meeting. *Semi-bored* with Brian. *Not-bored* when he read the file for the first time, *semi-bored* when he read it again, *three-quarters-bored* on the third reading. After that – the fourth, fifth and sixth readings - just *bored*, at least for all statistical purposes. *Bored* in the evening, save for about twenty minutes during *The Simpsons*. Then bed. You only went to sleep because you were bored. A quick calculation suggested he was bored for about 75% of his day, and by extension, his life. And he was a secret agent. God knows what being an accountant or a solicitor was like.

As usual, after the acknowledgement of the pathological boredom came the guilt. What the hell right did he have to feel bored? Who did he think he was? At least do something useful, something like *Aider L'Impuissance* – although not exactly that, because it was 100% phoney. Bloody typical.

He had to snap out of it. Maybe visit Jersey's Gerald Durrell zoo – if there was time. He loved animals, even slugs and flies and worms, although they all made him want to cry when he thought about them long enough, the things they had to put up with. But hey, that was the universe.

The plane landed. He hoped Annabel hadn't come to meet him. *Where have you been, John? I've been having an awful time, Tariq say's you're entirely to blame, and by the way, I love you.* He scanned the airport. No one he could see. But the car was there, a black Mercedes. She might be sitting inside, plotting.

Drizzle fell in waves. He ran from the plane to the car and got onto the back seat. Apart from the driver, it was empty. The upholstery smelt new. They drove to the Hotel Alfonso at a leisurely speed. So far he hadn't seen any protesters, not one. Mind you, the plane had approached the island at low altitude from the northwest, so he'd got no sort of view of anything much Jersey-related at all. Maybe later today.

The hotel was a four storey pre-war building with hulking bay windows, pilasters and a gabled roof. Like all such, the interior was based on a suburban lounge circa 1956. There were aspidistras, chandeliers, and low teak tables with local-attraction brochures on. After signing the register, he went straight upstairs to his single bedroom, where a chair and a chest of drawers and a view of the sea awaited him with dour expressions. Then the sun burst through the clouds, a rainbow appeared, and he had the unexpected feeling this mission was going to be a success.

He tried to look inside himself, discern his feelings. Was he bored now?

He didn't know. He noticed the red light flashing on the hotel phone next to his bed. Beside the handset, a card said, 'To access your messages, dial 745, then enter the password, 555.'

"This is Tina," a young woman's voice said. "I'm the Chief Minister's secretary. Welcome to the island, Mr Mordred. The Minister hopes you had a very pleasant flight, and that you enjoy your stay. He has reserved a time slot for you this evening at five. Assuming you get this message soon after you get in, it should be around two-thirty pm now. If for any reason you cannot attend, or you need anything, please don't hesitate to get in touch. We look forward to seeing you."

He deleted it. Two and a half hours, lots of time. Maybe this would be a good time to make an excursion. See if he could find any actual protesters.

He rang down to reception and asked them to call him a taxi. Ten minutes later, he climbed onto the back seat of a Cassidy Cabs saloon with an old man in sunglasses and a cloth cap behind the wheel.

"Where to?" the old man asked, in an American accent. "Sorry, they wouldn't tell me on the phone."

"I'd like you to drop me at the protest."

He looked hard into his rear view and pulled out into the traffic going eastwards. "You're a reporter," he said neutrally.

"No, a salesman. I'm just interested. Once in a lifetime experience to see something a bit unusual. Something beyond the everyday."

"Sure, 'beyond the everyday'. It's *that* all right."

"Is it affecting business?"

"In a good way, yes. All those extra people. The supermarkets are having to race to renew their stock. They're doubling their orders at the wholesalers'. Mind you, once the violence kicks off, it'll be a whole other matter."

"What violence?"

"It's inevitable, that many people, no proper johns. Sooner or later, they're going to get tired and grubby. Then they'll get irritable. I give them a week at the outside. After that, there'll be looting."

"From what I've heard, they're mostly middle-class discontents with jobs to go home to. Looting's probably not their thing."

"No disrespect, but that's not how these things work. It's never the majority. It's the small number of hangers-on with nothing to lose. You always get them. And they're nearly always out of control. Look at Altamont, sixty-nine."

"Before my time."

"Big rock concert. Started off cool, ended up a kid got killed."

"Well, let's hope history doesn't repeat itself."

The driver laughed. "That's all history ever does. First time as tragedy, then as farce. Haven't you heard?"

"What do you think of the protests? I mean, personally?"

"Love 'em. But then, I'm an unreformed hippie. Fantasy Fair and Magic Mountain, Monterey, The Stones in the Park, Woodstock, Altamont, Vancouver, you name it. If it was worth going to, I was there. And out of my head, mostly." He laughed. "I'm a walking, talking, cab-driving piece of goddamn history." He peeped the horn twice and stuck his fist out of the open window. "*Viva la revolución,*" he said, and laughed again. He saw an old lady at a bus stop. "*Hey, baby, I said,* Viva la revolución!" he shouted at her. She smiled and waved in a way that suggested this was a regular occurrence.

They drove in silence the rest of the way, down deep country lanes, up gentle inclines and down into shallow valleys. Above, the sun and a clear blue sky. Mordred was surprised by just how big the island was. He'd never really thought about Jersey before, but he had it down in his mind as somewhere so small you could see one side from the other. Even the size of Saint Helier struck him as larger than expected.

After a few moments, he heard something outside, and rolled the window down. A rock band. He still hadn't seen a single protester. Maybe there weren't any. Perhaps it was some deranged publicity stunt by the Jersey Tourist Board. Designed to stop visitors? Or encourage them? He didn't know.

The car pulled to a stop. As far as Mordred could tell, they were in the middle of the countryside. What was going on?

"This is as far as I go," the driver said. "Climb to the top of the hill in front of you, and you'll see it. I'll stick around if you're only going to be five minutes. Otherwise, you'll have to excuse."

Mordred paid. "I'll ring you when I need picking up. I'll wait here."

"It may not be me who returns, but I'll tell them where to find you."

"Is it big? The demonstration?"

"Hey, big, small, in between, it's all relative. You judge. I'm from Texas originally. Nothing's big in my world except Lone Star State stuff."

"Have a good day."

"*Viva la revolución.*"

The band was much louder now, although he still couldn't hear what they were playing. Something folksy. He hoped this wasn't going to be too much of a disappointment. The more people there were, the greater Hannah's chances of coming out unscathed when the violence kicked off – assuming the taxi driver was right and it was inevitable. Knowing Hannah, it would be two hundred or so pop stars and music execs – all friends of hers – and a man named Aubrey with long hair and a 'way' with a twelve-string acoustic guitar. They were probably hiding out here, in the middle of nowhere in order to keep a lid on how few of them there really were. The words, 'ten thousand', where Chinese Whispers were in play, might translate as anything. It hadn't occurred to him before, but he might even be able to persuade the lot of them to get on the next boat out of here. For their own safety. *I don't disagree with your message*, that's how he'd begin. World War O; bloody hell, what a farce.

The music got louder the higher he climbed. After a minute and a half, he reached the summit and looked over into … something he couldn't believe.

The whole landscape, right up to the horizon, was covered with people and tents. Hundreds of multi-coloured Jolly Rogers mingled with hundreds of scarlet Real Alternative flags, all at different heights and flapping proudly together in the afternoon breeze. To the right, the sea was dotted with surfers and flotillas of boats. In the distance – so far away as to be almost invisible – a band stood on a stage singing *Hard Times of Old England*. There must be close to a million people here, maybe more.

Suddenly, for the first time, he understood what World War O meant. That it wasn't hyperbole. It was real. It was here, now, right in front of him.

His head span. How the hell was he meant to find his sister in this? let alone someone like Peter Decristoforo, whom he'd only seen in photos? It reminded him not so much of a rock concert, but of Kumbh Mela, a gargantuan Hindu festival-cum-pilgrimage once every three years. Obviously, it couldn't be anywhere near that big, nothing could, but it was spectacular.

No point in staying. He wished he'd asked the driver to wait now. He had to be at Jeremy Pownall's at five. There wasn't even time to walk halfway across here before then.

Maybe there was no point in remaining on the island, full stop. How could he go between his sister and the Chief Minister if he couldn't even *find* his sister? And of course, it seemed unlikely she was in charge of *this*. The very notion of anyone being 'in charge' of it didn't seem to make sense. It was too big. She'd probably made one or two inspiring speeches at the beginning and the media had hailed her as head honcho. If so, they'd have done it as much for their sake as hers. They needed someone to go to, and if she was willing and able, why not?

Maybe he was being ungenerous.

No one seemed to have noticed him arrive, and he didn't suppose anyone would see him leave. New people turning up then departing was probably so commonplace you didn't even register it once you'd been here any length of time. Of course, once you got to the other side of the hillock – the side he'd scaled – you lost sight of the others, which would explain why everyone was over here.

He took out his phone and called Cassidy Cabs. A woman answered. He was about to explain who he was – he hadn't taken the driver's name or given his own – when he noticed what looked like a massive disturbance in the crowd, about two hundred yards downhill to his left. People were running away, screaming. They were being chased by bulky men in leather jackets wielding baseball bats. One of those fleeing – a man - tripped. A pursuer grabbed him, pinned him to the ground and began punching him. It was like watching a pack of wolves charge at sheep. Everyone trying to get away. No one resisting. Terror swept backwards like a Mexican wave, and so quickly that those on the receiving end, deep within the crowd and therefore safe for the time being, probably had no idea what they were terrified of.

Suddenly, Mordred was running. He grabbed the baseball bat from the man who was pummelling his victim, and so deftly that he didn't appear to realise he was no longer holding it till it swung round and smacked him unconscious. Four others were pushing into the crowd, trying to get space and leverage for a wide-arc swing. Mordred grabbed some men from the crowd and put them to service pushing the culprits from behind, so that they fell over under their own weight. He hit them hard as they tried to get up, and passed their weapons into the crowd. For a moment, the tide looked as if it was turning, but the men in the assault's forefront saw what was going on. They regrouped and turned on Mordred. One protester tried to defend him, but he was too slow. Then, it was a great basketful of punches and kicks and head butts. To begin with, Mordred didn't feel pain. He just felt angry.

Then he didn't feel anything at all.

Chapter 12: In Bed With Jeremy Pownall

When he woke up, he was on a raised bed. Hospital smell, hospital décor, but enclosed by four walls – he seemed to be in his own room. Tariq sat on his left, Annabel on his right. Tables stood to each side with flowers on, and daylight came through a frosted window. He didn't know how badly he'd been beaten, but his arm was in plaster and he felt painful all over. The door opened and a doctor entered before either of his friends had chance to say anything.

"How are you feeling?" he asked Mordred.

The sort of question that deserved a smart-aleck response, but he couldn't muster the energy. "Not very good," he said. "I think I may need to be sick."

"That'll be the pain. You *are* in pain, I take it?"

Mordred nodded.

"I'll get you something to ease it," the doctor said. "Meanwhile" – he reversed a step and leaned around the door frame – "nurse, get Mr Mordred something to be sick in, please."

A nurse appeared and a cardboard bowl was produced. Mordred retched. The doctor returned with two tablets and a glass of water. Mordred's hand shook as he took them. He lapsed back into unconsciousness.

When he awoke, Hannah stood next to him. The light was subdued and the curtain had been removed. She was crying and wringing her hands. Soraya held her supportively from behind. "Those bastards, those bloody bastards," Hannah said, while her friend shook her head grimly. Then Soraya took her smartphone out and started taking pictures of him. "Smile," she said. Hannah cried some more. Then Soraya balanced a parrot on her finger, and they all went outside into the darkness to set it free.

The third time he awoke – was it the third? – Annabel and Tariq were there again. They stood on the same side, holding hands. They were dressed formally, as if on their way to a dinner.

"I think he's coming to," Annabel whispered. "John, can you hear us?"

"You're getting better," Tariq told him. "You should be well on the road to recovery in a day or so."

"What happened to me?" he asked.

Annabel looked like she was going to cry. "He's actually awake!" she exclaimed.

The door opened. In came a tall, well-to-do looking man in a suit. He strode over and loomed behind Annabel. His hair was all but extinct, and he had large 1970s-style glasses with tinted lenses. "Good to see you making such solid progress, John," he said.

Mordred tried to connect this man with the doctor of however-long-ago, the one with the two tablets, but he couldn't make the congruence. Perhaps he was a consultant of some stripe.

"I'm Jeremy Pownall," the man said. "The States' Chief Minister. It's good to finally meet you."

"Hi," Mordred replied. He didn't offer a handshake. He wasn't feeling strong enough.

"Sorry you got caught in the crossfire."

"What do you mean?"

No one spoke. Pownall looked upwards. "What do I mean?" he eventually said to himself, as if it was something he'd already considered, and its unexpected reopening might be to his advantage. "I see, I see."

Another man appeared, this one much smaller and stouter. He closed the door behind him.

"This is my lawyer – the States' lawyer – Mr Pettigrew," Pownall said absently.

Mordred had no idea what was going on and felt too whacked to ask. He stopped looking at any of the people in front of him, and let his eyes focus on their preferred object, the frosted window.

"You see, the thing is," Pownall said, "those men who hit you were employed by a company based in Bermuda, but only registered in Saint Helier, and whose actual address, on the Avenue de l'Opera in Paris, is part of the 'Jersey Settlement' …"

Mordred drifted out of consciousness. When he came to, Pownall was still speaking. "And so that's why I think it would be a very bad idea for you to sue us," he said. "In a word, we're not responsible."

"Could I speak to a doctor?" Mordred asked.

"In theory, *we* could just as easily sue *you*," Pownall went on. "This was our plan for bringing the protests to an end, and you scuppered it. Not a pretty plan, true, but you can't make an omelette without breaking eggs. The idea was to hurt a few people – not as badly as you got hurt: not nearly as much: we're all very sorry about that – and frighten a good deal more. Thus we'd whittle the demonstration down to its hardest of hard core supporters, then play the waiting game. Winter would break them, if nothing else … Which all sounds very unkind, I know, but politics isn't always about choosing the good. Sometimes, there are only two evils, and you have to choose the lesser. The alternative is that the protesters overrun the island, and we become a metaphorical leper colony of asylum-seekers and hippie dropouts. Crime and unemployment shoot up, investment flees, the bottom falls out of tourism, and, goodness to me, it's the Dark Ages again."

Mordred sat up. He wasn't feeling as bad as he'd thought. "And how did I 'scupper' that?"

"You were being filmed," Pownall replied. "An hour later, you were on every news broadcast in the world. People – the protesters, above all – said we were responsible. And then someone took a picture of you *within this very hospital*" – he looked at Annabel and Tariq – "and that made matters worse."

"We've been through this," Annabel said icily. "It wasn't us."

"My sister was here at my bedside," Mordred said. "At least, I think she was."

Pownall looked like he'd been punched. "Your - ?" He turned to his lawyer. "But I - "

He obviously couldn't say *what he*. Presumably, he didn't want Mordred to know. But the remainder of the sentence was obvious. *… gave strict orders that she wasn't to be admitted here under any circumstances.* Words to that effect. "Where's Doctor Smythe?" he said, under his breath. He left. His lawyer followed him.

Annabel leaned over Mordred and whispered in his ear. "'But I gave orders that if she could once be separated from her followers, she should be arrested on sight'."

"Can we get you anything, John?" Tariq said. "Anything at all?"

Mordred smiled. "How's the honeymoon going?"

"Horrible," Annabel said. "Still, that's the Realm for you. Never know when it might need defending next."

"How the hell is *this* 'defending the Realm'?" Tariq asked. "More like defending the rights of big corporations to shaft everyone, right, left and centre."

"Tariq's a little bitter," she said. "As you can tell."

"As I have the right to be," Tariq said. "I was expecting sex, sunshine and scuba diving. The three S's. Instead of which, this."

"Fair point," Mordred said. "I'd be indignant in your position."

"Which you're not," Tariq said. "Don't forget that."

Annabel rolled her eyes.

"How long have I been here?" Mordred asked.

"A week," she replied. "You've got a broken arm, a couple of minor fractures, two black eyes, and most of your body's purple. Apart from that, you're okay. What the hell made you wade in like that?"

He laughed. "Vernon Johns: if you see a good fight, get in it."

"I'm not going to ask who 'Vernon Johns' is," Annabel replied. "Pownall will be back in a moment."

"He's probably got the place bugged," Tariq said. He began looking under the bed. "I'm not joking."

"How's World War O been getting on in my absence?" Mordred asked.

"Mostly over," Annabel said. "Switzerland and Luxembourg still can't secure their borders, Germany's in trouble now, and the City of London's far from out of the woods, but most of the offshore islands are 'fully ship-shape', as they say. Thirty fatalities, including two policemen, and up to two hundred injuries. UN Peacekeepers helped fleeing protesters onto boats in Singapore and the British Virgin Islands. Quite a few demonstrators are facing prosecution in their own countries."

"Still, they can say they were there, I suppose," Mordred said.

"Scant consolation if you lose your job or end up in prison," Tariq said.

"No one thinks it's the end," Annabel added. "Quite the opposite. But then, that's what they always say: *it ain't over, I'll be back*. It's good media fodder."

"If you call something 'World War O'," Tariq said, "you'd better have a Plan B. Pretty humiliating if it's all over in two or three weeks. Believe me, it really ain't over."

Pownall returned, trailing the doctor and the lawyer. "I wanted an expert opinion on your progress," he told Mordred, resuming where he'd left off as if nothing from Annabel or Tariq could possibly have moved the conversation on in his absence, "and Doctor Smythe didn't seem to be around, so I went to find him. It turns out that your condition is very serious, and probably deteriorating. We need to keep you here at least a week longer. And we should really inform the press. The perpetrators need to realise the seriousness of what they've done."

"'We'?" Mordred said.

"Doctor Smythe. *He*, I suppose, technically, although I'm in charge of the island, and I see you as my guest. So that makes 'he' a 'we'."

"I suppose we should really tell my family too," Mordred said. He was feeling a lot better now. "They'll probably want to visit."

"I think that's an excellent idea."

"Especially my sister, Hannah. Then we can grab her and boot her off the island."

Pownall smiled. "A true meeting of minds. John. For her own good, obviously. I don't want her to get hurt any more than you do. I don't want *anyone* to get hurt. Okay, let's stop dissembling here. Your condition isn't serious. You're not deteriorating. But am I right in assuming you'd be prepared to help us by pretending? She needn't ever know the truth, of course. No one would tell her. As far as she need ever be concerned, you were actually at death's door."

He was about to say no, but something stopped him. "Just give me a minute," he said, instead. "I need to think."

Actually, he could see Pownall's point. Looked at rationally, it was a solution, possibly even the best available. The protesters had made their point; lingering wasn't going to help that. By the sounds of things, whatever little they'd built had collapsed everywhere else. If Mordred left the hospital with a clean bill of health, the media would forget anything had ever happened to him. Pownall would then resume normal service, sending the heavies in to terrorise what remained of the crowds, only with instructions to be a bit more cautious this time: hit people where they don't bruise as easily. If he stayed put, in bed, everything might be easier to disassemble.

"What you've got to remember," Pownall went on, clearly determined to ram home his advantage, "is that the protesters have got it all wrong. Jersey isn't a 'secrecy jurisdiction'. It may have been once – I doubt *that* even, though I'm willing to concede it for the sake of argument - but not any more. Even in the past, it was probably only a few rotten apples. Nowadays, we've got FATCA – the United States Foreign Account Tax Compliance Act – plus there's a UK version, *and* we've got tax information exchange agreements with thirty-five other countries, with more in progress. How *could* anyone hide funds here, John? The truth is, *all* of the British crown dependencies are fully compliant with all international financial standards. The protesters are living in a fantasy world, pure and simple."

Tariq put his hand up. "Could I just say something?"

Pownall turned to look at him as if whatever it was, it couldn't conceivably be of any value. He shrugged. "Be my guest," he said coldly.

"Okay, the plan, as I understand it, is to use John as bait to lure his sister in. Once she hears he's deteriorating, she won't be able to keep away, for compassionate reasons. So she'll visit the hospital, probably with a friend or two, under cover of night, and you'll have personnel in the wings, waiting to apprehend her."

"Very perceptive," Pownall said. "That is indeed 'the plan'. Welcome to the exact conclusion we reached five minutes ago."

"What's the problem with it?" the lawyer asked.

"So what happens next?" Tariq asked. "You put her on the first plane out, I assume?"

"So fast, her feet won't touch the ground," Pownall replied tetchily.

"In that case, once she gets to Heathrow, she's going to start texting and tweeting. The protesters are going to find out what happened to her. There'll be outrage. They already think you've set a bunch of thugs on them. Now, they're going to think you abducted their leader when she went to visit an ailing sibling. How does that make you sound? How does it make Jersey sound? Imagine a crowd that size, descending on Saint Helier with clubs and rocks. Is that what you want?"

Pownall and his lawyer looked at each other. Pownall shrugged. "Okay, so let's say we keep her on the island," he said. "We take away her mobile and lock her up for a while, during which time we move post-haste to clear the resistance."

Annabel hooted. "What does 'Clear the resistance' mean? And what counts as a 'while'?"

"We could fly her back to Heathrow," the lawyer said, "and take down the island's communications network for a limited period. Prevent her from telling her sob story, and allow us to deal with the remaining problem in our own way."

Mordred held up his hands and gave a shocked laugh. "Okay, gentlemen, I'm afraid you can count me out. I'm going to say no."

"But – *what?*" Pownall exclaimed. "I thought you'd already agreed, it's the perfect outcome. Everyone wins!"

"With respect," Tariq said, "the devil's in the detail. It sounds a little as if you're making it up as you go along."

"You may not like my sister," Mordred said, "but, as far as I know, she's a pacifist. Removing her may not be in your best interests. I'm assuming there's nothing personal at stake here."

Pownall coloured. "*Personal?* What do you mean?"

"She has called the Chief Minister and the Lieutenant General a lot of names," the lawyer said. "Some of them quite indecent."

"Her bark's worse than her bite," Mordred said. "Why don't you arrange a meeting with her? I could set it up."

"Because there's nothing to discuss," Pownall said firmly. "I've spent the whole of the last few days with the most influential people on this island and abroad, trying to reassure them that nothing's going to change. If I meet with her, it sends out all the wrong signals. No, you don't compromise with bullies. The only language they understand is this." He put his palm up and shook his head. "The word 'no'," he explained, as if the mime might not be clear. "*No*, you're not welcome; *no*, we're not listening; *no*, we won't; *no*, we can't."

Mordred smiled. "Obama, but in reverse."

"Not how I'd choose to put it myself, but very well."

"As I understood it," Mordred continued, "my purpose in coming here was to act as a mediator between you and the protesters. Now you're saying that's not the case?"

"You only negotiate with someone for two reasons," Pownall replied. "Either you're in a position of weakness, or you hope to gain something only they can supply. If someone broke into your house and sat down on your sofa, John, you wouldn't enter into 'talks' with them. You'd call the police. That's what I've done."

"Okay, so I'm surplus to requirements."

"We wanted you here so you could explain to them how stupid they're being. Tell them about FATCA. Show them our thirty-five TIEAs. Get them to go on our website and see how transparent we are. It's all there. All they have to do is look."

"There are also some very unflattering things on the internet," Mordred said. "Some of them written by people who live, or have lived, here."

"Cranks. Every society has them."

"You also seem to be in *Private Eye* a lot."

"I don't read those sorts of magazines, thank you. Anyway, whatever anyone says: if it's negative, it's either a mistake or a lie."

"So you want me to be your propagandist, effectively."

"In a word, yes."

"That's not something I can confidently do. I don't know enough about Jersey."

"You can take my word, can't you?"

Mordred smiled. "I've never taken the word of any politician in all the time I've been alive. Until fairly recently, I didn't even vote."

"Then we have nothing more to say," he said frostily. "Thank you for visiting our island."

He turned his back and left. It took his lawyer a moment to realise what had happened, then he followed suit. They didn't close the door behind them. Tariq did that.

"We'd better get you out of here, John," Annabel whispered.

Mordred suddenly saw what she was thinking. Pownall wasn't finished yet. All they had to do was keep him here, and they didn't necessarily need his consent do that. Sedation would be the easiest means.

Annabel's phone began to ring. She took it out of her bag and looked at it irritably. Then her expression changed. She answered. "I believe he's gone for good," she told the caller after a minute. She listened some more and passed the phone to Mordred.

Edna's voice. "Hello, Sir. We've ID-ed the guys who attacked you, and guess what? They're among a group of goons who've got the building surrounded. My guess is, they're waiting for you to leave so you can meet with an 'accident' that'll put you straight back in again. Stay where you are. Annabel and Tariq will remain with you. I'm awaiting help."

She put the phone down.

"Don't worry, John," Annabel said. Tariq reached over and took her hand.

They heard footsteps approaching, and all three tensed slightly. Pownall come back for something? The door opened brusquely.

Doctor Smythe. But he was accompanied by two young men in denim jackets. Mordred didn't recognise them, yet he got the strong impression they recognised him. They weren't nurses. They were large enough to obscure the doorframe.

"Is there a problem?" Mordred asked.

"Visiting time's over," Smythe replied.

Chapter 13: Fish & Chips and the Sea

Doctor Smythe's appearance at the head of two strongmen was something Brian would have loved. Especially his 'visiting time's over', which was a baddie-witticism worthy of the Old School. Annabel casually took out her phone and dialled. She raised her finger to ask Smythe to be quiet a moment, then put it to her ear.

"Oh, hi!" she said. "Is that you, Gabrielle? That's right, it's Annabel again. I wonder if you could bring the car round? Unfortunately, we've got to leave … I know, but Doctor Smythe's just arrived with two men … I don't know. I'll find out." She put the phone on her knee and turned to Smythe. "Who are these two men, Doctor, if you don't mind my asking?"

"I'm not obliged to answer that question," Smythe replied. "As I just said, you have to leave."

"Because I think I recognise them."

The two men looked at each other and grinned. They came forward with their hands folded in front of them. Annabel put her phone in her bag and stood up.

"I don't suppose I'm allowed to discharge myself?" Mordred said, behind them. He tried to swing his legs over the bed, but was too weak.

"Stay where you are, John," Annabel said.

"The Doc says you've got to leave," the first man told her.

Somehow – Mordred had seen it once before, but even then he'd found it difficult to believe his eyes – Annabel's right leg left the ground and travelled upwards in a one-hundred-and-eighty degree arc, the last portion of which lay directly through her interlocutor's chin. His head snapped backwards and so did he. Almost simultaneously, she drew a gun from her handbag.

"Visiting time's just beginning," she said sweetly. "Get on the floor, please, face down."

Smythe and his accomplice took a moment to register what had happened – they even looked at each other for confirmation - then did as she told them.

"Put your hands on the back of your head," she continued. "And interlace your fingers. I don't want to have to tell you anything twice. This gun doesn't make enough of a noise for anyone outside to hear, but believe me, what it does do, it does well. And I won't hesitate to use it if I think you're trying to be clever. Tariq, there's a roll of duct tape and some cord in my bag. Make sure these gentlemen can't move, if you would."

As Tariq got to work, she took the phone from her bag with her free hand and placed it against her ear again. "I know, I'm really sorry, but I think it's sorted now. We've agreed a little bit of an extension to visiting time. The bottom line is, I don't think John's going to be able to make it unaided, and we need to get out now, preferably through the back entrance. Keep in touch."

She put the phone down and sat on her chair while Tariq bound the prisoners. When they were beyond the possibility of escape she returned the gun to her bag and refreshed her lipstick. Then she stood up again.

"We'd better get going," she said. "Tariq, you bring John."

Tariq was going to make a great husband. He just heard and obeyed.

Mordred tried to help as much as possible. It ought to be possible to make his legs go, for example. He hadn't often been in a state where he found it difficult to move his limbs before. By way of compensation, he apologised. Now he was upright, he felt woozy. Try not to black out, for Tariq's sake.

Suddenly, they were passing occupied beds. He had no idea what time of the day or night it was, but no one seemed to be asleep. Once or twice, they passed nurses. Because Annabel looked as if she knew what she was doing, and because she was dressed in a suit with an official visitor's badge, no one stopped them.

Edna was waiting for them at the end of a darkened corridor, after what felt to Mordred like an hour and a half, but was probably no more than five minutes. She seemed agitated, even for a junior agent. He hoped she wasn't going to start Sir-ing him again. There were limits to being Sir-ed, and when the Sir in question was in pyjamas and not quite right in the head, that was one of them.

"Don't 'Sir' me," he said, when she was within range. He hoped he'd whispered it.

"What?" Edna replied.

"Ignore him," Annabel cut in. "Where's the car?"

"Follow me," Edna said.

They went down another two miles of corridors, taking the best part of a fortnight. Edna snapped down the horizontal lever on a fire door. There was a rush of cold air and they were outside. A long road running left to right, a car, late afternoon sunshine, gulls, the smell of fish and chips and the sea.

And two men prostrate, on either side of them. They looked just like Smythe's two buddies, like the men who'd attacked him back at the protesters' encampment. Except they weren't moving. Could Annabel have shot them while he wasn't looking? Doubtful. Not her style. She liked to threaten and kick, not fire. Her pistol probably wasn't even loaded. She was like him, in that respect. Like him, only better.

"Not my handiwork," Edna said, indicating the two men.

"We'll discuss it later," Annabel said. "Do you know the roads well enough to drive?"

"Like the back of my hand," Edna replied. She got behind the wheel. Annabel sat shotgun. Tariq hauled Mordred onto the back seat and got in beside him. The car screeched away.

"What do you mean, 'not my handiwork'?" Annabel asked.

"They were like that when I got here," Edna said. "I thought you must have done it. Anyway, somebody loves us."

Annabel turned round as they went through an underpass. "What do you want to do, John? Wake up, you've been drugged."

He remembered the two tablets. "They were just painkillers," he replied.

She smiled. "In the light of subsequent events, I doubt that."

The strange thing was, he'd felt quite lucid during the time Pownall was there. Perhaps the getting up and moving around had caused the drugs to work more deeply into his system. Or perhaps they really were painkillers, but with drowsy side-effects. Most likely that, yes. No point getting paranoid.

"We could call London and get you out the same way you came in," Annabel was going on. "Pownall's got no pretext to keep you here, and we're secret service anyway. We'd cancel any warrant for your arrest, even assuming he could cook one up, which is unlikely. Realistically, in other words, he couldn't and wouldn't object to you leaving."

Mind over matter. Now he was at rest again, at least some of his former clarity seemed to be returning. He was going to be okay. He *was* okay. "You don't have orders to bring me back?"

"Not yet," Annabel replied. "Obviously, Tariq and I will have to leave, whatever. We've burned our bridges."

"My own orders were to liaise between the protesters and the Chief Minister."

"True," Tariq said, "but given that we've just taped a senior Jersey medic and one of his associates to the floor, and kicked the other unconscious, I think we can assume you won't be welcome *chez* Pownall for a while. You're coming with us."

"You're not taking deniability into account," Mordred replied.

"What do you mean?" Annabel said.

"I didn't kick him unconscious," Mordred answered, "you did. I was doped up. And Smythe and his associates weren't acting on Pownall's orders. They were in someone else's pay. There's no reason at all why what happened should come between two rational men dedicated to the grim art of *realpolitik*."

"Bloody risky game," Annabel said. "Pownall's got all the cards, and, as we've just heard from the horse's mouth, he doesn't want to negotiate."

"That may change. I'm not saying I'll go straight round to his house and ring the doorbell."

"What do you think, Edna?" Annabel asked.

"John's sister's here," she said simply. "My understanding is, she's trapped."

"*Trapped?*" Mordred said.

Edna nodded. "I wasn't going to say anything, but since it appears you're determined to stay, and none of us is opposed to that in principle, I guess you might as well know."

"Be more specific," Mordred told her.

"The protesters are in the northwest of the island, backed up against the sea. They're surrounded by a line of guys who look suspiciously like those you fell foul of. My guess is they're in Pownall's pay, but they may not be. There are lots of people in Saint Helier with the money and connections to raise a private army. And the determination to deploy it. They take this 'World War O' business very seriously. And they don't want to lose the opening rounds anywhere."

"How are we going to get in, if they've got the camp surrounded?" Mordred asked. "And how did you get out?"

"She's a spy," Annabel said, "that's how. Don't be patronising. And you'll get into the camp the same way. Assuming you're stupid enough to still want to."

"Sorry, Edna," Mordred said. "I'm trying to think of too much at once."

"You need to reconsider," Annabel said.

"Not unless you've got a new set of reasons," Mordred replied.

"How about this then?" she said. "They almost certainly won't even beat up your sister. She's the leader. Once it's all over, she's the first person the media will go to for a sound bite. It's going to look bloody terrible for Pownall if she's covered in bruises. No, they'll put a net over her, then handcuff her, maybe even sedate her, and she'll get home three or four hours later, foaming at the mouth but unscathed. Whereas you've already been beaten, and some of these guys have probably got a grudge against you, and you're not someone anyone would go to for a quote. You could easily be killed."

"I can look after myself," Mordred said. "and I've got Edna. Just to be clear, she's an Olympic gold medallist. She's quite capable of looking after me and herself."

"I think you're asking a hell of a lot of her," Annabel said.

"Maybe we should talk about Edna in the second person," Tariq said. "She is actually in the car."

"You're being an idiot, John!" Annabel rarely showed emotion, so she was clearly upset.

"Look I - "

"It would be perfectly possible for me to punch you unconscious right now, and bundle you onto the plane. I'd do it for your own good."

"But you wouldn't," he replied.

"You think not? Why not?"

"You'd have done it by now. The reason you won't, is because you could be wrong. Theory's one thing, practice another. We both know something might happen to Hannah, even against Pownall's supposed will. And you think that if you knock me out and bear me away, and something *does* happen to her, I'll never forgive you. I'll never speak to you again."

Her face crumpled somehow. It looked like someone had just piled a shovelful of snow on top of it.

"Even though," he went on, "I probably *would* forgive you, because I'd know you did it for the right reasons. We're friends, and that means a lot to both of us. But you daren't risk it."

She wheeled round abruptly to look out of the windscreen. She wiped her eyes - or that's what it looked like: she had her back to him, so he couldn't tell for sure.

As he expected, she recovered quickly. She took a hand mirror from her bag, and looked at herself. She re-did bits of her face. When she turned to face the back seat again, it was as if nothing had ever happened.

"Tariq?" she said.

"That's okay," Tariq replied glumly.

"I'll do whatever you want," she told him. "If you want to get on a plane and leave, we'll do that. If you want to stay, we'll stay."

"What if *I* want to get on a plane and I want *you* to stay?" he asked.

"That's not going to happen. You're not entitled to make up my mind for me. If you leave, so do I. This is our honeymoon and I love you. I'm not going to let you go your own way without me, not even for John. I mean it."

Tariq seemed to fill with light and joy. "We'll stay," he said. "I don't want you to choose between your husband and your friend. Besides, John's my friend too. Always has been, always will be."

"The feeling's mutual," Mordred said.

"It's settled then," Annabel said. "At least between the three of us. Edna, how about you? Could be dangerous. You can go if you want to."

Edna beamed. "I only joined up for the danger. I got tired of running."

As they left the capital and entered the country roads leading inland, they noticed something odd. Every half mile or so they kept passing the same man. Or that's what it looked like. Dressed and built just like the men who'd beaten Mordred up, and exactly like those mysteriously lying on their backs outside the hospital just now.

"What do you think it means?" Mordred asked Edna, as they passed the fourth.

"I don't know," she replied. She put her foot down slightly. "But I've a feeling we'll find out before long."

Chapter 14: Beware Ye, Men With Drums and Pointy Sticks

Edna knew of a little hill they could climb and look down on some of Pownall's men if they wanted. When they reached the top, there wasn't much to see. Ten or twelve ex-squaddie types slouched on the ground, talking. Four tents, some clothes slung over a line, a smouldering fire. Further up, the undergrowth was dense in places, so there were probably more men just out of view.

"How many do you reckon there are in all?" Mordred asked quietly. Physically, he felt a lot better now. But worry had set in.

"I reckon no more than a hundred and twenty," Edna replied. "Although that many well-trained men, of their size, constitutes quite an army."

"It's a lot, relatively speaking," Annabel agreed.

On the way back down, Mordred wondered what his sister was doing to prepare. She must know something about what was coming. She wouldn't be sitting idle. Driving sharpened stakes into the ground was a first measure. Everyone who'd ever done History at school knew about that. Then get some rocks to lob, set up an ambush. And if they had one or two carpenters in their number …

Assuming she knew. But she might not.

"Have you met my sister?" he asked Edna.

"I believe she thought I was a camp spy, sir. Someone planted by Pownall with a view to gathering information about the demo."

He stopped and turned to face her. "Okay, look, I'm very flattered that you keep calling me 'sir'. It shows a healthy respect, I suppose, for the time that I've been with MI7, and that I'm an officer, and so on. But I want you to stop. I never called Alec sir when he and I were and the position you and I are in now, and I never called Annabel ma'am. I don't want to come across as a trendy progressive, but from now on, I want you to call me John. Just John. Okay?"

She nodded. "Right."

"Sorry if that sounds like a rant. It wasn't meant to be. You're doing a great job as far as I know, and you've a very professional approach."

"Thank you."

"Rewind. Why does she think you're a camp spy?"

"Because *I* found *her*, not the other way round. I said I'd read somewhere she was once called Mordred and I just wanted to know if she was related to this person I'd once dated - "

"I assume she then asked you all about me."

"That's right."

"Bloody typical Hannah. How did it go?"

"I told her the things Brian went over in his briefing. That you're a vegetarian. And that your bank account's virtually empty at the end of every month: how you've got to pay for electricity, gas, water, plus support Battersea Dogs' Home, the Donkey Sanctuary, Orangutan Foundation, Greenpeace, Shelter, Amnesty International, Christian Aid, Save the Children, The RSP - "

"Anything besides my utility bills and charitable commitments?"

"That's all Brian seemed to know about. He thought they were good conversation pieces. In the event, all Hannah wanted to know was where, on your body, you had a particularly big mole."

"How the hell would *she* know anything like that? She was bluffing."

"She's your sister. She must have … er, seen you naked at some point?"

"About thirty years ago, maybe. Bloody hell. Anyway, I could have had it removed – assuming it even exists: I've never seen it."

They got back in the car, Mordred and Annabel swapping seats so that she and Tariq were together in the back, and Mordred was up front. Edna looked depressed.

"It's not your fault," Mordred said. "It's Brian's. He should have done a bit more research. Like, say, asked me about myself, or looked at my file or something. Can I ask how you reacted when Hannah asked where I'd got a mole?"

"Like I wasn't going to answer a question like that. If she didn't want to know me, that was her loss."

"Textbook. Well done."

"Thank you."

"When you see her again, you're going to be with me. How are you going to act?"

"Like she insulted me, so I don't trust her. I like you a lot, or I used to, and maybe I could again, but I don't like *her*. She asked me where your mole was. Weird."

Mordred laughed. "Now look, we're friends, okay? I mean, genuinely, in the actual, real world. That's the only way to be in this game. I don't know who invented the ranks stuff, but I'm guessing it was probably Bismarck or Kaiser Wilhelm or maybe Mussolini. It's got no place in the modern world."

"Understood." She smiled. She seemed genuinely happier now.

He looked out of the window. Evening was coming on, and the sun lay low on the horizon. The sky was all different shades of blue, and birds glided about haphazardly like they knew they'd done all the breeding stuff and now it was just time to have fun. The trees were a darker shade of green, heralding night. The road even more so. Apart from World War bloody O, it was a perfect summer's day.

He'd never taken that much notice of the Olympics or of athletics, but he'd seen Edna a lot on the TV till recently, and he'd seen her pick up her MBE. It was all over the internet, and on the front page of all the papers. What the hell was she doing sitting within ten feet of a loser like him? How the hell had they ended up with *him* having to tell *her* not to call *him* sir? Why was he having to tell her he was her friend, like *his* friendship, in comparison to *hers*, was some boon, hugely in demand? Of course, the celebrity stuff

– and she was a celebrity: a real one – was all so much nonsense, but even so. Even so. He was no one. She wasn't. She was someone. Suddenly, she was quite mysterious.

"Can I ask you something personal?" he said.

She shrugged. "Since we're friends."

"You're Edna Watson. Everybody knows who you are, even me, and I'm not the sprinting type. Added to that, you're tall. I know you pulled that stunt on Alec last year, but surely people must know who you are wherever you go. When you met Hannah, for example. Didn't she immediately say, 'Bloody hell, it's Edna Watson'?"

"I just tell them we're distant cousins. Our ancestors came from the same part of Africa."

"And they believe that?"

"Obviously, I can disguise my voice, re-do my hair, and so on. In the end, they've no choice. The point is, I wouldn't be any worse off if they found out I *was* Edna Watson. MI7 didn't hire me as a disguise artist. They hired me as Edna Watson. I can gain admittance virtually anywhere in the world if I want to, anytime, just by virtue of who I am. And if you're my relatively insignificant boyfriend, no one will notice that you've disappeared – that as a matter of fact, you're cracking a safe in a completely different part of the building – because they're so dazzled by the woman who broke the world two hundred metres sprint record in 2013."

"What if your boyfriend's caught in the act?"

"I only met him recently. Actually, come to think of it, I know very little about him." The car drew to a halt. "It's right here," she said.

They all got out and walked up another shallow incline, this time a field with cows in. When they reached the top, they found themselves looking at another group of men of the same type as those they'd seen encamped only a few moments ago.

"They weren't here when I left," Edna said.

"Is there anywhere else we could try?" Annabel asked.

They got back in the car and drove a little farther down the road until they came to a gap in the hedge. They pulled so far onto the verge that they all had to get out of the same side. They walked grimly to the top of the slope and looked down. More men. Five in all, sitting playing cards.

Mordred shook his head. "This is ridiculous."

"From what I've heard," Edna said, "they don't mind you going in. It's when you try to leave that they become obstructive."

"You mean, they try to stop you?" Tariq asked. "Why would they do that? Surely, fewer people will make their job easier when they finally do launch an assault."

"Leavers could be journalists," Annabel said. "Or they might be on their way to muster reinforcements. Same if they turn newcomers away: those newcomers might put two and two together and run for help."

"That doesn't make sense," Mordred said. "Everyone within the camp's got a phone. You could post your journalism or call for assistance that way."

"Assuming there's a signal," Tariq said. He took his mobile out. "Which ... there is." He frowned. "You're right. Something doesn't fit."

"If they're Pownall's men," Edna told Mordred, "they've probably been instructed to keep an eye out for you. They might let us three through, but you're a different matter."

"We'll have to chance it," Mordred said. "I can't see we've much alternative. Five of them against four of us."

"Two of us," Annabel said. "Tariq can't fight, and you certainly can't."

"How far is the protesters' camp from here?" Mordred asked.

"About a hundred metres," Edna replied.

"Did you exchange phone numbers with anyone in there?"

"A few people, but I suspect that now I've left, your sister's view that I'm a spy has prevailed. I left for reasons unspecified, and now I'm outside the perimeter trying to get in. How does that strike you?"

"Maybe not promising," Annabel admitted. "But then you tell them all you left to meet your boyfriend, who just so happens to be the beloved only brother of the almighty Boudicca."

"We need to put a story together," Mordred said. "Gabrielle, you joined the camp, then you met my sister. Despite how objectionable she was, she started you off thinking about me again, and you realised you still liked me. So you phoned me. I flew in all the way from London because I couldn't resist the romantic temptation of Gabrielle Duchamp and the moral obligation to stand by my sister in her moment of adversity. When I first arrived, I tried to come to the camp. I hired a taxi to take me there, but the crowd was too big. That's when I got beaten up. Then, this afternoon, I discharged myself from hospital and rang you because I couldn't wait for us to be together again. We agreed to meet in Saint Helier, so we could find each other easily, and because I needed help getting from A to B."

"And where do Tariq and I fit into this?" Annabel asked.

"You're on honeymoon," Mordred said. "You thought it would be romantic to join the protests, and you met Gabrielle by chance while she was waiting for me – where?"

"The Potter's Inn," Tariq said. "On the seafront."

"And you offered us a ride in your car in exchange for our – Gabrielle's – help getting you in."

"Why would we think we couldn't get in?"

"You made a preliminary excursion. The sight of all those roughnecks put you off. You didn't want to risk ruining your honeymoon."

"Heaven forbid," Tariq said.

Edna already had her phone out. "Hi, Simon. Yes … I'm outside the camp with some friends facing five very strong looking men. I - " She looked at her phone then at the others. "He's hung up," she explained.

"When were you last in there?" Mordred asked.

"This morning."

"Okay," he said. "I know what you're thinking, but you're almost certainly wrong. The camp's too big for something like 'Gabrielle's a spy' to have become a received wisdom. Unless it's shrunk significantly since I was last there."

"Of course it has," Annabel said. "You've been out of action for a week. You didn't think the world was just going to stand still, did you?"

"By how much?" he asked.

"No one knows exactly," she said, "but at its largest, it was estimated at about a million strong. It's probably not more than twenty thousand now. Proof, if any were needed, that terrorism works."

"Even so," he replied. "Twenty thousand's a lot. I hadn't thought of this till now, but the reason Simon 'hung up' was almost certainly not because he thought Gabrielle's a camp spy, but because his battery's virtually dead. Probably everyone's is. In that case, there's no need for Pownall or anyone else to interfere with the signal."

"So in sum," Annabel said, "no journalism's getting out, and they can't call for help. They're like fish in a barrel."

"The point is, no one's coming to *our* rescue either," Mordred said. "We either do this ourselves, or not at all."

They looked at each other. Two against five. Not very good odds, probably even when the five weren't built like gorillas.

"We don't have to fight our way through," Annabel said eventually. "How about me and Edna distract them and you sneak through somehow when they're not looking?"

"How are you going to do that?" Tariq asked. "And how are you going to get in once John and I are inside? Assuming we make it."

"All you've got to do is cross that little strip of field there," Annabel said. "Seven seconds, that's all it should take, no more."

"I'm serious," Tariq persisted. "I'm not leaving you till I know what you've got in mind."

"Very well," she replied. "More tall tales. I'm an estate agent and I was driving the famous Edna Watson round the island, hoping to sell her one of our more upmarket properties. Yes, that's right: this is actually her! Unfortunately, the company car broke down, but you can see the house from two hundred metres on, and since it's such a lovely evening, we decided to walk to that point. You'll have a look under the bonnet for us? Oh, how kind. Here are the keys. Yes, I know there are protesters over there, but we'll be fine. Edna can take care of herself, and so can I. We'll call you if we need you. Thank you so much."

"Sounds roughly pukka," Mordred said. "Especially if they're letting people in anyway."

"Thank you so much for the praise," she replied. "Now, we're going to go this way. You go that. Wait till we've got their attention, then move. We'll meet up again in ten minutes. If you can't see us at that point, switch your phones on."

They split up. Mordred and Tariq walked beneath the lip of the slope so they couldn't be spotted and emerged on the far side of a clump of shrubs. They could just see Edna and Annabel. They already had the men's complete attention, so crossing the border zone was easily done, and not even that nerve wracking.

Then minutes later they re-united on the edge of the protesters' camp. Annabel was laughing.

"What's so funny?" Mordred asked her.

"None of them spoke English," she said. "We had to use sign language. Mind you," she went on, suddenly becoming serious, "you should have seen what they had in the way of kit. Long, thick poles, sharpened into points. Anyway, they're 'fixing' our car."

"Did you see the drums?" Edna asked.

"What drums?" Annabel said.

"Under tarpaulin. Lots of them. Bass and snare versions, like you'd get in a military band."

They all looked at each other. Eventually, Mordred threw his hands up. "Sorry, I don't have a theory. Sherlock Holmes might know what to make of it. I don't. Anyone else?"

"Maybe they've got something inside?" Tariq said. "The drums?"

They all looked at each other again. They shrugged.

"Now I *definitely* don't have a theory," Mordred said.

Chapter 15: Hanging Loose With the Coal Tars

When Mordred tried to recall how he'd imagined the camp in advance, he couldn't, except for vague notions of trenches, spiked stakes, people arming themselves for battle. A sense of urgency born of fear. Ramparts, barked orders, chain gangs passing boulders.

What he actually found was very much what he'd seen on his first visit only vastly scaled down and in the twilight of a rapidly descending sun. Annabel had been right. People must have left in their droves. He remembered the Chief Minister: *we'll whittle the demonstration down to its hardest of hard core supporters, then play the waiting game.* Pownall must have been attacking fairly continuously to reduce it to this size. Or maybe not. Perhaps most participants had never been that committed. Maybe they'd been voyeurs or poseurs. Not impossible, by any means. People were like that, some of them. They'd just leave out of boredom, in search of another thrill somewhere else.

While the number of bodies had sharply decreased, the number of flags and pennants looked to have stayed the same. The mass departure gave them a more concentrated effect, making the whole camp look more entrenched, more self-assured.

Which it almost certainly wasn't. Everything else looked as lazy as an old folks' Sunday afternoon. Mostly, people sat or lay on the ground beside their tents doing nothing, or they drank, ate or conversed. They all looked glum. One or two had guitars. There was a collie dog sniffing about, and litter. Lots of litter. Two women greeted Edna as they passed, as if she'd never been away. No one seemed bothered by Annabel's skirt-suit. More disturbingly, no one seemed bothered that they were about to be pulped by hard men with a grudge against light and life.

Which could only mean one thing. They didn't know. He had to find his sister, quickly. Twenty thousand people, a lot to get through. He needed to start asking. Annabel, Edna and Tariq obviously had the same thought. They spread out.

Might as well start where he was. A man and a woman, about fifty, both in sunglasses and T-shirts, lying by a ridge tent, smoking.

"Excuse me," he said. "I'm looking for my sister, Hannah Lexingwood. Do you know where I might find her?"

The man laughed. "A lot of people here, mate. I don't know everyone's names."

"She's supposed to be in charge, that's all."

"No one's in charge. Not as far as I know. It's free admission. Chill out."

"She's made a lot of speeches. Tall, thin, long blonde hair, slight Geordie accent. Last time she was on TV, she wore a lot of silver jewellery, including a fairly distinctive hairband that used to belong to her grandmother."

"She have any tattoos?"

"Some kind of butterfly on her ankle, I think. Or moth, I don't know."

The man laughed. "What kind of a woman's going to have a *moth* tattooed on her ankle?"

"I don't know. She's in the music business."

The man laughed some more. "And that explains it, does it? Hang on, no, I do remember someone with a moth now. Was it a White-Shouldered House Moth, or was it a Case-Bearing Clothes Moth?"

Mordred smiled. "Very funny, yes. Do you know where Soraya Snow is, then? From Fully Magic Coal Tar Lounge?"

The name clicked immediately and he pointed. "About five hundred yards in that direction. No need to keep asking. Just follow the unearthly radiance. And the journos, saddoes and hangers-on."

"Thank you."

Annabel returned with Tariq. "She's over that way."

"Okay, let's get Edna and head over."

Wherever in the universe Soraya was at any one time always buzzed with an intense nervous energy. It was three times as crowded as the next spot along in any direction, and twice as noisy. To be at its centre had to be hell; but after a while, you probably accepted it as normal. What was puzzling wasn't those who wanted to attach themselves as satellites – after all, appearances were always deceptive – but those who, having succeeded, wanted to remain.

He saw Hannah from a hundred yards away, and she saw him. She sat on a deckchair with Soraya and four highly photogenic young men – the Coal Tars – before a tent large enough to stand up and walk around in, and which Mordred vaguely recognised as her Glastonbury one.

Hannah had once explained Fully Magic Coal Tar Lounge to him over dinner. She'd taken them under her wing in 2010 when their sales were in freefall, their manager had just dumped them, and they were a hotchpotch of boy-band-plus-1-girl, heavy rock outfit, and traditional-folksters. Under her expert guidance, Olly became the troubled rebel, and she encouraged him to do things that would land him in court. Gaz was the quiet one, given to reading and writing poems. Elliot was the musical genius, the creative brains and the composer. Paul was the fun one, with something of the demented child about him. Soraya was their combined lover, sister, mother, and guardian angel, famed for her vocal originality and power. She kept them on a short leash through majesty of soul, stupefying beauty and vigour of personality. No one could defy her, nothing could contain her. During a short-lived stint on *The Voice*, she'd been 'let go' after two weeks for 'artistic differences' with the production team, and similar only-half-explained brouhahas accompanied her wherever she went. This 'formula', Hannah said, was what had given Fully Magic Coal Tar Lounge both serious critical acclaim and ten UK number one hits in just five years. Another eighteen months at the outside, and they were expected to crack the US.

Right now however, they looked a million miles away from any sort of fame, notoriety or even common purpose. In fact, they looked close to expiry.

Lugging Hannah's tent all the way over here must have been hell, unless she'd got someone to do it for her, which, knowing her, she probably had. But then maybe she'd been here all along. Maybe they all had. He'd first encountered the camp somewhere on what he believed was the northeast of the island. Maybe it hadn't moved, just shrunk around a pre-existing point. She got up and ran to him and threw her arms round him.

"Thank God you're here!" she exclaimed. She wiped her eyes and laughed. "I mean, not that you can do anything, but just – that you came. I'm just so glad you're here!" She drew back so she could look at him full on. She brushed more tears away. "Thank you for coming. It's really, really nice to see you."

Not what he was expecting at all. He was grinning and emotional too. He'd been expecting her to be angry. *So, I suppose you've come to tell me how stupid I'm being!* And to have to retaliate in kind. *Don't you realise how* worried *everyone is?* She was tanned. Her hair had gone an even lighter shade of blonde, almost white, and she looked a lot like the wise old queen of the woods. He hugged her again. "It's good to be here," he said into her ear. She was almost as tall as him, but he could feel her bones, and somehow, in his embrace, she seemed withered and vulnerable.

Except for the bump. She stepped back and patted it. "Did Tim tell you?"

"Sure did."

"I suppose you think I'm stupid, but it's for the baby I'm doing it. I want him or her to inherit a better world. Funny, I wouldn't even have thought of coming here if I wasn't pregnant. I'm telling you, John, it's true. Crazy, crazy hormones."

"I didn't know you were having a baby," Edna said.

Hannah seemed to catch sight of her for the first time. "Oh my God," she said. "You're with – is this? It's Gabrielle. Shit, sorry. I didn't know. I'm paranoid. I'm really, really sorry."

"No problem," Edna said.

"You kind of brought us back together again," Mordred said.

"You don't understand," Hannah said. "It wasn't that Gabrielle's intrinsically suspicious or anything. It's just … I always thought you were gay."

"What made you think that?"

"The mysterious 'Alec' you're always out with. And when I got you and him together with Soraya and Shula, neither of you called them back. Soraya's *still* waiting by the phone. Believe me, she's *not* going to be pleased to see you. You don't fail to return her calls and get to live. I know what you're going to say: 'Alec's just a friend'. But I don't see how you can be mentioning Alec every time I ring and never mention Gabrielle or Soraya *once*."

"The mystery of me," he replied. "Anyway, Gabrielle and I are back together again now. At least until the next time."

She turned to Edna. "I want to know everything about you. How you met, where, when, what you used to do on dates - "

"Where John's mole is," Mordred cut in.

She blushed. "Okay, I made that up."

"Have I got one, yes or no?"

She hooted. "How the hell would I know?" She rounded on Gabrielle again. "Sorry, we're close, but not that close."

"He didn't have one when I knew him," Gabrielle said. "I'm pleased to report, he hasn't now."

"So all's well that ends well," Mordred said. All this talk about moles would definitely make a good spy novel. "Meet Annabel and Tariq," he went on. "They're on honeymoon. We met them in Saint Helier."

Handshakes were exchanged. "I take it you're not staying," Hannah said, looking the skirt-suit up and down.

"Tariq's parents secretly followed us on honeymoon with the intention of making us an impromptu 'visit'," Annabel said. "'Surprise, surprise!'"

"I've already apologised I don't know how many times," Tariq said awkwardly. He gave Hannah a sheepish grin. "You can't choose your mum and dad, though."

"This isn't what I'd choose to wear on my honeymoon," Annabel went on, "but they love the idea that their son's married an 'old fashioned girl who knows how to dress'. It was all I had that was smart and didn't need ironing. I can't even remember how or why I packed it. Anyway, when we met Gabrielle, we'd just waved my in-laws off."

"They're going to be a bit peeved if they find out you've come here," Hannah replied.

"Fair's fair," Annabel said. "I accommodated them. They've got to learn to do the same for me."

"Hear, hear!" Tariq said. They kissed.

"Well, let's go and meet the others," Hannah said. "John, Soraya's going to be *so* jealous - "

Mordred laughed. "She kept calling me Jim, as I remember."

In front of the tent, six deckchairs had been arranged in a circle. Mordred didn't know the members of Fully Magic Coal Tar Lounge by sight, but these guys looked like musicians: sharp colours, loose clothes, lots of accessories. The odd thing was, Soraya didn't dress at all like any of them. She was more of a straight pop star: short, tight dresses, heels and heavy make-up. But then that was what being a star was all about. You had to stand out from the crowd, the crowd being everybody, but especially your own band. You kept them in place that way. They knew that if there was a split, you weren't dependent on them for your tricks. Mind you, they'd been together for ages now, no exits, and they didn't call themselves Soraya *and* Fully Magic Coal Tar Lounge, so she couldn't be a prima donna.

They were all drinking lager from cans. Behind them, young people stood doing nothing, like supplicants in a Greek frieze. One of the band went into Hannah's tent and returned with four more deckchairs. He set them out. Introductions were made, everyone sat down. Silence fell.

"This is my brother, John," Hannah said, "and his girlfriend, Gabrielle. His two friends, Annabel and Tariq, who are on their honeymoon."

The band and Soraya didn't say anything. They looked darkly at each other.

"You do know what's about to happen, don't you?" Soraya said eventually. "Hannah, you did tell them, didn't you?"

"I was just about to," Hannah said.

Soraya took a deep sip from her can. "We're sitting here trying to get drunk," she said, "because in a few hours' time, we're going to get our heads smashed in. Hopefully, booze will dull the pain."

"I'm not drinking," Hannah said.

"We've got a place to hide your sister till the worst of it's over," one of the band members told Mordred. "They won't find it. She'll be safe."

"You mean there's going to be *more* gangs breaking in with clubs?" Mordred asked.

"The mother of all incursions," Hannah said. "Unfortunately, we're utterly trapped. Have you ever heard of Jeremy Pownall?"

"Jersey's Chief Minister?" Mordred replied. "He came to see me in hospital. Said he was very sorry I'd had such an unpleasant visit. Left a bunch of grapes and said he'd heard I was the brother of the great leader, and would I speak to her on his behalf, get her to see reason. Seemed like a nice enough guy."

"I've never had the pleasure," Hannah said coldly. "What was his 'message' exactly?"

"He said you're living in the past. Jersey's bound by FATCA and its UK equivalent, plus thirty-five – I think it was thirty-five; it may have been more – tax information exchange agreements. He thinks you're living in the past. Jersey's fully transparent nowadays, and you're a very silly girl. You should stop what you're doing and pack your bags immediately."

"How did he know you were coming here?"

"Stop being suspicious," he replied. "I guess he thought that originally, I'd come to see you. His men stopped me the first time, but quite reasonably, he probably thought I'd try again. I'm not his spy, if that's what you're implying."

"Sorry, I didn't mean it to sound like that," she said.

"Well, what do you say? I take it you're not leaving?"

"Legislative compliance doesn't mean actual compliance, John. You read *Private Eye*. You know for a fact that Jersey and Guernsey are in there week in, week out, never in a good way. Next time you see Pownall, ask him how he *knows* there's no financial secrecy here. Because if something's secret, you don't know it's happening. That's what the word means."

"He'd probably ask you how you know it *is* happening," Mordred replied.

"And I'd tell him we've passed that point now. Look, they're all 'mending their ways' now, John, all of them. Their greed nearly demolished our society. We rescued them. We were forced to. Even though we were the ones they'd been fleecing. Then, once the ship was back on course, they just went back to doing what they'd done before. The very stuff that caused the crisis. No one went to jail, no one apologised, no one even admitted any wrongdoing, and of course the culprits and the politicians went on cosying up to each other. Somewhere along the line, though, they realised that there's a big group of people out there – we call ourselves the 99%, John: you're one of us, whether you know it or not - who hate them. So: they decided to do a bit of PR. In the form of new 'regulation'. Nothing real. Just cosmetics. And that's where Pownall comes in. So if you want to know how I'd respond to his little 'how do you know it *is* happening' line, I'd tell him to stick it up his arse."

"Pownall's just a sock puppet," Soraya said. "It's not his private army that's coming to get us. The bankers have hired the men, and they'll take care of the press and the legal claims afterwards: make sure everything's settled out of court and the newspapers play it down or spike it."

"We hate them and they hate us," Hannah said. "They've even boxed us in so we can't run away. We've got to stay here and be beaten up. Spectacular finale to WWO. Trebles all round on the floors of the Stock Exchange. Maybe open after regular trading hours, transmit it live."

"Shouldn't we be doing something to prepare then?" Mordred said. "Defensive measures? Why's everyone just sitting around?"

"Because we can't afford to up the ante," Hannah replied. "What have we got here? Things to throw, that's all. Sticks and stones. The trouble is, if we use those, we might just succeed in beating them off, if we're lucky, but they'll come back tomorrow with something bigger. A few actual guns, maybe. I don't know whether you've heard the rumours, but there are supposed to be lots of firearms on this island. Sooner or later, we'll lose. The longer we draw it out, the worse it'll be. No one here's a skilled fighter anyway. No, we might as well take our pasting and live to fight another day."

"It would be better if you could withdraw, say to another part of the island. Have you tried talking to the guys that have you surrounded?"

"We can't 'talk' to them, John. They don't speak English. I'm pretty sure that's why they've been put there. No possibility of our negotiating with them, and off they head back to Eastern Europe when they've done their job. By the time the local police get round to doing anything about the violent crimes that are going to be committed here tonight, the criminals will be long gone."

Bloody hell, talk about a doom-monger. Mind you, it all fitted together, and they seemed pretty certain that tonight was the scheduled eve of destruction. Finally, however, he was in familiar territory. As MI7's resident languages expert, he might hold the key to a breakthrough.

"You know very well that I can talk to these guys," he told his sister.

She smiled. "Yes, I forgot about your uncanny knack for foreign tongues. I wouldn't bother, though. I don't want you getting hurt."

"She's right," Annabel said.

"Look," he went on, "I don't have to go over there on my own. We can go in a group. If they've been put on holding duty, there'll be some prearranged signal for the attack, and they're not going to want to sabotage that by moving in too early. That would reek of indiscipline. We'll rig me up a little white flag, and six or seven of us can go over. Gabrielle and Annabel have already spoken to them – I say 'spoken to': made contact with - and they didn't bite. It's worth a try. Come on, anything's got to be better than just sitting here."

"Jim's right," Soraya said.

"We might be able to buy them off," Mordred said.

Hannah hooted. "With what?"

"Soraya."

"Er, shit," Soraya said.

"Her autograph and a few selfies. It's worked before. Come on, she's global."

Hannah put her hands in her hair.

"Yeah, okay," Soraya said. She shrugged. "Nothing ventured, nothing gained. Me versus Hannah's baby – no contest."

They were about to move when there was a commotion, stage left. Everyone stood up and looked. Downhill, some way towards the ocean, an old man was making his way doggedly towards them, his eyes fixed on the ground as if directing every bit of his attention to keeping a sure footing. For some reason, his appearance was the occasion of a tangible dread written on the faces of Hannah, Soraya and the band members. Soraya sat down again, as if her legs wouldn't support her. She uttered an 'Oh, God'. Hannah leaned over her brother and whispered, "One of our spies in Saint Helier".

It didn't take him long to close the gap between them. Mordred recognised the taxi driver who'd brought him to the camp on the day of his arrival on the island. He was out of breath and red in the face.

"They're setting off to come here at eleven sharp, right after the pubs close," he said. "Probably about a thousand of them, armed mainly with clubs. No guns. They've been told to go easy, but that doesn't mean anything. You need to get everyone out and away. What are you still doing here?"

"We're surrounded, Kit," Hannah said. "We're trapped."

"Okay," Mordred said, "this has gone far enough. It's eight o'clock. That means we've got three hours till they set off from Saint Helier and probably four till they arrive and start kicking us all over the island." Annabel handed him the little white flag she'd made from a stick and the tail of Tariq's shirt. "Thank you," he told her. "Now, heads held high, let's all go and beg for mercy. Perhaps if they're confronted with a pregnant woman, they'll think again."

Chapter 16: The One With All the Men In

The nearest point of the encirclement was past the camp, across a small field, through a row of shrubs and down a shallow slope. Mordred tried to take the lead, but Hannah skipped up and linked arms with him. "Give me the flag and I'll let you do the talking," she said. Her voice trembled. She didn't add anything. Though getting there took no more than three minutes, everyone's boots filled with lead, their bodies with adrenalin and their brains with endorphins. When they arrived, they were both high on natural chemicals and sluggish with despair.

Twelve men in leather jackets and jeans stood up in mild surprise and turned to face the surrender-party. Mordred waved his white flag and smiled. He'd have to say his speech again in whatever language they spoke, but he might as well rehearse it. Give Hannah and her friends a flavour.

"Nice evening," he said. "I'm John, and these are my friends from the camp across the way. We've come out here to ask if you'll let us out. We realise we've lost. We don't want anyone to get hurt. We're willing to leave the island, if necessary. You've nothing to gain by hurting us. We've got a pregnant woman among us, as you can see. Probably more than one, given the lack of TV on an evening."

The men looked at each other. They seemed annoyed by their own puzzlement. "We don't speak English," one of them said.

Mordred smiled. "Luckily, you don't have to," he replied in Lithuanian.

"Hey," the same man replied in surprise. He grinned. "Whoa. Was that - ?"

"Me speaking your language," Mordred said.

He didn't expect what happened next. They all came over and started shaking his hand, slapping him on the back and laughing like he was an old friend.

"Not before time!" one of them said, a giant with a round stubbly head, a double chin, and a high-pitched voice. "I'm Vincas Samauskas. I'm in charge here. What's your name?"

"John Mordred. I don't get it - "

"Are you in charge in the camp, John?"

He didn't really know what was going on any more. "Er, I can be. If you want."

"Because in about three hours, you're going to be attacked."

"I know."

"You *know?* How?"

"We've got a spy in Saint Helier," Mordred replied. "A taxi driver."

"Hang on, I recognise you. You were the guy they beat up. We thought you were still in hospital."

"I received an early discharge."

"We banged a few heads together outside, stop them making away with you. Why isn't anyone inside the camp *doing* anything?"

Mordred scratched his head. "Who *are* you? If, er, you don't mind me asking?"

"We were sent here by Mr Decristoforo. To protect you."

This took what felt like a full minute to sink in. Mordred felt his head blow off and his breath vanish within his chest.

"What is it?" Hannah said anxiously. "What's going on, John? Say something."

"They're here to look after us!" he said. "My God, they're not going to attack us, they're here to defend us!"

"You need to start working," Vincas said. "We've got shovels and spades and stuff. All you need. Get your manpower together. No one behind you need get hurt tonight. Just do as we say."

Trenches were dug, spiked stakes were driven into the ground, people armed themselves with clubs and spears made from dismembered trees, and prepared for battle. A sense of urgency reigned, born of excitement. Ramparts were erected, orders barked, and chain gangs passed boulders from the beach over a mile away. At eleven, the news was bellowed round the camp that a one thousand-odd strong militia had set out from Saint Helier. Vincas and his men were all in the camp now. In the last couple of days, they'd seen the enemy running reconnaissance missions, and knew the three or four points by which they'd attempt ingress. They fortified them with concealed defenders.

The Lithuanians' orders were transmitted through Mordred to a network of adjutants, who took them to all corners of the twelve fields the protesters occupied. At half past eleven, news came in that the assault force was halfway there. The drums were brought out, and fitted to PA speakers driven by diesel generators. Men began to play them, another one joining the throng every five minutes, until the noise was deafening.

"Put the fear of God into them!" Vincas shouted. *"They know we know they're coming!"* He laughed. *"If you were among them, how would your knees feel right now?"*

"WHAT?" Mordred shouted.

"I SAID - " He gave a dismissive wave. *"You'll be able to hear this all over the island!"*

"My ears are bleeding!"

"If that's the worst that happens to you tonight, I've done my job!"

One of his men came up, cupped his hands and shouted something in his ear. He stood up, beaming.

"They're starting to turn back!" he shouted. *"We've been harrying them all the way from the capital. Rocks thrown, clubs swung, all out of nowhere. That and the drums – they're giving up!"*

Mordred smiled. He laughed. No one here was going to die. Everyone was going to live. They'd won, with hardly a shot being fired.

"Where are you going?" Vincas shouted.

"I've got to tell my sister!"

Another drum joined the reprise, at God knows how many gigahertz. Trumpets sounded. Now it really was impossible to hear.

Three days passed. Summer seemed to turn overnight to autumn. The air grew colder and the breeze from the sea a little less friendly. It felt like soon they'd be looking up at V's of geese flying south for the winter. Mordred didn't know whether you got that here. Did they pass over Jersey on their way to Africa? He hadn't been recalled to London yet. Maybe he'd stay long enough to find out.

The presence of Decristoforo's reinforcements had obviously reached Pownall. No more was heard of his militia. Presumably, he was sensible enough to realise that tit-for-tat could be the end of everything for everyone. He'd said The Waiting Game was his Plan B. Winter would achieve what amateur soldiers couldn't.

Mordred asked Vincas about himself. He owned a private security firm in Vilnius, guarding compounds at night, the rich and famous at home, money on its way from A to B. He'd met Peter Decristoforo about a year ago, after the old man invited him to England to discuss 'a large scale project'. He hadn't gone into details, but did provide enough in terms of a first class flight to and from Heathrow, three days' accommodation at a top London hotel, a chauffeur-driven car and a variety of paid-for outings, to convince the Lithuanian that he meant business. It turned out that what he wanted was what Vincas had just provided: a hundred strongmen to defend a protesters' encampment on Jersey. *Be ready for the call.*

Which meant Decristoforo was one of World War O's prime instigators. Mordred reported back to MI7, and the search for him was upgraded to top priority. Vincas claimed not to know where he was and within a few hours of talking to Mordred, he and his men disappeared, leaving all their equipment behind. According to hearsay, they left in ten big rowing boats from the east of the island like a band of Vikings desperate for Denmark.

Hannah knew that spies could still be anywhere, so she was careful to keep news of the departure to herself and her immediate circle. Theoretically, the camp was wide open to attack again, but there was a new confidence now, and, for a few days, humiliating defeat no longer looked a possibility. Thanks to the generator, mobile phones could be re-charged. Food in varying quantities arrived from sea, from foraging and from sympathisers in the surrounding villages.

Then the trickle of people leaving turned into something more. Four days after the Lithuanian exodus, and from a combination of causes including boredom, hunger, lack of running water, fatigue, the cold, low morale, the camp had shrunk by three quarters, and its end looked in sight. Suddenly, there were more flags than there were people, and the depletion showed no signs of slowing.

At last, even Hannah seemed to realise the game was up. She sat outside her tent with Mordred one sunny evening and watched a pair of seagulls glide over.

"How long do you think it'll be before Pownall sends his men in again?" she asked. "Not that he'll need to now, but I'm sure he'll want to give us a whipping before we leave. Just to console himself."

"We'd better get you out of here then. You're not a ship's captain. You don't have to go down with the vessel. And to be fair, we are trespassing on someone's land."

"It'll be fabulous to see Tim again. And get a proper shower."

"There's still the City of London. Apparently, resistance is still going strong there. But then that's because the mayor insists on dealing with it in-house … so I've heard."

"Are you and Gabrielle serious?"

"We have our ups and downs. I don't know."

"Are you sure you're not gay?"

"As sure as I can be."

"Because everyone will be all right with it, you know. In the family, I mean. Even mum and dad. Obviously not Gabrielle, but that's why I'm asking. I wouldn't want her to get hurt because you're in denial."

"I'm not in denial."

"I don't understand why you're not serious about her then. She obviously likes you, and she's really attractive, and she's a nice person, and she's intelligent. Is it because she's taller than you?"

"That's it, yes."

"Sorry, I'm prying. I'll be quiet now."

"Okay."

"She's related to Edna Watson," Hannah told him. "The Olympic sprinter."

"I know."

"Sorry, I said I'd shut up."

They sat in silence for a while. The sun beat down, the air filled with gorse scent, and a single bird repeated a refrain. Somewhere in the far distance, a ship's horn blew.

"I've been thinking about what Pownall told you to tell me," she said.

"Oh?"

"Maybe he's right. I don't know, I'm not a financial expert. Maybe Jersey *is* completely transparent now. The point is, why should anyone believe anything any of them say any more?"

"Let it go."

"I can't. It's their arrogance."

"Here comes Kit, the magic taxi-driver."

She looked in the usual direction. Just as before the attack, he made his way painstakingly towards them, looking at the ground. Newsflash from Saint Helier. They had radio access out here, but often Hannah's spies would be so far ahead of the game, information would arrive at the camp before it arrived anywhere else. Mordred put out an extra deckchair and Hannah opened a can of lemonade.

"Bad news," Kit called out, as soon as he was within speaking distance.

"Come and sit down," Hannah said. "Have a drink."

"Have you heard the weather forecast?" he asked.

"No, but it's a very nice evening."

"There's a hurricane on its way."

Hannah laughed.

"I'm not kidding," Kit said. "Why would I joke about a thing like that? You're completely exposed up here. You need to split up and find shelter. Barns, cattle sheds, anything. Go into the towns, sit down somewhere. A pub or something. You can't stay here."

Hannah walked away a short distance. She sighed desolately and put her hands on her head. "Have either of you ever read the Book of Job? Where, right at the beginning, a series of messengers arrives with bad news?" She did an imitation in a low voice. "'The Sabeans attacked and killed all your servants'; 'a bolt of lightning burned up all your sheep'; 'your house fell down'. I feel like I'm him. 'Pownall's put together a militia and he's coming to get you'; 'all your supporters are deserting'; 'there's a hurricane on the way'. Sorry I laughed."

"I can see the funny side," Kit said unconvincingly, "when you put it like that." He drank his lemonade.

Mordred sighed. "I suppose we'd better tell everyone."

"And bid them good bye," Hannah said. "This is just the excuse everyone needs to leave. It's everyone for himself with a force twelve gale in the offing."

"Pownall seems pretty convinced of that too," Kit said. "He came for a look at you all this afternoon, from just over there. Brought two of the other ministers with him in one of our cars. Last glimpse of the rebellion. This was the forecast they'd all been waiting for, apparently, something once-in-a-lifetime. He's got a direct line to the Met office in London. Gets to hear the good news early."

Now that Mordred looked, there were dark clouds right down on the horizon in the west. Angry looking slabs of cold, granite-bottomed steam, shooting electric flashes. Yes, you had to hand it to them: they did look quite Biblical. Very like the Book of Job.

Soraya and her band were coming up the slope. They'd been in the sea since four that afternoon, and they'd taken to wandering round the camp in their underwear unless it was cold. They seemed permanently depressed now, like they'd ended up in jail but they didn't know how. Every day Soraya's fans brought her supplies from mainland France, so she wasn't hungry. None of them were. "I'm losing my mystique," she said one morning as she stood in the ocean eating baked beans from a can with a tablespoon. "Sooner or later, people are going to start seeing me for who I really am." Even so, photographers still came from Rennes, Le Mans and Paris, risking their lives in fragile-looking boats, just to take a few shots of her.

"What's going down this evening?" she asked sardonically. "God, I'm bored. Never again. Never be a protest queen no more, no more, never protest no more, oh Lord."

"There's going to be a hurricane," Hannah said.

"Yeah, sure."

"I'm not joking. Look." She pointed to the clouds.

"Sure. I'm not an idiot."

Hannah laughed. "What are you talking about? I never said you were."

"I know what a hurricane is, girl. It's wind. And I know what wind is. It's air. And air's see-through. So don't go taking the piss. I'm fed up enough. If it wasn't for the fact that you're carrying my child - "

"God-child," Hannah corrected her.

"Hannah's not joking," Kit told Soraya. "The thing about moving air, baby, is that it moves other things. Like clouds. And it moves them in certain ways so you can tell from a distance how fast that air's moving, and that you'd better shift your sweet bippy if you know what's good for you. I'm from the USA. We have hurricanes all the time. And believe me, wonder gal, that *is* one. If I was back where I came from, folks'd be battening down the hatches now."

"So she's not just saying that to cheer me up?" Soraya said, wide-eyed. "There really is going to be one?"

"You bet your sorry ass," Kit said grimly.

Soraya looked as if she'd won the lottery. She extended both her arms and looked emotionally at the sky. *"Whoo-HOO! Thank you, GOD!"* She stood on Hannah's deckchair and addressed the camp. *"Hey, listen up, everyone! Great news! THERE'S GOING TO BE A HURRICANE!"*

Suddenly, everyone was standing up, whoo-hoo-ing and giving thanks to whatever deity they believed in. The excitement-drought had finally come to an end.

"Does anyone in Britain actually know what a hurricane is?" Kit asked.

"Only what we've gleaned from *The Wizard of Oz,*" Mordred replied.

Chapter 17: Putting the Wind Up 'Em

God knows why, but Hannah wanted to make sure the flags were safe before she ordered a general evacuation. They uprooted them, tied the collection in little bundles, and secured them beneath a hawthorn where the lip of the incline provided a natural wind-break. Then she and Soraya went round the camp like a couple of town criers, leaving Mordred to find the people he'd come with.

He found Tariq and Annabel on the beach at Plemont. He'd only seen them infrequently since his arrival, but they seemed to be enjoying their honeymoon now, and, oddly, the hurricane news affected them much as it had Soraya. Annabel laughed and hooray-ed. She and Tariq got up and followed him, as if she thought he must have a plan.

He couldn't find Edna at first. He and she had spent a lot of time together holding hands, or with their arms round each other. He had no idea what she really thought about him, but he got the feeling she found this particular job oppressive and him objectionable. For her sake, he tried to avoid her when there was no necessity for them to be seen canoodling, and luckily, she'd made a few friends so she was never at a loose end.

Nevertheless, when news of the hurricane came, she was the first person he thought of. Even though it was obvious she could take care of herself – better than he could in many respects – he felt an inexplicable over-concern for her safety. He found her sitting in a field playing cards with three of her girlfriends.

"Your boyfriend looks a lot older than you," one of them – a small woman with pigtails and a Nirvana T-shirt - whispered in French.

"I've just lived a rough life," he replied in the same language. "I'm only nineteen really," he added.

"It's the heart that counts," Edna said. "What's up, John?"

"Apparently, there's going to be a hurricane," he said.

The blood drained from her face. She stood up, clutching her cards. "Oh my God." She looked towards the camp. "Does everyone know?"

"I believe so."

"There doesn't seem to be much urgency. How far away is it?" She looked to all horizons and spotted it. "About an hour. Ninety minutes at the most. Come on, we'd better get to shelter."

"Where?"

"I know places. I've been using my time here wisely. I thought we might need to hide if Pownall attacked again. But we need to get packed and get moving now. Right away."

"You're in charge," he said. "I need to get Hannah and Soraya and tell them."

Edna took over. Over the course of here-quarters of an hour, she found shelter for about a hundred people, heading east towards Grève de Lecq, but ultimately, the magnitude of the task defeated her. Altogether, the camp was still nearly five thousand strong. When the locals heard five thousand souls were on the move and headed their way, they switched off the lights in their homes, set their dogs barking, bolted their doors, padlocked their gates.

But not everyone was that scared. Priests and helpers from St Martin arrived on foot outside the barracks at Grève and led a hundred people to shelter in the Roman Catholic Church forty-five minutes away on La Grande Rue. The vicars of Saint John's and Saint Mary's took another two hundred between them.

Which still hardly dented the problem: four thousand seven hundred still to accommodate. At least, in theory: Mordred reckoned a large number had left to fend for themselves, heading west, or south, or for Saint Helier. If you were at the back, you would. If you had any sense, you wouldn't hang around waiting for your 'turn'. This was Anarchism. Do as you feel. As they kept telling him, *no one's in charge.*

"If you can get to the capital, there are at least five churches willing to put you up there," the vicar of Saint John's said. They stood in a car park overlooking the beach at Grève. Waves battered the coast and fired spume into the dark sky like fireworks. The wind was already force eight or nine.

Saint Helier was about two and a half hours away on foot.

"I've run out of options," Edna said.

Hannah ran up, clutching her backpack. "We've had an offer!"

"How many people do we still have to accommodate?" Mordred asked.

"Clive and Gareth are at the back! About a thousand!"

"What on earth happened to the other four thousand?"

"I don't know! They're adults! We can't run their lives for them! If they want to leave, that's their business!"

"What if they walk into the sea?"

"For God's sake, John!"

Edna put her hand on his arm and turned to face him. "Let's get the remaining people to safety, John. If you want to go and look for the others afterwards, I'm happy to come with you, but I wouldn't recommend it. What have we got to do?" she asked Hannah.

Hannah produced an old man in a wax jacket, apparently from out of nowhere. "It's an hour's walk!" she shouted. "This man knows the way! All we have to do is follow him!"

Mordred smelt a rat. Pownall's work? "Where the hell on this island could there possibly be safe shelter for over a thousand people?" he asked her.

"The old war tunnels," the man said, before she could reply. "About four and a half miles southeast of here. Under Jersey law, they belong to the person whose land lies over them. I'm just his tenant. He specifically asked me to come and get you."

"I don't suppose he's got a name, this 'landlord' of yours?"

"Of course he has, sir. Can't see that it's relevant, though. You probably won't recognise it anyway. Don't you want to get these people to safety?"

"What is it? His name?"

"It's Peter Decristoforo. Some kind of rich scientist, lives abroad, hasn't been seen here for years. I swear to you, he told me to make myself known. That's all I'm doing. You can take it or leave it. My wife says I shouldn't be out at all."

Mordred stepped back a pace. "Yes, yes, of course. Sorry. You go ahead."

Edna took his hand, slung her haversack back over her shoulder and smiled. "Nice that you care, John. Now come on."

They arrived at the tunnels three-quarters of an hour later, battered, wet and slightly dazed, just as the wind hit force ten. This wasn't the tourist entrance, rather it was further inland, and outwardly much less well preserved. A double door, about the width of two people, opening onto a long metal ladder. They climbed down into a wide, high horizontal cylinder with a floor extending about thirty metres in both directions to where it turned beyond view. The whitewashed walls and the strip lights gave the whole thing a blinding effect. One-time operating theatres and medical centres led off on alternate sides at forty foot intervals. A smell of cooking. At the far end of the tunnel's northern extension, food was being laid on, or so the farmer had told them. Two sheep and a cow, slaughtered that afternoon, plus home-made bread and boiled potatoes. After an hour, it was served. Mordred made himself a potato sandwich. Most people then fell asleep as the storm raged impotently above and outside.

Chapter 18: The Return of Fenella

"Psst!"

Mordred awoke to find himself lying on Edna's chest. She lay asleep too and had her arms round him.

Two inches from his nose, with her index finger upright on her lips: Hannah. "Ssh!" she said, as if her exact meaning might be unclear.

He sat up drowsily, and looked at his watch. 3am. He felt Edna arise behind him. On either side of them, stretching up and down the corridor, hundreds of people, asleep, like a scene from the London underground during the Blitz.

"Follow me," she said.

She was pretty energetic for a pregnant woman, he had to give her that. Where was she taking them? They tip-toed in between the bodies, up the exit steps and out into the darkness. The worst of the storm was over now. The wind still raged, but not as strongly as before, and the sky was clear. The stars sparkled like they were intensely alive.

Across a field lay a house with a light on. Hannah had an electric torch and led the way. When they stepped through the front door, the farmer was waiting for them. They wiped their feet.

"Just wanted to invite you all up for a drink," he said. "This the last?" he asked Hannah.

"Well, obviously, I'd like to invite everyone," she said, "but these are my best friends. This is my brother, John; his girlfriend, Gabrielle."

"I'm Jacques. Come this way."

They went into the living room. A sofa, two armchairs and coal fire affair, with wallpaper, a mantelpiece with Wedgwood flower vases and Royal Doulton figurines, a thin fitted carpet and a ceiling low enough for Edna to have to stoop slightly. An old woman sat on the sofa, presumably Jacques's wife. She stood up.

"Welcome to my home," she said. "We're not all on Mr Pownall's side. Just because we didn't come out and trumpet our support, doesn't mean we weren't with you. Sorry it's over, but there's always next year. Have a brandy. Or two. And feel free to use the shower at any point," she concluded bluntly.

"Thank you," Mordred said.

Annabel and Tariq were there, sitting on the floor against the sofa, in front of Soraya and two band members. Annabel's suit had been washed and rewashed in water from the reservoir so often that it looked like it was falling apart, and Tariq looked like a tramp. They didn't look unhappy. The Coal Tars sat on hard chairs probably requisitioned from the kitchen. The man at the far end of the sofa stood up. Hannah took his place. Soraya put her arm round her and laid her head on her shoulder. "Hi again, Jim," she said.

"My wife and I are going to bed now," the farmer said. "That'll free up two seats. We just wanted to meet you. Take what you want from the fridge. Mr D says he's paying."

"Who is Mr D?" Soraya asked.

"A supporter," the farmer said. "A scientist. Our landlord. I don't really know very much about him. Good night."

"I suppose we should all start booking flights now," Hannah said, when they'd gone.

"So it's definitely over," Mordred said.

"We started off about a million strong," she replied. "then, before the storm, we were down to about five thousand. There's about nine hundred people left in the tunnels. On the way here, they were all talking about going home. If we try to regroup, we'll be lucky to muster fifty. So: *finito*, yes."

"We did a good job," Soraya said. "You should be proud."

"If only Tim could have got in. The irony is, he managed to get leave just as they closed the airport to visitors."

"They'll have to re-open it soon, though," Gaz said. "It's crippling the local tourist industry."

"It's a trade-off," Hannah said. "The tourist versus the finance industry. No contest."

"Even so, there's a hell of a lot of pressure from local businesses to start readmitting visitors," Elliot said. "Some tourist companies have threatened to sue the Jersey States."

"The banks will talk them out of it," Olly said. "Find a 'middle road'. Call me a cynic."

Hannah yawned. "It's academic now. Do you want a brandy, Gabrielle? John? Help yourselves, as you heard."

"I've got a confession," Soraya said. "We've been cheating."

Gaz rolled his eyes. "I told you not to tell her."

Soraya shrugged. "All right, you tell her then. You're better at stories than me."

"Tell her what?" Hannah said.

Gaz sighed. "Okay, okay." He clicked his tongue and rolled his eyes. "In between rehearsals, we've recently been spending a lot of time messing about in the sea. The French have been bringing Soraya gifts since we got here, but about a week ago, yeah, we're all way out from shore and this bloody great trawler comes over. They've got a *nous aimons Soraya* card they're holding up, and they're all shouting stuff at her. None of us speak French, and they don't speak English. Anyway, she's like, 'Have you anything to eat?', trying to tread water and mime feeding herself. So, anyway, they toss her a load of fish, then she's attacked by seagulls, and then they're all apologetic like they really didn't know *that* was going to happen, and next thing you know, they're hauling her onto the deck, and she's making them get us on board too. Cut a long story short, we got a bloody good meal out of it. Then they're back the next day, and the day after that. Then it was a luxury yacht owned by a Russian, and we had caviar and truffles and champagne. Then it was a motor launch - "

"That was the day before yesterday," Soraya said. "It was the guys with the omelettes you're thinking about, then it started getting like, fifteen, twenty boats a day. There's only so much you can eat. Three boats every twelve hours, that's my limit. Breakfast, bit of lunch, candlelit dinner. Me and the guys. I won't go aboard if they can't accompany me."

Hannah laughed. "I wondered why you were always in the water. I thought you were avoiding me."

"There's a reason I have to tell you this," Soraya said. She'd looked a little awkward throughout, but now it became obvious.

"Go on," Hannah said.

"Yesterday evening, it was another yacht. Just one, and not even too big. They seemed to know what we were up to, cadging grub. They sailed over, and a young bloke came out, about thirty-five, with an old woman – his mum, I assumed. They were very polite. No nudge-nudge, as-the-actress-said-to-the-bishop shit, and they'd already prepared some food. It smelt scrummy, whatever it was. Anyway, we went aboard as usual, and we all sat down to dinner. Turned out the young man and the old woman were just servants. The yacht's owner was a woman of about my age in a black dress called Fenella. Very, very posh, but in a Spanish kind of way, if you know what I mean. Very nice. Anyway, the point is, she knew all about you, Jim."

Mordred had seen this coming only halfway through. "What did she want?"

"She says it's urgent you return to London."

Hannah looked mortified. She was trying not to look at Edna.

"That was the actual word she used," Soraya said. "'Urgent'."

Edna smiled. "It's okay," she said. "It's a mutual friend. I know her through John's place of work. Fenella Salvaterra, she's called."

There was an awkward silence. No one believed her, that was obvious. They thought Mordred was hiding something. From confirmed homosexual to two-timing womaniser in the space of a few days had to be some sort of record.

"She didn't ask about *you*, Gabrielle," Soraya said. "Maybe she thought Jim was alone here."

"Did she actually *call* me 'Jim'?" Mordred asked.

Edna took his hand. "John and I have an announcement to make," she said, and smiled. "Although not that kind of announcement. The fact is, I've been lying about who I am. I'm not Gabrielle Duchamp. I'm Edna Watson."

He could see what she was doing. She knew he'd been blindsided, and she was tossing the biggest firework she could find to create a diversion.

"Er, what's going on?" Hannah said, after more silence. *I'm Edna Watson* seemed to have passed over everyone's heads as imperceptibly as a mote of dust in the stratosphere. Presumably, they couldn't process it, so they thought they'd misheard it.

"Who did you say you were?" Gaz said.

"Edna Watson," she said. "The sprinter."

The disbelief was still total. "And this relates to the woman in the boat ... how?" Hannah said.

"It's complicated," Mordred said. "Last summer, Edna was booked to do a bit of advertising with one of the businesses we're partnering, and the project supervisor wanted someone connected to one of the collaborating companies to escort her round Paris. There are only a few guys in all the firms put together of her age, and my charm and good looks, so we held a raffle. I won. We gave her a *nom de plume* and a bit of a disguise to stop her being mobbed, and the two of us spent more time together than was strictly contractual. Afterwards, we went our separate ways, but she realised she liked me. Hey, it was mutual, okay, but she's a cut above yours truly, so I tried to put her out of my mind. Fast forward, she saw you, Hannah, on the TV, and read your maiden name in a magazine. She thought there might be a chance the two of us were related, and came to Jersey to find me. I saw Edna on TV after she'd arrived in Saint Helier, and I guessed what must have happened, only I didn't have her phone number. Fenella, the woman that owns the advertising company did, though. She's a friend of Edna's and she agreed to put in a word for me at work, get me a bit of leave to come here and follow my heart, so to speak. Anyway, here I am, here Edna is, and it looks like my leave of absence from London has become a bit of a problem, so I probably ought to leave."

"Right," Hannah said, drawing out the vowel. "I didn't understand a word of that," she admitted. "You're saying this is Edna Watson."

"The real deal," Mordred replied. "Although she can carry on being Gabrielle Duchamp if you like."

"It's entirely up to you," Edna said.

"Okay," Hannah said, as if, even now, she was only prepared to accept it for the sake of argument.

Edna smiled. She took out her passport from her haversack and passed it over. Everyone looked at it without speaking. A kind of awe fell on the room.

"Wow," Hannah said, completely converted. "How do we do it? Us Mordreds, I mean. We seem to have a knack for attracting major celebrities. Me and Soraya, Julia and poor Chapman Hill, and now you and … sorry, I almost said 'Gabrielle'. Edna. Wow."

"Don't tell anyone outside this room, please," Edna said. "I don't want the full on star-treatment. I don't like it."

"Amazing," Annabel said. "Edna Watson."

"What a honeymoon," Tariq said. "First, Soraya Snow and the whole of Fully Magic Coal Tar Lounge. Now Edna Watson. No one's going to believe us when we get home."

"Let's drop it now," Mordred said. "Talk about something else."

"Like what?" Hannah said. "What could possibly top this?"

"What we're all going to do tomorrow?" Mordred said.

Hannah shrugged. "Pownall's apparently laid on free ferry rides for those who want to leave. I might take one of those, or I might get a plane..Do you know what I regret most?"

"That you didn't come swimming more often with us," Soraya said. "I tried to get you to."

"Not that," she replied. "The litter. Somehow, I thought we'd pick it all up before we left. Now it's probably halfway to Belgium."

"We were supposed to stay long enough to perform our Up Yours, Pownall concert," Soraya said. "Which means we've lost face."

"We can come back next year," Hannah said. "Mind you, it won't be the same. And realistically, we won't, will we? I'm really sad to be leaving. I love this island. John, did you know that some of our ancestors come from here?"

"Nope," Mordred replied. He was still thinking about Fenella. What did she mean, 'urgent'? Why hadn't Ruby Parker contacted him, if there was a problem? But a problem for Fenella Decristoforo-Salvaterra might not be a problem for MI7. Still, he couldn't ignore it.

Hannah switched her phone on. She suddenly glared at it as if it had offended her, and swept down. Her expression changed. She looked scared.

"What's the matter?" Mordred said.

"They're looking for me," she said.

Soraya sat up. "Who? Who is? Pownall?"

She read from her screen. "*Arrived in Saint Helier two hours ago. Stay away. Men asking for you by name.*" She opened another. "*Lots of Orcs demanding to know where you are. Very scary. Be careful.*" And another. "*Had our faces compared with picture of you. Don't try to exit this way.*" And another. "*Lots of men whose sole aim seems to be to find you. For God's sake, stay put.*" She put the phone into her lap. "Oh, shit."

"They can't do anything, can they?" Soraya asked. "This is the UK, isn't it? It's a free country … supposedly."

"Jersey isn't part of the United Kingdom," Annabel put in. "We're just responsible for its defence."

"Technically, I suppose it can do anything it wants," Gaz added. "And since it's a well-known secrecy jurisdiction, all Pownall needs to perfect his trap is to declare a state of emergency. Of course, given that there's just been a hurricane, he has the perfect pretext."

Soraya nudged him hard. "You're scaring her."

"I'm scared myself," he replied. "Can't you see? This affects all of us."

"We need to get back up to Plemont," Soraya said. "Phone for a trawler. I've got their numbers. Don't worry, girl, we're not leaving without you."

"That'll mean crossing the campsite again," Paul said. "Pownall will occupy it as soon as the wind dies down. Forget it."

"He might want to," Elliot said, "but there'll be too much damage in Saint Helier and all over. It'll be *real* emergency time, not the vanity-type he's been used to. *The protesters are giving us a bad name.* Not that type. We might stand a chance, if we're quick."

"I'm dead beat," Soraya said. "I've just walked God knows how far through a bloody hurricane. Now it's the middle of the night and I'm not even asleep. Don't ask me to walk back now. No way."

"It's out of the question anyway," Mordred said. "No trawler's going to risk a trip to Plemont at this time, in this weather, even assuming all those you added to your French Fishing Boat Contact List escaped storm damage. We probably need to wait till tomorrow afternoon at the latest."

"Do you really think we can all get out that way?" Hannah asked. She laughed. "What am I saying? They're probably not even looking for you. They're never going to risk abducting a major British celebrity. It's me they want."

"Let's not get this out of proportion," Mordred said. "I can't see them disappearing a pregnant woman. They probably just want to give you a stiff warning and ask you a few questions, maybe even prosecute you for trespassing."

"We don't need to get me out," Hannah said. "We need to get lawyers in. Lots of them, to defend me. If they're determined to keep me, fine, but I'll see them in court."

"You still don't get it," Soraya said. "If they've got their own laws here, who's to say they ever have to let you be accompanied by a solicitor?" She turned to Mordred. "Yes, they may well be going to slap her wrists and that's all, but we can't afford to think that way, Jim. We've got to prepare for the worst."

"Fair point," he said. It was.

"If they've got people out looking for her, they probably mean business," Tariq said.

"We need to get a showered and sleep now," Hannah said. "We're probably safe here for the time being. We'll work out exactly what to do in the morning when we're less tired."

Her words were final. The brandy, symbol of a job well done and an ordeal over, had hardly been touched.

After they'd all bathed, they stole back into the tunnel. It wouldn't be good if everyone woke up and discovered they'd gone; panic might set in. But then, it probably had already, a controlled version.

One by one, beginning at dawn, eight hundred people turned to each other and quietly announced their intention to leave. It was agreed they'd done a good job, the best possible, but that, in the nature of the beast, complete victory had never been possible. With each new confession, the process of letting go became easier. The wind had died to a murmur now, and, when the sun was finally fully above the horizon, the leavers went their way. By the time Hannah awoke at ten, only a handful of people were left. The rest were halfway to Saint Helier.

"I feel like a doomed Shakespearian king," she said, and laughed.

"We'll give it another two hours and we'll leave," Mordred said. "Soraya's been on the phone to her friends in the fishing business. Edna helped her overcome the language barrier. We think. They can be here at about three this afternoon."

She looked around. "We've still got about a hundred people," she replied. "They're not all going to fit on a trawler."

"Pownall's men aren't looking for them. They're looking for you."

"I can't just leave everyone."

"Er, yes, you can. If they get hit, they get bruises and black eyes. If you get hit, you might miscarry. It's too late for heroics."

"There may not be many people left, John. But these are the most dedicated, and Pownall's men are going to know that. Do you really think they're going to let them off with a scolding? Not likely. Weeds come in many types. You've got to be most brutal with the most persistent."

"Look, I'll stay behind with them," Mordred replied. "You're not capable. Don't think I haven't noticed you being sick into a hedge every morning."

Hannah hooted. "Don't think *I* haven't noticed that you were in hospital till recently and your left arm's still not functioning properly."

"Luckily, I'm right handed. Look, if something happens to you and you lose this baby, you'll never forgive yourself."

She sighed. He was getting through. "Do we know where these tunnels lead?" she asked.

"Annabel and Edna did a recce this morning. The south-facing tunnel goes nowhere. According to the farmer, it used to join the tourist *Hohlgangsanlage* farther south, but it collapsed mid-section in the nineteen fifties, effectively creating two independent portions. North, it extends about a mile, then joins a natural cavern which could lead as far as the sea, no one knows. You'd probably have to be a potholer to brave it, and Decristoforo hasn't been admitting explorers."

"What about from the other direction? If there is a cave on the northern shoreline, and it leads here, wouldn't someone have made the journey?"

He shrugged. "They probably have. They'd know they were trespassing, so they wouldn't advertise it."

"I'm just wondering whether it would be possible for us to go that way, rather than overland. Might save us being spotted."

"We don't know if it even leads as far as the sea. The farmer says he thinks it used to, but 'thinks' and 'used to' aren't very helpful. Even if it still does, there might still be fifty foot sudden drops, or the cave exit might be underwater, and of course, we'd be travelling in complete darkness."

"Apart from my torch."

"Which is rubbish, incidentally."

"So what's your plan? We just traipse up to Plemont and await Soraya's trawler?"

He looked at the ground, folded his hands and put them under his nose. He thought. "It's funny you should mention a plan," he said at last, looking at her and smiling. "Because I've just thought of one."

Chapter 19: The Power of Imitation and Echo

"Thanks for the offer, John," Hannah said, "but I really don't need you complicating matters right now. This is serious."

Annabel came up behind them. Mordred was having increasing difficulty recognising her: she looked like she'd been dragged through a hedge not just backwards, but forwards and sideways, and so many times she'd ended up wearing it. Her hair was spectacular. It contained leaves. "Could I have a word with you, John?" she asked. "In private?"

Hannah looked as if here was a new piece of evidence for a hypothesis she'd forgotten - her brother the womaniser – and withdrew with a scowl.

"What's the problem?" Mordred said.

"Keep your voice down. Tariq's gone for a drink of water. I just wanted to tell you again: sorry for what happened at my wedding. I never want you to mention it."

"I thought we'd already agreed that."

"I love Tariq now. I didn't think I could, but I do. And I don't love you. I thought I could, but I don't. I can't."

"That's fine. I just don't understand why you married him when you weren't sure."

"Because people kept telling me: 'nobody's ever certain, everyone gets the jitters'. I thought I was just normal. But obviously I'm not. In any case, I do know now that I love Tariq. For certain."

"Okay. Like I say, I can be very discreet. It never happened."

"It's not really you I'm worried about."

It clicked. "Oh, I see. Alec, yes. Well, as a matter of fact, I've already spoken to him. Right afterwards. His actual words were, 'As far as I'm concerned, it's forgotten'. So sorted."

"You're joking."

"Think about it. I like you, and so does he. Obviously, we're going to try and limit the damage."

She beamed. "I thought it might be all over Tracy Island by now."

"Believe me, Alec's passed the point in his life where swapping gossip for attention seems like a good trade."

"I know that this seems like a trivial thing, given what we're up against, but it's important to me. More than anything."

"Understood," he said.

"In that case, let's get back to the matter in hand. Did I just hear you say you had a plan?"

"A very good one. However, verily I say unto you, no prophet is accepted in his own country. Hannah's not interested. Yet."

"You don't need her consent do you?"

"Unfortunately, she's an integral part of it."

"Tell me. I'll pass it off as mine."

He grinned. "I like the way you just assume it'll be good enough."

"You're hardly an idiot, John."

Five minutes later, Tariq re-joined them and the three of them went to find Hannah. She was in the room where the food had been served, sitting on a low table, eating a crust of stale bread. "Where's Edna?" she asked.

"She'll be along in a minute," Annabel said in a distant tone. "I needed to have a word with John, I'll be having a word with Edna in a moment, but right now, I need to speak to you."

She stood up. "What about?"

"The truth is, Tariq and I are not who we claimed to be. Our meeting with Edna in Saint Helier was no accident. We're bodyguards. When her representative at the British Athletics Race Agency Service discovered where she was, she despatched Tariq and I to look after her."

Hannah pointed from Annabel to Tariq and back again. "So you're not …?"

"Husband and wife? That part is true, and it's also true that we're on your side. We came to Jersey with open minds – looking after one of the greatest sprinters Britain's got isn't incompatible with supporting either party in the dispute – but we've come round to your way of thinking. Even if we hadn't, given that Edna's clearly attached to John, and John's determined to remain with you, we need a plan of action to stop people getting hurt. I'm pleased to say, I've got one."

"I'm, er, listening …" Hannah said.

"We've got to think ourselves into Pownall's shoes. He's trying to find us. He knows a lot of people have given up the fight and reached Saint Helier, or possibly Gorey harbour in the east, depending on which way they came in. He'll know there are others still out here. They'll be his priority. He's probably posted lookouts, and if they're effective, they'll already have intercepted the leavers and be questioning them. It's unlikely anyone'll rat us out, so they'll have to resort to other measures. They'll confiscate a phone or two, or fifty, and read the messages. So what you need to do is text as many people as you can, and tell them where we are. 'Good luck, don't let on we're in the war tunnels at Poingdestre Farm'. Not quite that crass, but equally reckless, or so it must appear. When Pownall's shock troops get here, we need something to lure them into the tunnels, then we'll close and bolt the doors on them. The electricity supply's probably controlled from the farm, so we should be able to plunge them into complete darkness once they're inside."

"How are you going to get them in?" Hannah asked.

"Simple. I'm going to go down there and pretend to be you. Tariq will be with me. Using the power of voice imitation and echo, we'll produce the impression that you're only one of several people down there. That you've been caught unsuspecting, in other words."

Hannah laughed. "And how are you both going to get out afterwards?"

"I'm not. At least not for a while. As you can see, there are rooms with reinforced metal doors leading off from the corridor on either side. Tariq and I will repair to one of those and lock it from inside. Then we're safe. It may be that each room's on a different circuit, and the corridor itself can be isolated, so hopefully, we'll have light in there, but, if not, we'll definitely have food and drink, enough for three or four days. The farmer's bringing it now. All we have to do is sit tight until reinforcements arrive from London."

"How's that going to happen?"

"What do you mean?"

"Reinforcements from London. Given that Pownall isn't allowing anyone onto the island?"

"She's got a point," Mordred said.

Annabel looked at each of them in turn. "Haven't - ? You've not heard?"

"Heard what?" Mordred said.

"The news. A few hours ago. The hurricane nearly tore Saint Helier apart. Thanks to Pownall's isolationism, those families reliant on tourism were already halfway to bankruptcy. Storm damage was the last straw. Early this morning, a big crowd marched on his house with torches and pitchforks, demanding an end to it all. Luckily, for him, his Waterloo coincided with ours, and his wasn't quite so bad. This morning, he went on TV and addressed the island, US President-style. *We've achieved 100% success in ending the protests. Our financial services employers remain fully committed to the island's future, and have agreed to compensate businesses harmed as a result of the stand-off. The emergency is now over. We have won. For that reason, and with true gladness of heart, I hereby declare our ferry ports and the airport open again to visitors with immediate effect.*"

"Three cheers for the iron man of Saint Helier," Mordred said.

"And yet he still sends his goons out to give us a mauling," Hannah said. "What was it the PM said in *Yes Minister?* 'In defeat, malice; in victory, revenge'? That just about sums Pownall up."

"The point is," Annabel said, "Tariq and I work for a high-profile security agency. And with the island welcoming guests again, they will send people to rescue us."

"I have to admit, it sounds like a good proposal," Hannah said. "There's only one problem. What right do *I* have to ask you to make that kind of sacrifice?"

Mordred rolled his eyes and threw his hands up. "For God's sake."

"Don't flatter yourself," Annabel said. "I'm doing it for Edna. You're taking her with you, and the two of you can look after each other. When the chips are down, she's pretty handy in a fight."

"You and Tariq are going to be inside the tunnel," Hannah went on. "Who's going to shut the doors and bolt them in?"

"That'd be me," Mordred said.

She grinned and shook her head. "Oh, no." She laughed. "No, no, no. No, John, no."

"Why bloody not?" he asked.

"Because you wouldn't be able to do it properly, you'd - "

"*I've just about had enough of you treating me like a complete imbecile!*" He didn't feel angry, but it was worth a try. "*Every time I propose something new, or try to strike out on my own, or show the slightest little bit of independence, you're down on me like a ton of bricks. I didn't ASK you to come here; I didn't ASK you to get pregnant. But now that you ARE pregnant, and you ARE here, THE LEAST YOU CAN DO IS LET ME HELP YOU OUT!*"

Obviously this was the last thing she was expecting, which meant it may have worked. She looked at him for a moment as if she'd never seen him be so cruel, and how could he, then burst into tears.

"*I'm sorry!*" she wailed, turning to Annabel and Tariq. She waved her face. "*It's the hormones! I'm not normally like this! I'm sorry!*"

Mordred put his arms round her and they hugged as she tried to rein herself in.

"Stop thinking," he told her. "Just follow orders for once in your life. You're going with Edna and I'm staying here, and I'll be okay. I'm sorry I shouted. I still love you."

She wiped her eyes while still flooding them with tears. "Don't – don't do anything too risky, will you?"

"No," he said. "Now go and find the others, and get moving. I'll meet you in a few hours at Plemont fields."

She looked at him mournfully, as if she might never see him again, then got up to leave.

"Not so fast," Annabel told her. "I need your clothes. And one more thing: don't call for a taxi. We think Pownall may be listening in on their offices."

Chapter 20: A Lovely Day For Arson

Half an hour later, he lay beneath a clump of gorse bushes awaiting Pownall's private army. The sun beat down from a blue sky, bees and butterflies visited, a plane scraped overhead.

The assumption was that they would be talking when they arrived, and that would alert Annabel and Tariq. At the very least, the sight of an open doorway would pique the gang's curiosity. The lights were on, so Annabel would see them as they entered. Even if they caught sight of her, she was confident she could fool them into thinking she was Hannah. Two seconds was the fastest it took to descend the ladder; another four seconds to where she and Tariq were. But only one and a half from where they were to inside the room, close and bolt the door with the heavy-duty chain and padlock Mordred had to hand.

. The problem revolved around how many men there would be. Too many, and the entrance would clog. Annabel would be safe, but the number outside the tunnel would prevent the trap being sprung. Now if he'd brought a gun …

But he hadn't. And anyway, how could he have kept it secret from his sister? The camp wasn't the sort of place you could keep heavy physical objects to yourself. After a few days, you had to compromise on privacy in all areas. And the longer you stayed, the worse it got. She'd have found it. *What's this, eh, John?* She'd have assumed that, being his, it couldn't possibly be real. She'd probably have shot herself.

Then he imagined Brian. *But you're a secret agent, John! It's your job to keep secrets, even in these sorts of conditions.* Be interesting to find out what James Bond would make of all this. In Brian's Glamorous World of International Espionage, places like the protesters' camp in north Jersey didn't exist. There wasn't any litter in 007's world. Even women like Soraya didn't exist there. Feisty women, yes, but not from council estates in Rotherham.

He hoped they wouldn't go to the farm first. By way of hiding out, Jacques and Glenda had gone to Saint Aubin's in their car, but their farmhouse wasn't necessarily safe from marauding raiders. If they broke in, Mordred would be forced to watch.

After just twenty minutes, he saw them. About half a mile away: thirty-two men making their way quickly up the country road towards the tunnel. Not your average troublemakers. Mordred had expected shaven heads, leather jackets and army boots. But even in this heat, some of them wore shirts and ties. They all looked young, well-groomed and slim to the point where they wouldn't have looked out of place in a men's fashion magazine. None of them spoke. They just kept their eyes fixed on the road in front of them, as if what they were doing was programmed into their brains and predestined to succeed. The local Wolves of Wall Street.

When they reached the farmhouse, they smashed its windows. Not angrily, but again as if it was something they'd long since decided would be a rational action. Someone threw something inside and within a few seconds, the whole building was ablaze. They surrounded it in a ring, and stood watching as it burned, clearly waiting to see if anyone would come out.

Bloody hell. He hoped they weren't going to do the same with the tunnel.

No, they couldn't. There wasn't enough flammable material in there. They'd have to go inside - wouldn't they? Of course they would. They'd think they'd got her cornered.

When, after about a minute, no one had emerged from the conflagration, and no one could have survived inside, they moved over to the tunnel.

"Is anyone inside?" one of them called in a singsong voice.

"Who is that?" Annabel replied. Tariq shouted something and she changed voices to respond while he was still mid-voice. Mordred had to hand it to them: it did sound like there was more than one person in there.

It was the closest Mordred came to seeing any of the thirty-two smile. A wave of satisfaction seemed to run through them, lighting their eyes and turning the corners of their mouths up slightly.

"Shall we go in?" one of them asked.

"No point," another replied. "She can't escape and she doesn't know it's us. She'll come out in a minute. I'll lie down behind the entrance, grab her once she's got both feet on solid ground. The rest of you, find yourselves hiding places."

Mordred felt his heart bubble up into his throat. They spread out. As he expected, one of them chose his spot. He managed to get a hand over the man's mouth and punch him hard enough to render him unconscious, but the scuffle had alerted those nearby. Half a minute later, after he'd knocked another one out and overturned two others, four men held him fast.

The throng parted for their leader, a small, thin man with side-swept hair and a blue tie. He was sweating. He looked Mordred up and down as if he could hardly believe his luck.

"Goodness," he said.

"Thanks for the compliment," Mordred replied.

"It's not praise in my world." He turned to the others. "Twist his arm out of its socket. When she hears him screaming it'll bring her out more quickly."

Mordred smiled. "I take it you're not used to working in bright daylight."

"I don't know what you mean," the thin man said.

"Well, let's say you're working in a warehouse. It's a pretty closed system. After a few preliminary checks, you can be pretty sure you're alone. Out here … well, that's the great thing about the modern day: everyone carries a video camera about. And of course, people can hide anywhere, do a little filming then send those pictures to Youtube, say, at the press of a button. Obviously, we knew you were coming, otherwise why would I be hiding here, and why would the farmhouse be empty? You've fallen right into our trap."

Everyone suddenly looked nervous. "You're bluffing," the thin man said.

Mordred smiled. "Well, we'll soon find out, won't we? In England, we call it second degree arson. I'm not sure what you call it in Jersey. But I'd advise you to cut your losses, because I'm pretty sure murder's murder wherever you live. You may be interested to know, incidentally, that my sister was born thirty-five years ago when my parents were on holiday in New York. She's got dual US-UK citizenship, in other words. The President tends not to like it when foreigners slay his subjects in foreign lands. If you do it on film, I wouldn't like to vouch for your futures. Any of you. Even Goldman Sachs probably couldn't get you out of that one."

"Beat him unconscious," the thin man said. "But don't break his bones. We need to have a conference."

They hauled him to his feet and held him fast. Two men took up position, one on either side of him and began punching him hard in the groin. He felt like his whole body wanted to exit through his mouth, then they dropped him. He rolled over and moaned softly. Mustn't yell for Annabel's sake.

Why hadn't they finished the job? Didn't they know he was still - ?

"Lie on the floor and put your hands on your heads!"

Edna. He forced enough recovery to discover what was going on. She stood some way off to his left with a revolver in her right hand and what looked like a compact submachine pistol in her left. The way one man was writhing about screaming, it was obvious she'd already fired. The others, including the thin man weren't taking any chances. One by one, they did as she'd commanded. She edged her way over to the tunnel without taking her eyes off them.

"You can come out now!" she shouted. "It didn't work!"

After a few seconds Annabel and Tariq emerged, looking as if they thought it might be a trap. They seemed to take in the burning building first, the men on the floor second, and Edna last.

"Is that a Steyr TMP?" Annabel asked admiringly.

"I don't know," Edna replied. "I'm not an expert. Yet."

"Where did you get it?"

"I burgled a house. Now, I want you all to crawl towards the tunnel and get inside. Don't try anything that'll make me hurt you again."

They made their way over to the entrance using their elbows and dragging their bodies. One by one, they disappeared inside.

The thin man was the last to go. When he was on the ladder he turned a grin on Edna. "You do realise this tunnel leads to the sea? We'll be out before you know it."

"*Go!*" she yelled.

He blanched slightly and disappeared from view. Annabel and Tariq rushed to close the doors and Mordred indicated the padlock and chain. He staggered to his feet, swallowing repeatedly to quell the nausea.

"Are you okay?" Edna asked, zipping the guns back into her haversack.

"Thank you for saving me," he gasped. "I'll be fine."

"Would you like to take a few moments?"

"There isn't time. We've got to get over to Plemont. Find Hannah."

"I've a taxi waiting," she said. "It's just across that field."

"A taxi? I thought Pownall had their offices bugged."

Annabel smiled. "It's not going to do him much good with his entire private army ten feet underground. The bigger problem is, how are we going to pay?"

"I burgled Pownall's house," Edna said.

"When?" Mordred said. "When did you get time to do that?"

"You spent a lot of time at the campsite talking to your sister," she replied. "I guess you thought I was off with my friends. Whereas in reality, I was out running." She put her arm round his waist to lend him support. "And sundry other things."

They piled into Kit's taxi and in fifteen minutes they were back at the former campsite. They found Hannah and her band of followers sitting disconsolately at the summit where her tent used to be. Now the storm had done its work, nothing remained to show what it had ever been. The sea was calm but empty: no sign of a trawler or anything else. Hannah stood up indignantly when she caught sight of Edna.

"Where have you been?" she demanded. "We were supposed to look after each other! We've been looking everywhere for you!"

"I was too worried about John," Edna replied. "Turned out you were right."

"What happened then?" she asked. She turned to Annabel and Tariq. "How did you two get out?"

"Give us a chance to catch our breath," Mordred replied. "Where's this bloody trawler?"

"It was damaged in the hurricane," Hannah replied. "We're stranded. At least for the time being. Soraya's got other contacts but none of them speak English. We were waiting for you, John. You're good at languages. Can you speak Russian?"

Always the same when someone asked you if you could speak such and such a language: whether or not to frame your reply in it. "Yep," he said.

"Good, well, go and bloody get Soraya."

"Where is she?"

"I'm guessing in the sea, looking for more food opportunities. We're all famished."

He looked round, trying to locate her somewhere nearby before making the long trek down to the beach. Then he saw something else. Where the land met the sea, about a mile east. Pownall's men emerging over the clifftop in numbers. They stood still for a minute, brushing themselves off, then they began to approach.

Everyone turned and to look.

"Shit," Hannah said. "Is that what I think it is?"

"That was quick," Mordred said.

"Don't worry," Edna said. "I've got the means to defend us."

"Unfortunately, I think they'll know you're not going to mow them down," Mordred said. "It may have worked when we had the element of surprise, but they'll have had time to think about it now. We need a different strategy."

"That's your problem, John," Annabel said. "Far too pessimistic about guns."

The men picked up pace. It was only a matter of time till they started running. Despite their expensive shirts and ties, they were that type. Desperate to fight.

"Excuse me," a genteel voice said from behind, "are you Hannah Mordred? Is this Plemont protest site?"

She turned to face a man none of them had seen before – fortyish with a bush hat, a hiking stick and a backpack. Behind him, about a hundred other people were coming up. "We're looking for the protesters' camp," one of them said.

This wasn't the only contingent of arrivals. Looking across the landscape, Mordred could see others – four all told, with others on the horizon.

"We've been waiting at bloody Weymouth and Heathrow for weeks," the man said. "Finally, Pownall's given us the green light."

For what seemed like a long time, no one said anything. The newcomers started pitching tents as if there wasn't a moment to lose in the rush for a good spot.

"You're … very welcome," Hannah said eventually, the truth apparently clicking.

In the distance, the men had slowed, apparently puzzled. They stopped. They stood watching for a while as the other new arrivals closed in and started erecting canvas, then one after another turned and exited south, towards Saint Helier.

Mordred gave a sigh of relief.

Over the next twelve hours, new people came and kept coming. The camp burgeoned again, as seasoned Occupiers washed in from battlefields where they'd been routed – Guernsey, the Caymans, Singapore, Hong Kong, Bermuda, Mauritius. They brought new skills, an increased sense of determination and a willingness to fight. At nine o'clock that night, Mordred counted seven hundred and twenty-one camp fires.

At ten, Tim arrived with a new tent and enough provisions for two weeks. Hannah cried. Tim cried. Mordred finally got the recall from London, just like Fenella's, marked 'urgent'. He left Edna, Annabel and Tariq to look after his sister and brother-in-law.

The following morning, Pownall resigned.

The plane took off, the land receded, and as they wheeled round to face Henley, he saw the Plemont encampment for the last time. Just a lot of people, that's all: except for the absence of a central stage, nothing to distinguish it from any summertime pop festival anywhere in the world. The rostrum would come, of course. Nothing could stop Soraya's Eve of the End of the World concert now. He hoped his sister would be okay, but he was sure she would. That established, he had to get back to London. It was 'urgent'.

Which raised the question, *what* was urgent? He'd been in Jersey for a long time now, relatively speaking, and Ruby Parker hadn't contacted him at all until yesterday. She'd have found a way if she'd wanted to. From what he'd been told, the protests still weren't over in London. But that wouldn't require his presence. What was it that Fenella Decristoforo-Salvaterra considered so serious that Ruby Parker had only just discovered? And were they even talking about the same thing?

He probably wouldn't find out immediately. He had no idea where Fenella was, even whether she was in the UK, let alone London, and unless she'd taken her concerns to Thames House, she'd probably have to find him.

He needed to sleep and eat. The latter would have to wait: MI7's overseas budget apparently didn't stretch to an in-flight snack, not even a Twix. But you could sleep anywhere. You didn't even need the right training. You just needed to be shattered.

He awoke when the plane bumped down on a rainy day in Henley. For a moment he thought he was back on the island. He looked across the airfield: another black saloon waiting to take him to a pre-appointed destination. Another meeting probably. He hadn't written his report yet, but he'd been in this situation before. When you had a lot to feed back and hardly any time, they usually sent a fully briefed stenographer with a list of questions and permission to interrogate. It never made for a comfortable ride, no matter how carefully you'd played it by the book. Too much ground to cover, too little time to explain the limiting factors, nuances, qualifications.

Thus, on the car's back seat, a man of his own age awaited him. Gwyn: they'd met once in the lunch queue. He had a notepad, a pen and a grim expression. "Welcome back to Britain," he said curtly.

"Thank you, Gwyn."

"You remembered my name." He seemed unimpressed.

"Fire away then."

He gave a 'time is of the essence' nod of agreement. "Describe your first meeting with the protesters."

They arrived at Thames House just over ninety minutes later. It was still raining, and there was a traffic jam on Lambeth Bridge with New York-style peeping of horns. Gwyn got out ahead and went straight inside. Mordred followed him without trying to catch up. Colin Bale stood on duty at reception looking disgruntled as usual. No sign of Gwyn now anywhere. Presumably, the report was so red hot it had to be studied and digested immediately.

"Welcome back, John," Colin Bale said, as if he had to.

"It's great to be home. When's my first meeting?"

"I understand your report's just gone upstairs. You're to go to the canteen, get something hot to eat and drink, and be ready for further debriefing in an hour. Someone will come and get you."

"So it may not necessarily be an hour."

"It'll be *at least* an hour, put it that way. After that, just try and sit quietly without causing any trouble."

"Is Alec around?"

"It's irrelevant, John. You know the rules. You're not allowed to talk to anyone before you've been debriefed. Interference with the memory, that sort of thing. Don't read anything, don't check your phone, don't surf the net, don't watch TV. The four don'ts."

"I've never heard them so handily lumped together before."

"My idea."

"The only problem is, with 'don't talk to anyone', it makes five."

"Don't be a smartarse, John. It doesn't suit you."

"Am I allowed to look at my watch?"

"Repeat, don't be a smartarse, John. It doesn't suit you."

"That's another don't … Sorry, sorry, I'm still slightly out of it. I've another question now, a genuine one. Could the firm please lend me some money for food? I'm skint."

"We're not idiots, John. It's on the house. Just order what you want."

"Thanks."

"Have a nice day."

He ate a butternut chilli and drank two cups of strong earl grey. Afterwards, he had a bowl of ice cream. He felt drowsy now and there were still thirty minutes left till he was called to an anonymous office somewhere to account for himself. At least. Was taking a nap a sixth don't? How many don'ts were there, really? And fancy Colin Bale missing the fifth one – don't talk to anyone - when he'd already mentioned it! How about 'don't leave the building'? Or 'don't look out of an interesting window'? 'Don't do a crossword' was obvious, but file that under the prohibition against reading. What about 'don't let your mind wander'? Or the opposite: 'don't think too much about your story'? After all, over-reflection could be disastrous. You might subconsciously start to iron out apparent anomalies, and something important might get missed. Maybe the psychologists had got it entirely wrong. Maybe the don'ts should be converted to dos, keep the data pristine. *Do* talk to Alec, *do* check your phone, *do* look out of a fascinating window. But that was MI7. Why allow people to do things when you could just as easily tell them not to?

Here she came. A young woman in a pencil skirt with a notepad. She arrived at his table without breaking stride and smiled. "John Mordred?"

"That's me."

"You're expected in Ruby Parker's office in five minutes' time."

He took his used crockery back to the serving hatch. The canteen staff were supposed to do it, but he liked to give them a hand. "Have you got any mints?" he asked Sandra, the middle-aged lady behind the counter.

She laughed. "We're a cafeteria, love, not a sweet shop. Thanks to you and Alec we've got crisps and biscuits now, but that's where we're drawing the line. We've got mint chocolate blancmange if that's any good."

"It's just, I've got a meeting in a few minutes' time and I didn't get to brush my teeth this morning."

She rummaged in her pocket and offered him a Polo. He thanked her twice and they laughed gently at her quip about smokers always having mints. As he left her for his meeting, he realised he'd unwittingly done a don't.

Gwyn was sitting in the corridor outside Ruby Parker's office. Standard procedure. You'd keep the stenographer to hand in case there were transcription issues, which there usually were. Mordred knocked and went in. Ruby Parker sat behind her desk, still reading what was presumably his report. She didn't look happy.

"Welcome back, John," she said as if saying those words was a formality that had to be got through.

"Is something wrong?" he asked.

"We'll come to that later," she said. "First, your report."

"I wondered why you didn't contact me earlier," he said.

"You went off-brief," she replied, "but not in a bad way. We expect agents to use their initiative, and when they do, I nearly always assume that they know more about conditions on the ground than I do. I try not to interfere."

"So I'm not in any trouble?"

"It says here that Fenella Decristoforo-Salvaterra made indirect contact with you, and told you to return to London as a matter of 'urgency'."

"Correct."

"You've no idea what she was referring to?"

"No. She didn't speak to me. She spoke to Soraya Snow."

"What do you think she meant by 'urgent'? You must have formed a theory of some kind."

"I assumed it was something to do with her father. Whose location is one major purpose of this investigation."

She harrumphed. "It may interest you to know that he's not in Britain. At least, not so far as we know."

"But I thought he'd been seen entering Heathrow."

"Someone was. And they had his passport. The cameras conclusively show that, despite appearances, it wasn't him, only a lookalike."

"Who would do a thing like that? Why?"

"We don't know. John, Phyllis has been abducted."

The words took a second to register. "My God. How? When?"

"Yesterday evening at 7.15 give or take a minute either way. Somewhere between Saint Paul's Cathedral, from where she'd just called in, and Barbican Tube station, where Ian was awaiting her."

"In the 'City of London', in other words. As opposed to real London."

"Obviously, the two aren't mutually exclusive, but I know what you mean, yes. Within the territory of the City of London Corporation. Two days ago, Norman Pruett, the Remembrancer, turned up dead on Dartmoor. Murdered, we think, although the post-mortem's still out. He'd been hiding out on a retreat at Buckfast Abbey, and according to the monks, apparently in fear of his life. Very uncommunicative, very jumpy, very despairing. I mention the fact simply so you know what may be at stake."

"They can't have killed her, surely."

"What makes you say that?"

"The two cases belong in different categories. By the sounds of things, the Remembrancer was running away from someone, and they caught up with him. Phyllis is another matter. You don't go to all the trouble of kidnapping someone just to kill them. You could do that with a bullet from a rooftop, or push her in front of the train at Barbican."

"Did the Lord Mayor contact you when you were in Jersey?"

"The Lord Mayor of London?"

"The same."

"No. What for?"

"He claims he did. Horvath, the private security firm he bought out to help him bring the protests to an end, say the same thing."

"Then they're lying. What were we supposed to have talked about?"

"A job offer. How you might go and work for them."

He laughed. "I hope you didn't give that idea any credence."

"I'd have contacted you earlier if I'd thought there was the slightest truth in it. The unexpected upshot is, the Lord Mayor has invited you to a meeting."

He paused slightly as his brain put the various pieces together. "To talk about Phyllis."

"That's one plausible assumption, and why you have no option but to attend."

"I assume everyone in the building's out looking for her."

"All those we can spare. And the Met's Special Branch. And now that I've read your report, and things in Jersey appear to be stable, I've recalled Annabel, Edna and Tariq."

"That's a lot of manpower. Enough to get a result, surely?"

"I'm not so sure. The City's a very secretive place, and not everyone with a stake in it feels any loyalty to this country whatsoever."

"So when's my interview with the vampire?"

"He asked to see you as soon as you arrived back in this country."

"Right now, effectively."

"Amber's got a suit ready for you. Take your time. I'll let him know you're on your way over, but it won't hurt to keep him waiting a little."

"Are we sure he didn't kidnap Phyllis as a way of pulling me out of Jersey? Because if he and Pownall have been in contact – if Jersey is part of the offshore 'spider's web' tax experts like Nicholas Shaxson say is run from the City of London – then he may have got the impression I was the one pulling the strings out there. If so, me showing up at his house will demonstrate that I'm no longer in that position. Maybe he'll let Phyllis go."

"Nice idea, but if that's all it is, and he does, how could he conceivably stop you returning to Jersey on the next plane out?"

"He could arrange for someone to 'meet' me at Jersey airport. Or even *en route* to Heathrow."

Ruby Parker rubbed her forehead once. "We're speculating. We don't even know for sure that Cavendish is behind Phyllis's abduction. It could be anyone."

"But no one's owned up to it yet, which is itself odd. Put it another way, if he's not going to offer Phyllis in exchange for me signing a job contract, why does he want to see me?"

"Think about it, John. He's definitely *not* going to offer Phyllis in exchange for your services. The City may have some of the world's most ingenious lawyers on a retainer, but even they couldn't make that sort of contract stick. No, it has to be something else. As to what, I think it'd be faster for you to go and find out than it would for us both to sit here hypothesising until we find something that makes sense. If it seems prudent or harmless, report straight back to me afterwards. Otherwise, sit tight and I'll find you."

He got up. "Understood."

Chapter 22: At Mansion House

Amber dispensed the suit she'd been holding and the information Ruby Parker rang over. The Lord Mayor was sending a car over. It would be outside the front of the building in ten minutes' time. Mordred showered downstairs, changed and combed his hair, then went to stand in reception with Colin Bale. Colin said hello, then ignored him. Ten minutes later, a middle-aged man in a suit and a peaked cap came in and asked for 'Mr J. Mordred'.

"Standing right there," Colin said, as if any idiot could see that.

"You're the man from City Hall?" Mordred said.

"If you'd like to follow me, sir, I'll show you to the car."

He seemed a lot nicer than Kevin, MI7's resident driver. He had a voice for a start. And he actually smiled as if he liked you. All an act, of course, but then chauffeurs should be actors. Everyone should. Complete brutal honesty was seriously overrated.

They went outside. On the double red lines by the bollards, a black Jaguar XE awaited. The chauffeur opened the back door and Mordred found a new copy of the *Telegraph* on the back seat. They pulled out silently into the traffic.

His phone rang. *Mum.* Bloody hell. Pick up – yes or no?

He pressed answer. "Hi."

"Our Hannah's just been on the TV again. Is she pregnant?"

"I can't really speak now. I'm at work."

"I'll take that as a 'yes'. Why didn't she tell us?"

"Maybe because she's trying to lead a revolution and she hasn't got her phone with her?"

"Then why didn't Tim tell us?"

"He wanted it to be a surprise. Besides, it's not his place, he's just a man."

"So you knew, but we didn't?"

"Correct. I was told not to tell you. She wanted the news to be special. And I can't do special, and neither can Tim. No one can, only Hannah. Look, I love you, but I've got to go now."

"I'll speak to you this evening. We're not finished yet."

She hung up. He liked the way she always referred to her children as *our* whatever-their-name-was, as if you might get confused about who she was talking about. Is that Hannah *my sister* you mean, or do you mean maybe Hannah *Arendt*, the mid-20th century German political theorist?

The driver didn't seem in any hurry. He didn't look for short cuts or change lanes or accelerate on amber. Mind you, the car was probably too expensive to take risks with.

He picked up the *Telegraph*. The headline: MPs' latest 10% pay increase compared with the 1% cap on public sector workers. "We have made the necessary break with the past," the chairman of the Independent Parliamentary Standards Authority said. Further down the page, two columns devoted to government attempts to repeal the Freedom of Information Act. On the other side, an article about how the woman with the fez and the golden armlet had been shortlisted for the Booker. Right at the bottom, and 'continued on p4': 'One Week Until "Illegal Pop Festival" in Jersey: The Countdown Begins'. Mordred read it from start to finish. Hannah got two mentions, Soraya seven, 'former Chief Minister' Jeremy Pownall, one. An unnamed representative from the Jersey States said the authority had decided to work with the protesters to provide 'a safe and peaceful experience for tourists'. Tourists. Well, at least they had a sense of humour.

The car drew to a gentle stop in from of Mansion House, a colossal, grey Palladian building, fronted by six Corinthian columns supporting a pediment, and accessible only by steps to either side. This part of London was mostly eighteenth century piles, but relieved in places by fashionable steel-and-glass or even postmodernist whimsy. Opposite, there was one entrance to Bank Tube station.

Mordred wasn't expecting to stop on Walbrook. He knew Mansion House was the Lord Mayor's official residence, but he didn't think he actually lived here. More probably, the Mayor wanted to underline his institutional prestige. Within the pediment, a frieze showed the City of London crushing its enemies underfoot.

Well, if this was to be an exercise in low-level intimidation or overawing, they'd chosen the wrong man. Take away the pretentious classical front and it was very little different to Thames House.

An old man in a suit awaited them. He opened the rear door and Mordred stepped out onto the street. The rain had stopped now, and the sun peeped out from behind low-lying clouds. A double-decker bus roared past.

"Just follow me, sir," the man said.

They mounted the steps, entered the building and walked through a long reception area with an ornate barrel vault ceiling, stained glass, and more columns. Then up a flight of stairs and along a carpeted landing.

They stopped in front of a broad white door. Mordred's guide raised his hand, extended his middle knuckle theatrically and knocked. He opened the door for his charge, ushered him in, and withdrew, shutting him inside.

The room was small in comparison with what Mordred had expected. It contained a long table at which men and women in suits sat in silence looking angry, with the Lord Mayor at their head. Behind and around the room, others sat on chairs, mostly with their legs crossed. Framed portraits of three previous Mayors hung from the wall, all looking embittered by something just out of view. A chair had been left at the foot of the table directly facing Ashley Cavendish, presumably for the newcomer. When Mordred entered, everyone turned to look at him: he guessed around fifty glares of varying intensity.

"Hi, everyone," he said.

No one replied.

"Sit down, Mr Mordred," the Lord Mayor said.

Mordred took the seat apparently reserved for him, interlaced his fingers on the table, and looked the Mayor in the eye. He smiled.

"I'd like to read you a short extract from a paper called 'Financial Services contribution to the UK economy'," the Mayor began, "written by a lady called Gloria Tyler and published by the House of Commons Library. Are you ready?"

Mordred shrugged.

The Lord Mayor put a pair of horn-rimmed spectacles on. "'In 2014, financial and insurance services contributed £126.9 billion in gross value added - GVA - to the UK economy, 8.0% of the UK's total GVA. London accounted for 50.5% of the total financial and insurance sector GVA in the UK in 2012. The sector's contribution to UK jobs is around 3.4%. Trade in financial services makes up a substantial proportion of the UK's trade surplus in services. In 2013/14, the banking sector alone contributed £21.4 billion to UK tax receipts in corporation tax, income tax, national insurance and through the bank levy.'"

Everyone hummed approvingly, as if Mozart had just slipped in to play a few chords on his way to the Albert Hall.

"I'm looking for someone called Phyllis Robinson," Mordred said. "She was abducted yesterday, and I'm really only here to find out what you know about that. If no one's happy to speak up, fine, I'll go. But I'll be back on my own terms."

They all looked at Mordred and at each other. Then most of them stood up and left, jostling him as and where they passed. The Lord Mayor was the last to exit. He closed the door behind him.

Mordred found himself seated at the table with just eight others – five men, and three women, all about a decade older than him - whom he recognised as Horvath employees.

A steel haired man with film-star features who'd been sitting next to the Lord Mayor smiled. "Let me introduce - "

"I know who you are," Mordred said. "I'm going to come and work for you, apparently. Now let's stop messing around. Where's Phyllis?"

"Are you wearing a wire?" the man asked.

"No. It's too unsubtle. I haven't actually joined Horvath yet."

"Would you mind us checking?"

"If you must."

He stood up with a sigh. A man and a woman came over. They patted him down. The man opened his shirt and looked inside. After about a minute they seemed satisfied and sat down. Mordred re-did his buttons.

"Of course, if MI7 was really good," he said, "we'd have put a spy among the thirty-odd people who've just been in here. He or she would have planted a listening device on entry."

They looked at each other. "You – MI7 - didn't, though, did … you?" their leader said, as if even he wasn't sure whether it was a question.

"It was mooted. I'm not saying yes. I don't know."

They took this as an indication that he was at least partly on their side. During the next ten minutes, they turned the chairs on their sides, one by one, to examine beneath, and upended the table. Two women crawled onto it for a closer examination.

The door opened and the Lord Mayor came back in. For a moment, he and they looked equally shocked.

"What the hell's going on here?" he said.

"I tried to stop them, but they wouldn't pay any attention," Mordred said.

"We're looking for listening devices," one of the women crouching on the upside-down table said.

"Why would there be listening devices?" the Mayor demanded

"We've received information that one of the people just in the room may have been a spy," the man with the steel hair said.

The Mayor looked like he'd been doused with a bucket of water. "*What?*"

"We've received information - "

"Those people are my friends! They're on our side! Where did you get this information?"

"From me," Mordred said.

Silence. Mordred expected an explosion of Mayoral fury, but the opposite happened. The Horvath employees sheepishly put the furniture back as it was and Cavendish looked as if his blood had stopped flowing and his eyes no longer saw. His arms hung by his sides. His chest became motionless.

Finally, everything was where it had been ten minutes ago. The Horvath employees sat down and the Lord Mayor came back to life. He went to sit at the head of the table. "I'll take it from here," he said. "Everyone out, except John Mordred."

They looked at each other as if it wasn't something they themselves would have advised, then did as commanded. They closed the door behind them. Mordred found himself alone with the Mayor at the opposite end of the table.

"I'm not going to get into a discussion with you about the value of the financial services industry," Mordred said.

"We're on the same side," Cavendish said.

Mordred smiled. "I doubt that."

"All right, put it another way. We want the same thing. We share a common interest. What we both want is to find Peter Decristoforo. You want to discover how he managed to blindside yourselves and GCHQ. I want to find him to put a stop to this blasted 'World War O'."

"You mean, by killing him."

"By putting the fear of God into him. He's very old anyway. Maybe frightening him will cause his death, I don't know. The point is, he facilitated this. Without him, it couldn't have happened. We're close to closing it down now, but it's not been easy. A lot of good men and women have suffered a lot of anxiety."

"About whether they'll get their bonuses this year."

The Mayor smiled. "Come, come, Mr Mordred. You know as well as I do that those sorts of things are ring-fenced. I mean, profits, shareholders, bad press."

"Let's get to the point, shall we? Where's Phyllis?"

"Phyllis …?"

"Okay, then. A different question. What happened to the Remembrancer?"

"Have you ever read a book called, *The Shock Doctrine?* Sometimes, a little chaos is good for business. It allows you to clear out your dead wood, and it creates new markets. I won't say World War O has been completely valueless, but it's outstayed its welcome now."

"It may not be over yet."

"Oh, it is. Even my friend Jeremy will be back within six months. The Jersey States will wait a while before politely informing him that they can't, in all conscience, accept his resignation. And he'll ever so reluctantly, but oh so graciously, accept the recall to public service. And it'll be December: freezing cold and windy; and the protesters will be but a distant memory."

"So nothing at your end's going to change."

"Obviously not. There's too much money at stake; too many players with too much power and no aversion whatsoever to being ruthless. You haven't seen anything yet, John. In the 'phoney war' – which is all it's been so far - things are always pretty restrained. People like your sister might well get an utterly mistaken impression of whom they're dealing with."

His phone rang. *Hannah.*

"Sorry, I've got to take this," he told the Lord Mayor. Looking back, he merely wanted to cock a snook at him, however, the Mayor didn't appear in the least affronted. His eyes glazed over and he went back into hibernation.

"How's things?" Mordred asked.

"Not good," Hannah replied. "A group of bloody newbies has taken over Mont Orgueil Castle on the east of the island."

"Like a sit-in?"

"That's the idea," she said. "Apparently."

"Shouldn't you be pleased? I thought that's what you went there for. To protest."

"I've come to realise what ought to have been obvious from the start. That the finance industry and the tourist industry aren't necessarily in cahoots. Driving holidaymakers away is just playing into the bankers' hands. The hoteliers and the bed-and-breakfasters and the vine growers and farmers and lavender growers and zookeepers are what this place has going for it. I actually told Martin Baker we'd open the pop festival to tourists. That was *my* word: *tourists*."

"Who's Martin Baker?"

"Acting Chief Minister."

"I don't understand why you're ringing me. I mean, it's great to speak to you, but I'm in England." Yes, something was up. She was about to drop a clanger.

"I'm just nervous, that's all. I was quite impressed with you while you were out here, John. You kept a calm head. I just wanted to sorry."

Yes, sure. And … ? "What's to be nervous about?"

"I'm going in to speak to the occupiers. Try and persuade them to come out."

"Good luck. You've got a good argument and a spotless reputation. I can't see them defying you. But be warned. These sorts of movements often work this way. They start off quite reasonable, then a bunch of 'newbies' comes in with borrowed anger and a more extreme approach, and before you know it, you've got bombs going off in shopping malls."

He heard her scoff. "I can't see that happening, John."

"No one ever can. Not at the beginning."

"Why are you telling me this? Do you actually believe you're helping, or something?"

"You just said you were impressed with me. I'm cashing in on that while it's still fresh from the oven. When you've completed this pop festival, you've got to come home. Quit while you're ahead, and make it clear you disown anyone who doesn't do the same. Get Soraya to back you up."

"Coming home then was always the plan."

"Don't let anyone dissuade you. Listen, if you're nervous about going in to speak to the protesters, I've got something that'll put it in perspective."

"Oh?"

"Mum saw your bump on the TV."

A moment's silence. "I know. I've got a phone now, remember?"

"How was she?"

"Angry at first, then less so. She said she'd spoken to you, and you helped."

He laughed. "That's not the impression she gave me. I've got to go. Best of luck in the occupied castle."

"John? One More thing?"

He sighed. Here it came. The impossible request, just as he thought he'd got away with it. "Yes. Go on."

"Sorry, I know you're at work. It's just, I want you to come to the pop festival. Edna's going to be here."

100% as expected. "I'll have to see. It's short notice. I don't know whether work - "

"You are still an item, aren't you?"

"'An item'. Like the 1940s."

"Funny *you* reproaching *me* for being old fashioned."

"She's too good for me, I'm afraid. I realised that when I got back to England."

"Oh, bloody rubbish!" she said contemptuously. "Listen, you'd better be here, work be damned. You've only got one life. You've got one shot at Edna, that's all. If you love her, be here. *Plus*, I'm singing two songs on stage with Soraya, and I need your support. *And* mum and dad are coming over."

"What?"

"It was the only way I could make it up to them. I told them you might meet them in Saint Helier."

"What?"

"Might. And don't say 'what' again in that high-pitched voice. I've got sensitive eardrums. I've got to go now. I've got a castle to storm."

She hung up. He blew air and put the phone back in his pocket. He'd almost forgotten where he was.

"That was your sister, from what I could make of your conversation," the Mayor said. "Well done. Wise words. Just what was needed."

"Let's cut to the chase. I was told you want me to come and work for you."

"We've put together a very generous package with John Mordred specifically in mind. Two hundred and fifty thousand a year, plus bonuses."

He whistled in an attempt to appear impressed. "What would I be doing?"

"Heading Horvath. It's about time the City had its own intelligence service. On a more day-to-day level: industrial espionage, spying on our competitors beyond the City. Weakening them where necessary with a view to opening new horizons. Not necessarily in person, of course. *The Shock Doctrine.*"

"Turning, say, non-profit ventures into commercial opportunities."

"Amongst other things. Creating a better world. The world of Milton Friedman and Friedrich Hayek. A single global market."

"Right, well, I'll have to think about it."

The Mayor drew back slightly "What is there to think about?"

"Firstly, Phyllis is my friend. However much I may want your job, I'm not the kind of person who likes to leave a comrade in the lurch. I need to find her before I commit to anything."

"What if finding her and committing to us were part and parcel of the same thing?"

Mordred smiled. "I rather thought they might be. Go on."

"I'm not sure I trust you completely, Mr Mordred. Not yet. Therefore, I'm going to set you a little test. A little something I –

we in the City – devised before you arrived back from Jersey. Something you would have had to do anyway, regardless of whether you agreed to come and work for us."

Mordred's phone rang. *Mum.* Bloody hell. Show respect for the Mayor – yes or no?

"Sorry, I've got to take this," he said.

The Lord Mayor looked a little more like he'd been cocked a snook this time. However, his life-signs still went to zero.

Mordred picked up. "Welcome to John Mordred's place of work," he said. "Please hold the line to hear him get the sack, live."

"Sorry!" She hung up.

He switched it off – what he should have done last time – and returned it to his pocket.

He turned to face the Mayor again. "I thrive on tests," he said.

Chapter 23: Just For the Sake of Argument

"So you want to know where your colleague 'Phyllis' is," the Lord Mayor said.

"Yes, please," Mordred replied. They sat alone upstairs in Mansion House, surrounded by chairs, and facing each other across a long table. The three former Mayors in the portraits regarded them like the ghosts of Christmas past, present and future, but without any festive or optimistic associations. They looked like they spent most Christmases slashing Wat Tyler to death.

"Let's say, for the sake of argument, I knew where this woman was," Cavendish said.

"Go on."

"And I also knew where Fenella Decristoforo-Salvaterra was."

This was a bit like being with Hannah. The surprises. "Keep going."

"You don't sound very taken aback," the Lord Mayor said. "Good acting. You probably need a skill like that in your job."

"So you've got Phyllis Robinson and you've got Fenella Decristoforo- Salvaterra. What are you going to do with them?"

"I'm not saying I've 'got' them."

"What *are* you saying?"

"I'm saying *for the sake of argument*, for God's sake. I thought I'd made that clear at the beginning. Don't try and trap me. It won't work."

"If, for the sake of argument, you were holding Phyllis and Fenella, then what, for the sake of argument, would you do with them?"

"For the sake of argument, I – we: we in the City of London – would hold on to Phyllis, while you rendezvous with Fenella Decristoforo-Salvaterra and persuade her to lead you to her father. Once you've done that, we would release Phyllis. For the - "

"But you'd kill Peter."

"In the last resort, maybe. But his internet-cloaking discovery probably has important commercial applications. We'd want to access that first. Better than it falling into the hands of terrorists, you must agree. To that end, we'd need to hold on to his daughter."

"I see, yes."

"I accept that, for the sake of argument, all this would be asking a lot of you, but you'd be the head of Horvath and obviously two hundred and fifty thousand pounds is a lot of money. You'd have to be prepared to go beyond the call of duty *all the time*."

"Yes, I appreciate that."

"The people at Horvath warned me about your conscience, by the way. 'He's pretty self-righteous', they said. They - "

"What? The people at Horvath said *that* about *me*?"

"Does it surprise you?"

"I thought they liked me."

"For the purposes of this discussion, they like you a lot. After all, you're going to head their organisation."

"Who specifically in Horvath said that about me?"

"I'm not at liberty to say. Does it matter?"

"Was it Tarquin?"

"Tarquin who?" The Lord Mayor frowned. "Wha - ? Horvath doesn't even have a 'Tarquin'."

Mordred nodded. "I see, yes. He's going by another name nowadays."

"*Who* is?"

"Sorry, I shouldn't have said anything. Forget it."

"I - "

"I'll deal with it on my first day in the job."

"Look, Mr Mordred, I'd like you to leave now. We both need time to think about this. I need to consult with what I hope will be your future colleagues; you need to consult your precious 'conscience'. In the meantime, tell yourself this: a developed sense of empathy, of justice and injustice, makes a person weak. It stops him or her getting on. Luckily, however, it's not indestructible. It can be overcome. I was once a 'good' man like yourself. I trained myself not to mind hurting others. Not to go out of my *way* to hurt people, of course. I'm no sadist. But life is essentially about trampling. Having it done to you, or doing it to others. In the end therefore, conscience is just an illness, like a bad dose of the flu. And like most such ailments, you can get rid of it. The difficulty lies in taking the first steps, because they're always the most painful." He stood up. "Good luck, Mr Mordred. There's a car downstairs waiting to take you back to Thames House. Say nothing about this to anyone, otherwise, I'll know. I'm the Lord Mayor of London. Like MI7, I have spies everywhere."

"Before I leave, I'd like to know how Phyllis is."

The Lord Mayor looked at him a moment then smiled. "You keep asking about her. Am I to assume there's something more between you than mere work relations?"

"In a word, yes."

"Just one word? Fine, play your cards close to your chest. I've always found that particular strategy works for me. Don't worry about her. She's not underground in a dungeon or anything like that. Quite the opposite. She's being very well looked after. Apart from the obvious restrictions on her movements consistent with her being a prisoner, I would imagine she's having a whale of a time. I wouldn't have it any other way. Contrary to popular opinion, not all financiers are ogres."

"At least, not for the sake of argument."

"Of course. Everything's hypothetical."

"Is she still in London? Just for the etcetera?"

"That would be foolish of whoever might be holding on to her. No, her gaolers have probably moved her out to the shires. The attic of a country house somewhere, maybe."

"So long as she's okay. I'm hoping to be able to persuade her to come and work at Horvath. Assuming you haven't been unkind to her, I think I may be in with a chance."

"You're a sensible man, Mr Mordred. It took me a long time to realise that you can always attract an attractive woman when you're as well off and well connected as I am, and you're perhaps going to be. Having said that, *intelligent* attractive women are different. Even with all my wealth and power, I still find attracting such women nigh on impossible. You'd do well to hold on to this one."

"I'll do my best."

"That is, if I don't beat you to her. As I say, her confinement isn't exactly onerous, and I'm very good at playing the charming host."

"I'd better watch out, I guess."

The smile fell from his face. "I'm joking, John. I'm too old for that. I'm only interested in money nowadays. Good luck with her."

"Thank you."

"Now, if you'll excuse me, I've work to be doing. As I say, your car's downstairs. We've got twenty-four hours. One day for you to decide whether you want to work for us, and … for us to make an equivalent decision about you."

"What happens if one or the other of us decides to say no?"

"Let me just say that since I don't actually know where 'Phyllis' is, I can hardly be held responsible for her safety. I hope nothing happens to her, but that's all I can do: hope. Have you tried calling the police, by the way?"

Mordred smiled. "I'll see you tomorrow, sir."

The same car and driver that had brought him to Mansion House returned him to his point of origin. On the way, he rang his mother. He apologised for cutting her off.

"And I'm sorry for shouting at you earlier," she said. "Obviously, it wasn't your fault. I just needed someone to vent my frustration on, and you're always so forgiving. I'm becoming a real bag."

"I spoke to Hannah," he said. "She may have given you the impression that I can meet you in Saint Helier. I'm not sure I can. With work."

"Oh, be there if you're there, John. We'll miss you if you're not, but we'll understand. Your father and I aren't *old*, you know. We're perfectly capable of looking after ourselves."

"I know."

"Just a piece of advice, though, honey. If you're at work and you can't talk, for goodness sake, *switch your mobile off*. There should be a red button on there somewhere. Just press it when you're not available, and press it again when you are."

"Yes, you're right. Thank you."

They said love you and hung up. Now for the main event. He called Hannah. Somehow, even in the monosyllable with which she answered, he could tell she was excited. In a positive way.

"Is Soraya around?" he asked.

"I'll pass you over," she replied. "The castle thing's completely sorted, by the way. Piece of cake. My God, isn't it *amazing*, John? We're all in tears over here! – Here, it's John. He just wants to say congratulations!"

Soraya: "Hi, Jim! Hey, guess what? I know your real name!"

"Er … congratulations?" Mordred said.

"I love you!" she shouted. *"I bloody love you! I BLOODY LOVE THE BLOODY WORLD!"*

"Okay, well … that's good."

Hannah again. "Isn't it *AMAZING?*"

"Listen, I've got a question for Soraya."

"What is it? Hang on. I think I know! Is it: *'why are you so wonderful, so utterly AMAZING?'*"

"No, it's: 'can you remember the name of the boat on which you met Fenella?'"

"What? It's a bad line! You'll have to speak up!"

"Look, what going on? What's happened that's so fantastic?"

"Haven't you heard? – Listen everyone: John just said congratulations to Soraya and *he doesn't even know what's happened!*"

Raucous laughter. Soraya again: "*I love you, man!*"

"Hi again, Soraya. Do you remember the - "

"Listen, John." Hannah again, doing her level-best to sound restrained. "'Name Me Your Stone Cold Name' has just reached number one in the Billboard Top 100. It's the *number one track* in the United States *and* the UK at the same time! We've finally done it! We've finally made it in America! Five years this has taken! Listen!"

She treated him to two seconds of Fully Magic Coal Tar Lounge drunkenly singing The Star Spangled Banner.

"Congratulations. Really great news."

"And before you ask, no I'm not drinking. Everyone else is. We're family. Soraya's going to be my God-mum, remember? I'm high on life!"

"*I love you!*" Soraya shouted in the background.

"Is there anyone else I can speak to? Anyone a bit more … grounded?"

"Listen, I'm putting Tim on. Tim and Jim, speak to each other. Whoo-*hoo!*"

"Hi, Tim."

"Hi, John."

"Are any of the Coal Tars vaguely sober? I need to ask a question about a boat they were aboard."

"Gaz is a teetotaller. Do you want me to put him on?"

"Hi, John," a bass voice said. "Welcome to Gaz. What can I be doing for you, this fine day?"

"Can you remember the name of the boat on which you met Fenella?"

"Who?"

"Out in the channel. She wore a black dress. About Soraya's age. 'Very posh, in a Spanish way'."

"Oh, *her*. Yeah, I remember. It was called Saint Martha's Pride."

Bingo. "Thank you. And congratulations on the number one."

Gaz laughed. "Vanity, vanity, saith the Preacher. All is vanity."

Afterwards, he put an urgent call through to Ruby Parker requesting that she recall all agents in the vicinity immediately.

Thirty minutes later, he sat at the head of a long table very much like the one in Mansion House, in a room that looked much shabbier than its counterpart. Ruby Parker sat to his immediate left. Karen, the minute-taker, to his right. Further down the table: Alec, Ian and Gwyn, and about twenty other faces he only half-recognised from seeing them in corridors.

He gave a blow-by-blow account of his meeting with the Mayor before proceeding to more general observations and conclusions.

"I asked him whether Phyllis was in London. He said no. 'For the sake of argument', her captors had 'probably' moved her to the shires. There was no necessity for him to give that sort of information away. He could just as easily have said he didn't know. I'm pretty sure he was lying. He wanted to make sure I'd be thrown off-track. And of course, his body-language also said liar. Long blink, look to the right, touched his nose. I'm pretty sure she's somewhere within the Square Mile."

"The trouble is," Ruby Parker said, "that's a lot of office-space occupied by a lot of very powerful people, and, being the City of London, it's technically out of our jurisdiction. I accept we're spies, but getting people into those places is a long-term project. We probably don't have the luxury of time."

Alec put his hand up and smiled. "I predict that John's about to divulge a plan."

"I very much hope someone is," Ruby Parker said.

"It's partly why I called everyone back to Thames House," Mordred said. "In twenty-four" – he looked at his watch – "twenty-*three* hours, I've an appointment with the Lord Mayor of

London to talk about a job offer. Within that time, I want us to have found both Phyllis and Fenella, but more importantly, I want to make ensure that's the end of it: no more abductions, no more trying to get their hands on whatever it is Peter Decristoforo knows, that's it. The City's complete withdrawal from any claim to an interest. And I'm going to force the Mayor to agree to that at our meeting."

"I take it this is the greatest plan the world's ever seen," Alec said.

Mordred went on. "What we need is a list of all the office-cleaning suppliers within a twenty-mile radius. Then we need to find out which have customers within the Square Mile. Finally, we ring up claiming to be a big City firm looking to employ a cleaning company on a lucrative contract. Ideally, we want to hire one that's already familiar with the Square Mile, and so appreciates its high standards. In other words, *do you already do business with other firms within the Square Mile?*"

"Negotiating a contract sounds like the sort of decision only the boss could make," Alec said. "Most bosses won't be available on a cold call."

"Depends how much money's at stake," Edna said. Mordred hadn't seen her come in; nor Annabel and Tariq. They were sitting at the end of the table.

"You can nearly always find someone in authority if there's enough at stake," Ruby Parker said.

Mordred continued: "Once we've discovered who does do business within the Square Mile, we arrange for them to be visited by a representative from Her Majesty's Revenue and Customs – which is to say, *we* pay them that visit. Officially, we're investigating money laundering in the City. We need to look at precisely the areas each firm is responsible for within that area: what buildings, what floors, what rooms."

"I'm sure we all see where you're going with this," Ruby Parker said.

"We're only investigating two point nine square kilometres," Mordred said. "It shouldn't take long. If we do it properly, we'll end up with an exhaustive map of which parts of the City are in regular use. The remainder – the parts where no cleaner ever goes – is where Phyllis will be. Since office-space in that part of London's at a premium, we should find ourselves with two, three, maybe four locations."

Everyone turned to each other and made approving noises. It was a great plan, really great. The best they'd heard for donkeys' years. Then he overheard someone tell her neighbour, 'His sister's the manager of Fully Magic Coal Tar Lounge'. Her neighbour nodded and made approving noises.

Alec had his hand up. "It's a good proposal," he said, "but it can be improved."

"Go on," Ruby Parker said.

"We can save ourselves the initial cold calling," he went on. "Thames House must employ a cleaning company in at least some areas of the building. Assuming that company's like any other, it must be looking to break into its competitors' markets all the time. We need to get hold of it and ask what it knows about its rivals' territories."

"We should probably ask that question generally," Mordred said. "To everyone we visit."

"We're assuming she's in some office building somewhere," Annabel said. "What if we're wrong? What if she's in a private residence?"

"It seems unlikely," Mordred said. "They must have taken into account the slim possibility – from their point of view – that we'd find her. If we locate her at a private address, the culprit's automatically identifiable. No one's going to risk that. With a commercial building, there's always inbuilt deniability. And don't forget: everyone in the City has a stake in this. Given that the Lord Mayor's involved, the strong likelihood is that they're working as a cabal, each prepared to cover for the others."

"All for one and one for all," Alec said. "You're making a lot of sense today, John, I'll give you that."

"If we really go all out, we could put together a comprehensive map within twelve hours," Ruby Parker said. "I take it we then infiltrate the cleaning staff and access the uncharted areas. That shouldn't be too difficult."

"See how well she's being looked after," Mordred said. "Assuming she's not actually being mistreated, we rescue her just before I go and see the Lord Mayor and I take her with me. Which brings me to the separate problem of Fenella Decristoforo-Salvaterra."

"Mightn't they be two puzzles solvable by a single method?" Alec asked. "If they think derelict office-space is a good place to hide Phyllis, wouldn't they hide Fenella there too? Why re-invent the wheel?"

"Because," Mordred replied, "as I've already said, they must have taken into account the possibility that we'd find her. If so, it seems unlikely they'd put all their eggs in the same basket."

"Okay," a twentysomething man at the front with a newly sharpened pencil said, "then how do we know it's not Fenella who's in the empty office-space, and Phyllis who's elsewhere?"

"Because I think I know where Fenella is," Mordred replied.

"You seem to know everything," the man with the pencil said sardonically.

"How's the spy novel coming along?" Mordred asked him.

He blushed. "I didn't – how did you - ?"

"Fenella arrived in this country in a boat called 'Saint Martha's Pride'," Mordred went on. "She had two servants with her. Since neither of them has yet been to the police, my guess is that they're being held hostage with her. And the best place for anyone to do that would be aboard the boat itself. We need to contact the British Ports Association in the first instance. But my strong suspicion in that they'll attempt to keep her close. That means Canary Wharf, Greenland, Poplar, Limehouse Basin, Saint Katharine Dock. Unless anyone objects, Alec and I will take the latter. We'll need to conduct all searches in disguise, because it could be Horvath that's holding her, and its personnel may recognise some of us on sight."

With the exception of the man with the pencil, everyone turned to each other and remarked on his perspicacity. He was an utter genius, that much was plain, what conundrum couldn't he solve when he put his mind to it? Then he overheard someone tell the man beside him that he once went out on a date with Soraya Snow. The addressee drew his chin back and made an incredulous noise.

"I need one more thing to make this plan work," Mordred said. "I need someone in this room who can do a passable imitation of my voice."

Everyone looked at each other.

"Your voice?" Alec said. "You mean *you*? John Mordred?"

"My voice. Is there anyone here around this table who's ever attempted to imitate me?"

Sheepishly, one by one, everyone except Ian, Edna and Ruby Parker put their hands up. Total silence.

Mordred realised he was blushing. "Well, that's enough to be going on with," he said.

Ruby Parker asked him if he had any more to add, then closed the meeting, stood up and began to assign responsibilities.

Chapter 24: So What About a Luxury Yacht?

"How the hell did you know Smarmy Steven was writing a spy novel?" Alec asked, as they left the meeting on their way to the canteen.

"Just a quick cup of tea," Mordred replied, ignoring him, "then we need to get moving."

They went along the corridor to the lift. Alec pressed the button. "Shouldn't we be getting over there right away? Saint Katharine Dock, I mean. Not the canteen."

"Amber's got ten disguises to put together at short notice. She's a perfectionist. It doesn't do to rush her."

"How did you know Steven was writing a spy novel?"

"You've just asked me that."

"And you didn't reply."

"Because *everyone* in this building's writing a spy novel."

"I'm not."

Mordred smiled.

"What?" Alec said.

"And you've *never* written a spy novel?"

"Never." The lift arrived. They stepped inside. "It was a screenplay, actually."

"I see. Plot?"

"In the late 1970s, a British agent – Jason Statham - goes to East Berlin on a mission. Can't get back, but manages to cobble a new cover ID together. Just about to escape when he meets a girl, Kate Winslet. Marries her and settles down where he is. Then the Berlin Wall falls, and Kate dies."

"It doesn't fall on top of her, does it?"

"Ha, ha. Anyway, suddenly, his British paymasters – Ralph Fiennes, Colin Firth and Jude Law - want to know why he didn't return, and they've got one more job for him, stop him being exposed to Fleet Street as a traitor."

"Sounds pretty good so far. What's the job?"

"Go to China on a business trip with a view to picking up intelligence about a nuclear missile. However, while he's there, he meets a girl-stroke-middle-aged-woman."

Mordred laughed. "A girl-stroke-middle-aged-woman?"

"A female. Vera Chok. But she's a double agent, of course."

"Then what?"

"That's it. I couldn't finish it. It became too complicated."

They stepped out of the lift and entered the canteen. It was virtually empty. Tariq sat alone at a table looking disconsolate.

"Bloody hell," Alec said under his breath. "I thought the two of them looked depressed in the meeting. Their marriage must be over."

"Whoa, hold hard. That's a bit of a leap."

"What's your theory then, Brains?"

"A tiff, obviously."

"This is Annabel we're talking about. She doesn't do conventional. Prepare to be shocked."

Mordred ordered two teas, a Wagon Wheel and a packet of pickled onion Monster Munch. They sat down facing each other, Alec beside Tariq.

"How's married life?" Mordred asked.

"It's over," Tariq replied.

Alec tore the Monster Munch open from top to bottom, exposing all the snacks on the dismembered bag. He nudged Tariq. "Help yourself."

"I'm fine," Tariq replied.

"John?"

Mordred put his palm up. "I've got my Wagon Wheel, thanks."

"What do you mean, 'it's over'?" Alec asked. "How can it be over when it's only just begun?"

Tariq wiped his eyes angrily, as if he had enough to contend with, without a possible song title. "It's impossible to explain."

Alec shrugged. "Well, it's none of our business, of - "

"I asked her to come to Australia with me. I thought we could make a new start, just the two of us, away from all this. I don't want her to get killed. I want to have children with her. But no, she won't go. Something's keeping her here. She won't say what, but I think I know. I think we both do, don't we, John?"

"Er, now wait a minute," Mordred said. "Last time I spoke to her, she said she was head over heels in love with you."

"When did she say that?"

"When we were in Jersey."

"What the hell would she tell you something like that for? What was the context?"

"We were down in the tunnel, and she was discussing my plan to get you both locked in a room together."

"That was *your* plan, was it?"

"Yes."

"She said it was hers!"

"She passed it off as hers, that's all."

"Are you sure the two of you weren't planning to get locked in that room together, and leave me outside?"

"I'm assuming that's a rhetorical question. Has it occurred to you that jealousy isn't a very endearing quality? That maybe that's what's putting her off?"

"No, never. That never occurred to me. I'm a stupid, stupid man."

They sat in silence for a minute. Alec crunched his Monster Munch.

Eventually, Tariq spoke. "Can I ask you a question, John?"

"If it's, 'Are you in love with her?'" Mordred replied, "the answer's no. Not 'no, you can't ask me a question', but 'no, I'm not in love with her'. If it's 'Do you think she's in love with you?' – ie, me - then the answer's still no. If it's, 'Do you think she's in love with Tariq?' the answer's yes."

Tariq sniffed. He scrunched his eyes and clasped his hands in his lap. "You're a good friend really," he said. "I'm sorry for doubting you. I know you don't want it; I know you haven't sought it; but she does love you. I know she does."

"Has she said she does?" Alec asked.

"No, but - "

"Well, she almost certainly doesn't," Alec said. "The truth is, John's just a boy, a thirty-one year-old child. Look at him, sitting there guzzling his Wagon Wheel. Can't even keep his mouth closed while he's eating, *and* he's got chocolate on his face. And me, with my Monster Munch. We're like a couple of primary school children. Can you really imagine Annabel going for that? She's a sophisticated woman. Cucumber sandwiches, canapés at the Ritz, won't go to Harlem in ermine and pearls. She's not going to want an infantile nerd like John. Or me. Not that I'm an issue, of course."

Tariq stood up. "Thanks for being so nice," he said. "But I'd better move on. Got some computers need fixing downstairs."

"It's just a tiff," Mordred said. "Believe me."

"I – I'd like to. But it's more than that." He left.

Alec waited till the double doors has swung shut, and let out a huge sigh. "We both know he's probably right."

"What? About it being over? No way."

"Remember what she told us two last year? That she'd been 'badly abused as a child'?"

"What about it?"

"It might explain why she wants to stay in MI7. The security, the secrecy, the access to guns. Don't forget, her dad's a violent man, and it was him that abused her. It might also explain why she balked when he mentioned kids. She probably got married thinking it would make her normal. Now she's suddenly realised what she's up against. And *he* doesn't know the half of it. I bet she hasn't told him about the child abuse."

"Why wouldn't she?"

"Like I say, she wants to be normal."

"Well, she's going to have to make compromises. I wonder if I should talk to her."

Alec scoffed. "Who do you think you are? Doctor Raj Persaud? No, leave them well alone, that's my advice. They've got to learn to resolve their own problems."

It was Mordred's turn to sigh. "I guess so."

"Drink up then, and let's get going."

"I'm not sure Amber will be ready for us yet, but okay."

"Do we really need disguises? Why can't we just get hats and sunglasses?"

"If you'd read the manual, you'd know."

"What 'manual'?"

"The MI7 Manual of Expert Spycraft, twenty-third edition, 2014."

"You're making it up. What's it say?"

"It states the obvious fact that two clearly connected men in hats and sunglasses are likely to attract suspicion."

Alec looked pensive, clearly trying to visualise the scenario. "The manual's actually right," he said.

Two hours later, they boarded the tube to Canary Wharf. Mordred had straight dark hair, horn rimmed glasses and a suit and tie. Alec wore the same, but with expensive men's jewellery. He had moulded polystyrene pads in both cheeks to make his face broader, and a not-quite-fat suit under his shirt. His hair was full and brown with a short well-trimmed ponytail and he had a suntan.

St Katharine Dock lay just north of Tower Bridge, and was overlooked by offices and expensive hotels. They arrived as rush hour began and strolled around the marina. A group of tourists had arrived to watch the opening and closing of the lock, and the smell of cooking from two dozen cafés and restaurants filled the air. The evening was warm and the sky blue and people in shirt sleeves and summer dresses dined al fresco. A jumbo jet passed noiselessly overhead at high altitude.

"Do you ever wish you had a boat?" Alec asked.

"Sometimes. But then I think: no, it's a lot of hard work and the sea fluctuates between being deadly dull and trying to kill you."

"What about a luxury yacht?"

"That's a type of boat. So no."

They walked on for a while. Some of the vessels had owners or caretakers aboard, checking masts, tying or untangling ropes, or sitting with friends or partners looking important.

"They say attractive women like luxury yachts," Alec said, "but when you think about it, that's got to be bullshit. Like all attractive women have exactly the same tastes."

Mordred shrugged. "Yet I can see the logic up to a point."

"You're being ironic, I take it."

"The truth could be that all human beings have a latent love of luxury yachts, but that it's disproportionately awakened in attractive women, because they get a disproportionate number of actual invitations to go aboard. Thus giving rise to the myth."

Alec chuckled. "Plausible, I suppose. The weird thing is, the main reason I'd want a luxury yacht was because I thought it was an attractive-woman magnet. So it's kind of circular."

"When I met the Lord Mayor, he said he found it quite easy to attract beautiful women, unless they were intelligent, when it was 'nigh on impossible'."

"What's your point?"

"Imagine Annabel or Phyllis or Edna or Ruby Parker or Amber. Do you think they'd clamour to get aboard your luxury yacht?"

Alec shrugged. "I haven't got one, but if your theory's correct, it's irrelevant. Their universal latent love of luxury yachts wouldn't be awakened until they actually felt the invitation in their hands. And presumably, until a little time had passed, so that what's now dormant could come properly to life."

"But you can't imagine it."

"I can't imagine lots of things about the lifestyles of the rich and famous. Doesn't mean they're not real."

"I think any sensible woman would want to know a man quite well before she agreed to go out to the middle of the ocean alone with him," Mordred said. "But if she gets to know him that well, she'll probably have made up her mind about him already, luxury yacht or not."

"I'm glad we had this conversation. I'll spend this month's salary on something else. Can I ask you about the case now?"

"Obviously."

"We know the name of the boat we're looking for. Do we know what it looks like?"

Mordred thought for a moment, and the point of the question clicked. "I hadn't thought of that."

"The abductors may have changed the name."

"It would have to be a professional job if they did. Nothing about these boats is allowed to look amateurish."

"How might a person go about changing the name of a boat? Do you know?"

"It would have to be done out at sea, or it would arouse the suspicion of the port authorities. They might not even be permitted to do it in harbour, I don't know."

"Repeat: do you know what the boat looks like?"

"I've no idea. I got the description from one of Soraya's band. I doubt they'll remember now."

"How is she these days?"

"Soraya? About the same."

"Does she ever mention me?"

"I think my sister may have told her we're a gay couple."

Alec took a deep, despairing breath. He held it for a second then released it to the four winds and looked at the floor. "Fine. I spy, with my little eye, something beginning with P."

"Ping Pong?"

"What?"

"Ping Pong. It's a Chinese restaurant. Over there, by Tower Bridge House."

"Follow my sight line, dummy. The answer's 'paint job'."

Mordred did as instructed. Three boats down from where they were standing: a large white motor-yacht by the name of 'The New Mary Rose'. Beneath that, a layer of uneven white paint, obscuring whatever had been there before.

"Bloody hell," Mordred said.

"Don't let's get too excited, John. It's interesting, but hardly conclusive."

"I'm not looking at that any more."

Alec gave a puzzled laugh. "So what *are* you looking at?"

"That old woman at the pizza outlet, other side of the dock. That's Maria. Definitely."

"Maria …?"

"*The* Maria. Fenella Decristoforo-Salvaterra's servant."

Chapter 25: The Tears of a Brian Penford

Soon after Mordred spotted Maria making a purchase in Pizza on the Dock, a team of six MI7 agents moved into the Guoman Tower Hotel on the south side of the marina and kept continuous watch on the freshly re-named Saint Martha's Pride. After three hours, they saw Fenella poke her head above the cabin for a few moments. Later, they saw Maria and Rory running errands in turn. They had to wait until midnight to catch sight of the hostage-takers. A man of about forty emerged on deck to smoke a cigarette. Then another man took his place and stayed there until morning, watching intently. Both were quickly identified as Horvath employees. They were probably dedicated, but not enough to kill hostages. A visit from a Scotland Yard swift response unit should put paid to them.

And yet it was important not to act prematurely. Mordred had an appointment with the Lord Mayor in fourteen hours' time, and the aim was to present him with something he couldn't wriggle out of. For that, he needed Phyllis.

At first sight, it looked like there was an alternative solution: just liberate Fenella and persuade her to lead them to Peter. But Mordred didn't think she'd do that. She might not even know where he was. If all MI7 did was rescue her from St Katharine Dock and she was unable or unwilling to cooperate with them, obviously that still left Cavendish with something to hope for. Wherever the old scientist was, the City might still succeed in getting to him first, and there was no telling what new stratagems Cavendish might turn his hand to in pursuit of that end. No, Phyllis was integral. And someone to imitate his voice. God, how humiliating that everyone in the building did impressions of him. Because that's what it boiled down to. Men and women, old and young. He'd probably have to hold auditions. Did that make it better or worse?

Fifteen hours away from his job interview with Cavendish, and Ruby Parker sent him and ten others down to the pods beneath the building to get some sleep. *Mansion House, 3pm sharp.* He was already beginning to have nightmares and he hadn't even fallen asleep yet. He expected to lie awake worrying, but in fact he'd underestimated how tired he was. He fell asleep with Ruby Parker's words ringing in his ears. *This is a team effort, John. Others can look for Phyllis just as well as you. The star part is tomorrow at three. For that, you need to be alert.* When he was awoken at eight by a gentle dinging, he showered, dressed and went straight to basement one where the most integral hub of Red Department was.

The first person he ran into was Annabel. "Well done, John," she said. "We've found her. This morning's cleaners, Pickthanks Office Hygiene, 5am. Top floor, Domine Dirige Tower."

For a moment, the news was so good he felt he must be dreaming. He looked at his watch. 9.05. Nearly six hours to go. Doubly brilliant, unless -

"How is she?" he asked.

"Fine, I think. Go and see Ruby Parker. I don't want to be seen speaking to you for too long because it might get back to Tariq."

"I spoke to him yesterday," he said. "I'm sorry to hear ..." He didn't know how to end the sentence.

"How was he?" she asked.

"Very, very upset."

Whether this was or wasn't what she was expecting, he didn't know. She looked emotional for a moment, then walked away.

Leave them well alone, that's my advice. They've got to learn to resolve their own problems. He continued along the corridor and knocked on Ruby Parker's door.

"Good news," she said, when he put his head round the door.

"I just heard it from Annabel."

"And from what we can discover, she's being treated very well indeed. We're keeping watch on her from Whitaker Place, the adjacent building."

"Excellent."

"On another matter, you'll also be pleased to know I've been running auditions. Your sound-alike."

"Yes, I suppose on reflection it doesn't make sense for me to do it myself. Most people don't have a very good grasp of what they sound like."

"And, of course, natural human vanity gets in the way. We all want to think we sound better than we do."

"Don't keep me in suspense then. Who's the winner?"

"It was a toss-up between Annabel and Brian. In the end, I gave it to Brian, because Annabel has other priorities."

He laughed. "Annabel and Brian? What about Walter, or Chris, or Marcus?"

"They may be about your age and build, but imitation's a tricky business. The upshot is, Brian's upstairs and waiting. I've a vague idea what you're planning, but I expect to see you back here before midday to finalise the details."

Brian was known to value courage as the crown of the virtues, and he exhibited it by coming into work every day in the same clothes. To his credit, there was nothing malodorous about him - presumably he bathed and visited the dry-cleaners on a regular basis – but thirty years in a tweed jacket and khaki trousers was a long time. What made it doubly odd was that he also valued glamour.

They met in a seminar room with a digital recorder between them. "Good to see you," Brian said in a voice clearly not his own. One Mordred vaguely recognised.

"Is that my voice you've got there?" he asked.

"Is that my voice you've got there?" Brian repeated.

"Because it doesn't sound anything like me."

"Because it doesn't sound anything like me. Sorry, John," he said, reverting to his own voice, "before you get annoyed, I've been practising by going the last eighteen hours in character. Obviously, I drew the line at dressing like you and adopting your mannerisms – I'm not Dustin Hoffman: I don't think either of us is – but I brought a colleague of yours along to verify the authenticity of my rendition."

"Hi, John," Edna said, from the corner of the room. He hadn't noticed her before.

"Hi," Mordred said. "What 'mannerisms'?"

"I was told by Ruby Parker that time is of the essence," Brian said. "Shall we get started?"

Mordred turned to Edna. "Is this what I *actually sound like?*"

"It's a nice voice," Edna replied. "What do *you* think you sound like?"

"In my own head, I sound like … I don't know. A normal person."

"It's what I'd describe as posh with a pinch of Geordie," Brian said. "A bit like Bob Ferris in *Whatever Happened to the Likely Lads?*"

Mordred grinned. Oh, well. He was what he was. Not Roger Moore, though.

"I take it you've got a script," Brian said.

"Two copies," Mordred replied. "Read it through first, then we'll go live. This should only take five minutes at the outside."

"I'll operate the recorder," Edna said.

"Am I allowed to make changes?" Brian said.

"No," Mordred replied.

"Because I don't think *you* would say this."

"Nevertheless, that's what I did say. It's the transcript of an actual conversation."

"Who's this other character then? 'L.M.'?"

"Lord Mayor. As in the Lord Mayor of London."

"Gotcha. And you're going to play him, right? Bob Wellington."

"Correct. Except it's not Bob Wellington. It's Ashley Cavendish."

"Who?"

"Ashley Cavendish. The Lord Mayor of the City of London. One square mile. Bob Wellington's only the Mayor of Greater

London. Six hundred and seven square miles. Just take my word for it."

"Are you sure you can do him, this 'Ashley Cavendish'?"

"I'm a languages expert. A lot of being able to learn different tongues lies in one's ability to imitate native speakers exactly. I've been honing my skills since I was ten."

"Can you do an imitation of me?"

"Can you do an imitation of me?" Mordred repeated.

"That didn't sound anything like me!"

"Defer to Edna."

"Sorry, Brian," Edna said. "That's exactly what you sound like. It was even better than yours of John." She apparently saw how crestfallen he looked, and added: "If that's possible."

"Look," Brian said bitterly, "don't take this the wrong way, but why can't you just do both parts? You must think you can do the Mayor – sorry, Lord Mayor - otherwise we wouldn't be here. And obviously, you can do you."

"It's more difficult than it sounds to convincingly alternate two voices when your audience is judging with their ears alone," Mordred said. "I'd have to be a much better actor than I am."

"Know your limits," Edna said. "The first rule of effective spycraft."

Brian sighed. "*Que sera, sera.* Let's get down to it then."

Edna pressed record, and nodded.

"So you want to know where your colleague 'Phyllis' is," Mordred said, in the Lord Mayor's voice.

Brian spluttered a loud guffaw. Edna pressed stop.

"What's so funny?" Mordred asked.

"He surely can't sound like *that!*" Brian exclaimed. "No one sounds like *that!*"

"I assure you he does," Mordred said.

"He sounds like bloody *Jabba the Hutt!* Play it back! Go on, play it back!"

Mordred didn't need to have it played back, but Edna obliged anyway. Brian was right. He hadn't seen it before. How could he have missed it?

Five minutes later:

Mordred: "So you want to know where your colleague 'Phyllis' is."

Brian: "Yes, please."

"Let's say, for the sake of argument, I knew where this woman was."

"Go on."

"And I also knew where Fenella Decristoforo-Salvaterra was."

Brian tried to say his next line. He quaked, scrunched his eyes, made his fingers rigid. Mordred laughed. Edna followed suit. She fell off her chair. Brian howled and slapped his thighs. He slapped the floor. He dribbled slightly onto the carpet.

One hour later:

Mordred: "So you want to know where your colleague 'Phyllis' is."

Brian: "Yes, please."

"Let's say, for the sake of argument, I knew where this woman was."

"Go on."

"And I also knew where Fenella Decristoforo-Salvaterra was."

Brian tried not to crack up. Mordred juddered, tears in eyes. Edna laughed. She fanned her face.

Everyone recovered.

Mordred: "So you want to know where your colleague 'Phyllis' is."

Brian: "Yes, please."

Two hours later, Mordred knocked on Ruby Parker's door.

"Talk me through your plan," she told him.

"We keep a close eye on Fenella and Phyllis until about 2.40pm," he told her. "Then we send in an armed team to rescue them. We know the two sets of Horvath guys holed up in Saint

Martha's Pride, and we know they'll come quietly once they realise the game's up. We know the same about Phyllis's captors. We need shock and awe, obviously, but we can do that."

"2.40 may be cutting it a bit fine," she replied. "Are you sure that leaves enough time for you to reach Mansion House?"

"Barring a serious traffic jam, yes, but even then, we're authorised to use the bus lanes. Plus Kevin knows the short cuts. Or at least, so he told someone else."

"And we bring Fenella here, right?"

"Plus her two companions. It seems the safest option in the short term. After I've seen the Lord Mayor, we can take her where we like. In terms of telling us where Peter is, she probably won't cooperate."

"We'll come to that in a moment. What are you going to say to Ashley Cavendish?"

"I'm going to show him Phyllis in the flesh, and tell him we've got Fenella, so he no longer holds any cards. Then I'm going to tell him I was recording him with my phone at our last meeting, and present him with this."

He took his phone out and pressed it. A tinny MP3 played.

"So you want to know where your colleague 'Phyllis' is."
"Yes, please,"
"Let's say, for the sake of argument, I knew where this woman was."
"Go on."
"And I also knew where Fenella Decristoforo-Salvaterra was."
"Keep going."
"You don't sound very taken aback. Good acting. You probably need a skill like that in your job."
"So you've got Phyllis Robinson and you've got Fenella Decristoforo- Salvaterra. What are you going to do with them?"
"I'm not saying I've 'got' them."
"What are you saying?"
"I'm saying for the sake of argument, for God's sake. I thought I'd made that clear at the beginning. Don't try and trap me. It won't work."

"If, for the sake of argument, you were holding Phyllis and Fenella, then what, for the sake of argument, would you do with them?"

"For the sake of argument, I – we: we in the City of London – would hold on to Phyllis, while you rendezvous with Fenella Decristoforo-Salvaterra and persuade her to lead you to her father. Once you've done that, we would release Phyllis. For the - "

"But you'd kill Peter."

"In the last resort, maybe. But his internet-cloaking discovery probably has important commercial applications. We'd want to access that first. Better than it falling into the hands of terrorists, you must agree. To that end, we'd need to hold on to his daughter."

"I see, yes."

"I accept that, for the sake of argument, all this would be asking a lot of you, but you'd be the head of Horvath and obviously two hundred and fifty thousand pounds is a lot of money. You'd have to be prepared to go beyond the call of duty all the time."

"Yes, I appreciate that."

"The people at Horvath warned me about your conscience, by the way –"

He pressed stop.

Ruby Parker stroked her chin. She took a deep breath. "And that's you and Brian, is it?"

"Yes."

"It's convincing, I'll give you that. You've both got the voices off. What are you going to do with it, once you've played it to him? How does it help?"

"There's nothing clinching enough to put him in the clink here, especially with the kind of judges we've got in this country. But circumstantially, it's enough to cause him serious embarrassment. All his 'for the sake of argument' qualifications are going to count for nothing next to the fact that he's talking about two women who've just been rescued from a captivity in which Horvath – the organisation now in his employ, and of which he explicitly offers me the headship - played the gaoler role. The Director of Public

Prosecutions may or may not think it's worth sending to trial. The press will have a field day. And we do know that apart from the dressing up and processing through the city once a year, the one thing the Lord Mayor hates with a vengeance is light on his domain."

"And yet for all its superficial power, the recording is a fake. If he calls your bluff - "

"Would you, in his position?"

She thought for a moment. "No, probably not."

"We're not doing anything immoral. Illegal, maybe."

"I have no problem with that, John. It's the poker aspect I find worrying."

"Cavendish is basically a wannabe Mafioso. It pays to call such people out. They're not good for democracy. This guy isn't, and he never will be. The sooner Bob Wellington soaks him up without remainder, the better."

"How many copies of the recording are there?"

"This one, and the one on the digital recorder upstairs."

"I'll arrange for that machine to be destroyed. I'll talk to Brian about confidentiality, although of course, he's already bound by the usual agreements. After this is over, whether it works or not, I want you to give me your phone and buy another. Charge it to expenses, obviously."

"Here's a consoling thought. Say Cavendish thinks to himself, 'that's not a real recording, he's bluffing', even so he's wise enough to know it'll disappear before his lawyers have subpoenaed it. The mere rumour of its one-time existence would be enough to inflame a million conspiracy theories, none of which do him any good whatsoever. In that unlikely event, I'd expect MI7 to cut me loose as a 'rogue agent', acting without the approval of the centre. I'd take the consequences, in other words."

She laughed humourlessly. "I'm supposed to find that 'consoling'?"

"There are things that can go wrong – one of Horvath's men might get trigger-happy, or there might be more security surrounding Phyllis than we anticipated – but, as plans go, this one's relatively impervious."

"That's what's troubling me. It's just a little too perfect. And don't forget, even if it works, it merely takes Cavendish out of the picture. It doesn't necessarily get us one inch closer to Peter Decristoforo."

"Sooner or later, he and Fenella will have to meet. We'll be waiting. I know that makes me sound a bit of a heel, but Cavendish was right about one thing. We don't want his invention – whatever it is – falling into the hands of terrorists."

"Good luck, John. I'm assigning Annabel to help you and the others rescue Phyllis. She's a black belt and she knows how and when to use a gun."

"I don't imagine it'll come to that, but thanks for the thought."

"And obviously, report straight back here after you've finished at Mansion House."

"Of course."

She must be pretty nervous. She didn't normally state the *blatantly* obvious.

Chapter 26: Ambush!

He met up with Alec and Ian for lunch in the canteen. They went downstairs for disguises and took the tube to Whitaker Place. Both it and Domine Dirige Tower, where Phyllis was being held, were within the boundary of the Square Mile, so nothing could be left to chance.

Whitaker Place was mixture of hotel, retail outlet, restaurant and office building. The hotel was at the top. They checked in at reception under assumed names and took the lift to room 376b, a luxury apartment with three rooms and an *en suite* from which four MI7 agents – Marcus, Mildred, Celia and Madison - kept watch on Phyllis with a telescope and a camera. She was handcuffed and chained to something below and out of view, but she didn't seem to be suffering unduly. Meals arrived promptly at nine, midday and seven, and she had a selection of magazines, which she spent most of her time perusing. There were cameras on the walls, and when she wanted to shower or visit the toilet, her chains were automatically unlocked, presumably by someone outside. When she'd finished, she put she chains back on herself. Presumably, they had ways of compelling her. Most of the time, she had the curtains closed.

"I assume we know who's operating her chains," Mordred asked. He looked through the telescope. Phyllis lay on the bed, staring at the ceiling. She looked miserable.

"Four Horvath staff," Celia replied. "We ID-ed them this morning. In case they won't cooperate, we've got bolt cutters, of course."

"Any guards?" Ian asked. "I mean, apart from the four Horvathians?"

"Difficult to tell," Mildred said. "You're looking at a building that's named after the City of London motto. It could be full of loyal foot soldiers. Alternatively, it could just be full of the usual nonentities."

"We can't afford to take anything for granted," Mordred said.

"I know," Celia said. "That's why we're providing armed cover. Just in case."

"Can't the police help out?" Ian asked. "I mean, this is a kidnap."

"City of London immunity," Marcus replied. "The Met could probably get away with it, but they're reluctant to get involved unless they absolutely have to. Don't like to upset the establishment. Never have."

"So we're on our own," Mordred replied.

"Unless you'd like me to call the army," Celia replied. "Joke. They wouldn't come out either. Yes, I'm afraid you're on your own. Still, you've got the advantage of surprise."

He looked at his watch. 1.30pm. Still a good hour and a bit to go. The tension was already getting to him, wearing him down. He'd imagined himself arriving at Mansion House full of beans, bursting into the building with a speech to hand about never to get out of your depth, Mr Mayor, we're always one step ahead, let this be a lesson, etc., etc. But he wasn't sure he could deliver it any more. Right now, he wasn't even that person. He was Highly Strung, Rather Manic Guy, that's who he was. Faced with a job of such importance that once he'd completed it, there was every chance he might just collapse in a heap. He sat down on the bed.

"Toilet's just through there, John, if you're nervous," Alec said.

"I'm good," he replied.

"Don't worry. I'll be there, and so will Annabel. They're not expecting us, but I've got a mental map of the building, and there are at least four fire exits if things go the least bit belly up. Everything's covered."

"This strikes me as much more the kind of thing the SAS do."

"It's your plan we're following, don't forget that."

"That's why I am worried. My plan, my responsibility. If it was your plan, I'd be having a whale of a time right now."

"I see, yes. Well, you're right, of course. It could be a bloodbath. Still, fingers crossed, eh?"

"You know I didn't mean it like that. Obviously I'd care if it was your plan. But you know what I mean."

"I've been in the army. So has Phyllis, and she won a medal for gallantry. We'll see you're okay."

He patted Mordred on the shoulder like he was an octogenarian, and went to the window to peer through the telescope. Mordred looked at his watch again.

1.32pm.

And 41 seconds.

42, 43, 44 …

Strangely, the more time passed, the more relaxed he began to feel, as if 1.32 and 41 seconds was his predetermined nadir and anything more than that had to be an improvement. More likely, once real things started to fall into place – the guns, Annabel, the two-way radios, Kevin, back-up personnel – his imagination found so much less room for manoeuvre that it eventually abandoned doom-mongering as too much of an effort. At 2.35, they left Whitaker Place in groups of three, Annabel, Alec and Mordred in the advance.

As soon as the agents attached to Pickthanks Office Hygiene had discovered Phyllis, at 5.30am that morning, they put a call through to Tariq. He arrived twenty minutes later and connected the building's closed-circuit TV to a surveillance monitor in a van parked around the corner from, and out of sight of, Domine Dirige Tower, and which the police had been instructed to avoid. For six hours, agents were able to observe employees entering passwords to computers and sending emails throughout the building and beyond. They were able to lip-read and so discover names, snippets of information, topics of the day. Thus it was that they were able to make appointments for four sets of three sales reps, between 2.25 and 2.45, all with people they knew would be out.

"Excuse me," Mordred said to the receptionist. "We're from TFL Insurance. We've got appointments to see Mr Gambon on the tenth floor. I was told you'd have a set of three passes ready. You're Tina, right?"

Tina smiled. She was about Annabel's age, short hair, in a skirt suit with a scarf. "Yes, sir. I'm afraid – I'm pretty sure Mr Gambon's out at the moment, but I can see your appointments with him on my screen."

"That's okay. He told us to wait for him outside his office."

"Yes, it says that here. I'll let him know as soon as he returns."

She handed three badges over, and a document to be signed. They went straight to the lift, passing two security guards who looked through and beyond them. Once they were in the lift, Annabel took her phone out and rang the team at Saint Katherine Dock.

"We're inside," she said. "We estimate five minutes to target, no more. Take this as the all-clear to move in at your own discretion. Repeat: you have the all-clear."

She put the phone away. She took her gun out, checked it and returned it to the chest holster beneath her jacket. Alec did the same. Neither of them asked him where his was.

They stepped out of the lift and turned straight left. Down the corridor, left again through the fire door and onto the stairs. Two flights and they'd be there. They removed their shoes. Annabel and Alec took their guns out. Their hearts hammered.

Then they heard an explosion from above. Not a major one: a controlled version, as of a door being blown. They exchanged puzzled glances and sped up.

Suddenly, they were on the corridor where Phyllis supposedly was. Smoke everywhere. Mordred was the first through. A bullet whizzed past his head and he rolled like he'd been taught. Someone screamed, "Get down on the floor!" It could have been anyone – man, woman, friend, foe. Annabel fired twice, then fell backwards into the fire-escape recess, apparently wounded. Alec ran forward. Mordred got up and, without even knowing how they'd got there or what they were doing, they were wrestling men with guns. Someone came out of Phyllis's room with Phyllis draped, apparently unconscious, over his shoulder. Alec's opponent took a few hits to the chest and stomach, and they seemed evenly matched for a short time, then the opponent got into his stride and smashed Alec into the floor. Blood seemed everywhere. Mordred battered his adversary's face and stamped hard on his head before he had time to get right, then went after Alec's man. He grabbed him as he was scrambling to his feet, and threw him against the window. Someone shot wildly again and half the glass smashed. Mordred's man fell against one side of the gaping hole, shattering yet more of the window, then recovered and renewed his attack, but Mordred was ready. He got a strong kick in, and to his half-surprise the man tumbled back against the glass – only now it didn't exist. He continued through to the outside, tried to get a handhold, and fell with a yelp. Nothing Mordred could do. Kill or be killed; well, he'd killed now, pity the people below. Then someone hit him hard in the stomach and he went down gasping, the fight all out of him.

He watched Phyllis getting borne away. He saw Alec lying unconscious. No movement at all from Annabel. He crawled to the fire bell and smashed the glass through. Then over to Annabel. Thank God, she was alive. She'd been hit but she was okay. A text message pinged on her phone. He took it from her pocket and read it.

Saint Katherine Dock mission aborted. Completely overwhelmed at last minute by hostile firepower, source/identity unknown. Please respond urgently.

He put her gun in his pocket. Possibly might some day need it.

The last thing he saw was a helicopter ascending from the top of the building.

Chapter 27: Seriously, Totally Peeved, Man

He came to as they were carrying him out of the building. He didn't know what MI7 protocol was for a mission like this: a double disaster where senior agents ended up seriously injured - or possibly dead: he didn't know exactly what had happened at Saint Katherine Dock. Whatever that protocol was, it probably didn't extend to where the evil happened on the doorstep of headquarters. God help him, this was the worst-beyond-the-worst case scenario.

Once that registered, he threw himself off the stretcher and careered into the road. Luckily, it had been closed off by the police or he might have been run over. Men and women shouted at him.

He spotted Kevin in the getaway car on the far side of them road. They made eye contact, and it was like love at first sight. They'd been enemies before, or something like it. Now they were two hearts beating as one. The next thing he knew, Mordred was in the back seat. Kevin screeched away. Neither of them spoke.

Mordred didn't consider himself a ferocious man, but there were certain times in everyone's life when the lust to violence overtook you completely. Had Kevin not driven when he said drive, he'd maybe have got out, riven him bodily from the front seat, punched him in the face, then driven off himself. But thank God, Kevin foresaw all that, must have.

The next person up for a plateful of punches to the mouth and stomach was the Lord Mayor of London. Kevin didn't need to be told where to go. Two minutes later, he squealed to a halt in front of Mansion House. Mordred had no idea what was going to happen next except that it would strongly resemble that scene in *LA Confidential* where the crusading police officer dangles the District Attorney out of a high window till he confesses.

He crossed the reception area without pausing to acknowledge the protests from staff. He could already sense security on its way. Always bloody security bloody guards, wherever you went. Them and receptionists – the twin pillars of every institution in the 21st century. Working-class people assigned to welcome or rebuff, and so preserve the everlasting facelessness of the establishment.

"Cavendish! Come out!" he yelled.

He took the stairs two at a time, and kicked open the door to each room. All empty. Not even any lower ranking lackeys. No one. Four guards were on their way over. He took Annabel's gun out and pointed it at them. They stopped and raised their hands.

"CAVENDISH!" he shouted at the ceiling, *"I'M HERE FOR MY JOB INTERVIEW!"*

He laughed. He must in shock, that was it. He'd been hit repeatedly on the head, his friends had been shot, he'd just killed a man and watched helplessly as the woman he'd been certain he was going to rescue was whisked away beneath his nose. He was completely out of it, my goodness, my, my, yes sir indeed.

He had to stop. He wasn't Violent Crazy Man, any more than he'd been Highly Strung Rather Manic Man two hours ago. He was John Mordred, pacifist. Okay, use the gun to get back in the car, then ditch it. Don't pull the trigger under any circumstances.

He held the guards transfixed long enough to get out of the building the way he'd come in. Kevin was waiting where he'd dropped him. He got into the back and they pulled away.

The whole of London was ringing with sirens now, but Kevin was so good at short-cuts, he hardly had to decelerate. A few minutes later, they were back in front of Thames House.

"I'll never, ever criticise you again," Mordred said. He put the gun onto the front passenger seat. "Get rid of this and you're at the top of my Christmas list. If you think it's a request too far, toss it out of the window as you pull away. I'll take care of it."

He got out, and Kevin screeched away. The gun remained untossed. Mordred silently thanked God for friends you didn't know you had.

He climbed the steps to Thames House and staggered over to Colin Bale. Rarely had he seen MI7's chief receptionist look so astounded.

"John – you're – shouldn't you be – ? You're covered in blood: look at you. We thought you'd gone to hospital!"

"Is Ruby Parker available?"

"Shouldn't I call an ambulance? I'd better -"

"I'm fine. I've just had a bit of an accident. Now, about the boss. Is she - "

"She's upstairs with Sir Ashley Cavendish, the Lord Mayor - "

"Yes, I know who he is. Tell them I'm on my way up." He half-regretted throwing the gun away now, but too late to go back: a pacifist he'd decided to be, and one he must remain. Besides, he was too tired to give anyone a pistol-whipping now. Give Jabba a piece of his mind, that was as much as he had the energy for.

He was halfway up the stairs when he realised he'd forgotten to ask where Ruby Parker or Ashley Cavendish were. This was a big building.

Well, you wouldn't want someone like him in the most sensitive areas, so that eliminated three-quarters. You'd probably want him where he'd already been. Where was it they'd first clapped eyes on each other? That's right. B14. Take the '1' out and it was B4. Where they'd met *B4*. He laughed out loud. God, he was turning into Alan Partridge. Brian would like it, though. *B4*. Good old Brian.

He couldn't quite remember where B14 was. Luckily, he could hear a row. A Ruby Parker versus Ashley Cavendish row. Hang on, Rube, I'm coming. He was hobbling. He'd been beaten up in Jersey, now he'd been beaten up in England. Status Quo: Beaten All Over the World.

B14! Yahoo! Search engine John Mordred. He opened the door and went in. As he expected, Ruby Parker and Ashley Cavendish in the middle of what looked like an old time cockney-style slanging match. Her with hands on hips, him arms extended, both with chins jutting out, eyes locked. They turned to look at him and seemed to lose all passion for attack. Then defence. Their mouths dropped open. He'd never quite seen the like before.

"I'm here to bring peace," he said.

Five minutes later, they all sat round a table. Colin Bale called to say an ambulance was waiting outside. Mordred told him to send it away. He didn't know whether the message was passed on. When he looked out of the window after fifty seconds, the road was empty.

"So it wasn't your men who abducted the abductees," Mordred said to Cavendish.

"No, for God's sake, *I've already told you -* "

"Stop," Mordred said.

The Lord Mayor's hands fell limp on the table.

"We agreed," Mordred said. "Yes or no, that's all. Yes? or no?"

"No," the Lord Mayor said.

"And you've no *idea* who they were?" Mordred asked.

"No."

He turned to Ruby Parker. "And you've no idea who they were either?"

"No," Ruby Parker said. She raised her hand. One of the rules was that, if you did that, you were allowed a single sentence.

"Go on," Mordred said.

"It wouldn't make the slightest bit of sense for me to send in a second team to attack my first team, and thereby send important members of my department to hospital."

Mordred turned to the Lord Mayor. "Ash?"

"I told you not to call me that," Cavendish replied.

"Sorry, I'm still only half in the room. But it's the best we're going to get. Can you see the sense of what Ms Parker's saying?"

Cavendish shrugged.

"I need an actual word," Mordred said.

Cavendish shrugged again. "Suppose."

"Okay look," Mordred said, "here's what we're going to do. The important thing here is that we both accept the other's speaking in good faith. Sir Ashley, you're only annoyed because you lost what you had no right to in the first place. You abducted one person and held another prisoner, and we possess the evidence to prove it."

Time for the showpiece. He took his phone out, put it on the table and pressed play. They listened to Mordred and Brian discussing abductions 'for the sake of argument'. The Lord Mayor seemed angry for a moment, then he withdrew into himself and his vital spirits appeared to flatline.

"Might not be enough to secure a conviction," Mordred said when it was over, "but future Lord Mayors certainly won't speak very highly of you."

Cavendish stood up calmly and went to the door. Before he closed it behind him, he turned to face them. "Well done, Mr Mordred and Ms Parker. You win. A good businessperson always knows when to call it a day. I'm sorry for the trouble I've caused you. I sincerely hope you manage to salvage something from the wreckage. Destroy the recording and you'll hear no more from me. As you rightly say, it won't be enough to convict me."

"Deal," Mordred said.

"Then we're done," the Lord Mayor said. "If and when all this comes to an end, I do hope we'll meet again. For lunch, maybe."

He left, closing the door behind him.

"I suggest we go to your office," Mordred said, "and get someone up here to conduct a sweep." He walked to the door and held it open for her. "Good try, Ash, if you're listening."

"You shouldn't be here," Ruby Parker said spiritlessly as they sat down in her office. "You should be in Accident and Emergency. At least get yourself checked out."

"We need to get to the bottom of what happened," he said.

"And how do you propose we do that?"

"You must have some theory as to who the perpetrators are. I know I have."

She smiled. "Who wants to go first?"

"I think you should."

"Very well, MI7 is composed of five very different departments, of which we, in Red, are but one. We overlap in places – we share a building and a canteen – but otherwise we have completely different remits. White, Red, Blue, Grey, Black. Take your pick. Since it's obviously not us, it could be any one of the remaining four."

"Whichever it is, there's a mole amongst us."

"That would probably be Steven Harris. 'Smarmy Steven', as Alec calls him. He transferred out just before the attack. We're not allowed to know where."

"It couldn't be White. That would be a step down. Maybe not in pay, but prestige-wise."

"He never struck me as caring too much about his reputation. Besides, we don't know that Blue, Grey or Black are any better."

"My guess is it's Blue. All those stories you hear about their military ethos. These guys seemed to know what they were doing. And they could fight. I don't know how I managed to kill one of them, but - "

"You *killed* one of them? How?"

"We were hanging out of a window. I can't quite remember who swung the last blow, but it was an unambiguous KOBEK: kill or be killed. He lost his grip and fell ten floors into the street."

"There were no reports of any deaths."

"Only someone in this building would have the power to cover that sort of thing up at infinitesimal notice. Which confirms what we've already agreed. It was an inside job."

"So where does that leave us? They're determined to get their hands on Peter Decristoforo, and they need Fenella to do it. They took Phyllis because they know we won't let it rest, and two separate pursuits effectively divides our powers in half."

"That's about the size of it," Mordred remarked.

They sat in silence for a while, listening to the fish tank.

"What if …" he said.

"Yes?"

"Sorry, I didn't mean to say that. I was just thinking."

"You might as well tell me. Whatever it is, it may lead somewhere."

"What if the whole thing's just one big smokescreen?"

"I'm not sure I follow."

"So far, what we've all been doing is trying to get our hands on Peter Decristoforo's Internet Cloaking Device. Think about that for a moment. Just stop worrying about the strategic advantages of having such a thing, or the harm it might do in the wrong hands, and especially about what it's allegedly facilitated: World War O. Just think about the thing in itself."

She smiled. "Okay ..."

"Doesn't it strike you as somewhat unlikely?"

"Actually, yes. Like a 'spy-fi' device."

"We believe in it because all these offshore financial centres got occupied and it was sold to us from the start as the *cause of that effect*. GCHQ didn't spot anything. The Joint Intelligence Committee didn't spot anything. The NSA didn't spot anything. What if, alternatively, everything came through as normal, but senior figures within those organisations decided to suppress information for reasons of their own?"

She laughed. "That's absurd. What possible reasons could they have?"

"That's putting the cart before the horse. Before we ask, what possible motive could x have for y, it might be a good idea to ask whether y actually occurred."

"That could entail an awful lot of wasted time. For something this unlikely. It involves diverting manpower from Phyllis."

"What's going to happen within the next thirty minutes is that your phone's going to ring, and it'll be Colin Bale. Alec and Annabel have reported for duty at reception."

"I'm sorry to say this, John, but you've been acting strangely - "

Her phone rang. He used his eyebrows to ask if she was going to answer. She picked up.

"They shouldn't be here," she told the caller after a moment.

"Tell them to come to your office," Mordred whispered.

"Send them down to my office," she said, and replaced the receiver. "Very clever," she said drily. "How did you know?"

"They both think I'm a sissy. The thought of them lying in hospital while I'm at my desk will have driven them crazy. Plus prematurely reporting back for duty when you've been injured in the line of duty's a universal trope of cop drama."

"I'm going to send them back where they came from, and order them to take you along."

"Why? I can see I'm beginning to irritate you. But put your ego aside for a minute - "

"I beg your pardon?"

"Sorry, that was disrespectful. But look at it rationally. Yes, I may be in shock. But so may you. You've just had a major intelligence operation go wrong, several agents injured, and a titanic run-in with the Lord Mayor of London. Probably neither of us is on our best form. But I got rid of Cavendish, and I've got reasonably good form with speculative possibilities. If Alec and Annabel want to stay here, don't patronise them by sending them away, put them to use."

"What sort of use?"

"Poring over documents."

"You'll have to be more specific."

"I want unrestricted access to all raw data from GCHQ for the last twelve months. Specifically relating to internet surveillance. I want an order from you, and possibly the Home Secretary - assuming you can twist his arm after what's just happened - compelling GCHQ to comply unreservedly with all my requests as a matter of top priority."

"You're talking about a hell of a lot of data. Are you sure you're qualified to distinguish the wood from the trees?"

"I can only try."

She considered. "I'll give you Tariq."

"I'm not sure putting Tariq and Annabel in the same room - "

"You're either serious about this, John, or you're not. If you are, it's an urgent matter of national security. It's not the sort of thing you let a marital squabble get in the way of. I'll give you the whole of his department, plus Edna and Ian. I'm doing this so that you get it out of your system, understood? You've got twenty-four hours, and I advise you to work in shifts. After that, I don't want to hear any more about it."

"Deal," he said.

You've got twenty-four hours. Alec and Annabel were going to love that.

Chapter 28: Things Pan Out

Annabel, Tariq and Alec came in to Ruby Parker's office in a group. Annabel had been shot in the chest, a rib deflecting the bullet. She walked like Frankenstein with a stick, but the heroic cop-trope was buried too deep for anyone, or even common sense sanity, to interfere. Alec was covered in contusions and cuts, but only Mordred had the cop-trope glory-look of being plastered in dried blood and bits of gore. Together they were cop-trope perfection and they looked like they belonged in an eighteenth century madhouse.

They went downstairs to Tariq's computer domain. After twenty minutes, everyone who'd been assigned to the task had arrived. Mordred explained his theory, and their brief, and what he was hoping to find, and asked if there were any questions. There weren't.

GCHQ didn't quibble. It sent over everything on request, although there was a distinct sense of Humouring The Children about some of their replies. At 7.30, someone's mobile rang. Mordred looked around, thanking God it wasn't his. *Mum*, that'd be the final straw. He checked he'd pressed the off button as advised.

Annabel answered, listened and put her hand over her mouth. She stood up. "Sorry, I have to make a return call," she muttered. "Good news. Fantastic news. Just excuse me a moment, please." She left the room.

They all looked at each other. Tariq gazed at his screen, pretending not to notice.

After a few moments, they heard her scream. Alec and Tariq got up and ran out.

"I'm finally free!" she yelled, somewhere in the distance. *"I'M FINALLY FREE!"*

She screamed again. Then it sounded like she was crying.

Everyone tried to ignore it. The morphine? having embarrassing side-effects? She'd had a brutal day and in a few hours she probably wouldn't remember anything. Right now there was too much else to concentrate on.

After a minute, Alec came back in. He slapped Mordred on the shoulder and grinned. "I'm pleased to report the al-Banna marriage is officially up, running and probably going to Australia," he whispered.

"What the hell just happened?" Mordred asked.

Alec chuckled. "Great news, completely out of the blue apparently. Her father just died in hospital."

Twelve hours later, patterns began to emerge. Leads were followed up, new discoveries were cross-referenced and the group began to re-divide the labour according to the emerging consensus. Grains of wheat appeared among the chaff. The demoralising effects of that afternoon's operational disaster were nullified by a growing sense that they were winning, and miraculously, without even leaving the building. Thenceforth, they worked shifts. Half the team went to the pods to sleep. At 5am came Mordred's turn. At eight, he awoke to the sound of a gentle ding. He pressed the release button and his bed ejected slowly from the wall.

Alec stood waiting for him, fully dressed. "I wasn't sure whether you'd be dead," he said, "the state of you."

Mordred was too beat for jocularity. He threw his legs over the side of the bed and felt like someone had spent the entire morning punching him. Was he going to vomit? No, probably not.

"Say something," Alec said.

"Like what?"

"That'll do. Get showered and dressed. Your orders are to cross the river to Saint Thomas's, get a full check-up, and when they give you the green light, go home and get some proper sleep. There's a car waiting to ferry you. It'll be straight in at the hospital, no hanging around in the waiting area. Everything's been arranged, courtesy of the Big Park. Report back here at eight. We've done it."

"Done what?"

"Remember four hours ago when we were all in Tariq's computer room? What we were doing then? That."

He couldn't be bothered to pursue it.

"It'll all be explained when you get back here," Alec said. "I'll be here too. Eight this evening. Don't be late. Put your alarm on."

"Bit of an odd time."

"See you later." He threw his coat over his shoulder and left.

Done what? It was pretty clear: Alec's body language screamed it out. He didn't know either.

Mordred washed and shaved painfully, dressed in the new clothes Amber had laid out for him and took the lift to the canteen. He sat next to Sandi from Accounts and ate a bowl of porridge with cream. She had her laptop open, eating a Pop Tart, occasionally stirring her coffee with one hand, and typing with the other. She was wholly engrossed, and didn't appear to notice Mordred at all. He couldn't help catching sentences out of the corner of his eye. *Do you really think that Russian piece of crap's gonna work on me?* and *Before they could stop him, he threw himself off Spasskaya Tower. Nadia screamed.* He looked around the canteen. Every second person with an open laptop, typing.

Kevin took him to Saint Thomas's at nine. As promised, it was straight in, straight out. He'd had a nasty 'fall', that was what the doctor told him. Stop drinking and clubbing was the hidden subtext. He was home at ten. He ate two paracetamol tablets and a stale Chelsea bun and crawled straight into bed.

He didn't sleep well. When you lived on your own, there was always the temptation to get up and wander round during bouts of insomnia. Go to the kitchen, put the TV on, read a bit of a magazine, surf the net, fiddle with your apps. No one cared whether you rested or not, and so what if you fell asleep later, at work? You were usually in a bad mood when sleeplessness hit, and work seemed as good a fall guy as anything.

He went to bed for the tenth miserable time at 2pm, and managed to stay there. At seven, his phone rang. It took him a moment to realise where he was. He picked it up and looked at the screen. *Alec.* Bloody hell. Mind you, anyone would be cause for irritation right now. Still an hour to go. He wanted to get ready at his own pace.

"Hi," he said.

"You ready to go?" Alec asked.

"It's only bloody seven o' clock. It's not for an hour."

"I thought we might grab something in the canteen first."

"I'm not even hungry. Where are you?"

"Outside your block of flats. I'm coming up the stairs now. I thought we'd get the bus over together."

"Why? Why can't we just meet there like any normal day?"

"I came over to see if you were okay. Ruby Parker's orders. I'm to 'keep an eye' on you. In a thoughtful, caring way. Also, I forgot to tell you this morning: you're to put your best suit on."

There was a knock at the front door.

"That's me," Alec said, "obviously. Knocking."

Another shower, another shave. Alec sat in his pinstripe suit and watched Channel 4 News, then they went downstairs and caught the bus. They arrived at Thames House with ten minutes to spare.

"I'm bloody starving," Alec said. "Why do you never have any proper food in your flat?"

"I tend to buy then eat, buy then eat. I don't store things."

"Why the bloody hell not? What if you get ill? Couldn't you just keep a few cans for emergencies? And what about guests? I know you're a vegetarian, but even a can of baked beans or spaghetti hoops or macaroni cheese would be better than nothing."

"Consider me warned."

"For your own good. Do you think there's time for something from the canteen?"

"If we're quick and there's no queue. Maybe a slice of pizza?"

"Even a single boiled potato would be better than nothing. Come on."

When they arrived, the canteen had just moved to its late menu and a new batch of food was being prepared. By coincidence, all that remained from the last sitting was five boiled potatoes. Julie let them have them for free.

"Put salt and a sachet of mayo on," Alec said, when they were eating. "They're surprisingly good."

Three minutes later, they knocked on Ruby Parker's door. Mordred looked at his watch. By a miracle, they were two minutes early.

"I might as well begin by apologising," she said, when they were seated. "To you, John. It turns out you were right, after all. There is no 'internet cloaking device'. Even saying those three words makes me feel slightly silly now. How we – I - can ever have believed it defies me."

"So what do we have instead?" Mordred asked.

"As you predicted," she went on, "an apparent conspiracy to withhold information about the protests until too late. The evidence is too glaring for them to deny, though I'm sure they'll try. We've three senior GCHQ executives, including the Director himself, two Joint Intelligence Committee members, one of whom is the chairman Sir Joshua Haines, and the really interesting odd one out, Sir Thomas Calderhouse. Of course, they must have liaised with the Americans, because it 'got past' the NSA as well. But that's out of our jurisdiction."

"What's so 'really interesting' about Sir Thomas Calderhouse?" Mordred said.

"I've suspected for a long time that he's the head of MI7's Blue Department," she said. "The Blue Maiden."

"Should make for an interesting interview," Alec remarked. "Given yesterday."

"I hope so," she replied.

"I still don't know why we're here," Mordred said. "And I'm not sure Alec does either. Why eight o'clock sharp? Why are we all wearing suits?"

"In a minute, we're going to get in a car and go across London," she replied. "There we're going to meet the six co-conspirators. The fact that they've asked to see me probably shows they're in panic. Their common membership of the same London club doesn't bode well for them either. We couldn't have known that at the outset."

"Do they know you're bringing us along?" Alec asked.

"I don't think I could do this without some back up," she replied. "But neither do I need to match person for person. I've enough cards in my hand. John's coming because he can see things I can't. You're coming because I trust your judgement."

"What do we expect them to say?" Mordred asked.

"As I pointed out earlier," she said, "the evidence is fairly undeniable. My guess is they'll want to cut a deal of some sort: concessions for silence. I haven't mooted anything yet because I don't know for certain that will be their approach. Obviously, the moment it becomes apparent it is, Phyllis is top of the agenda. We should even get Fenella Decristoforo-Salvaterrra. The most they're entitled to ask us for is time. We can sit on our findings for a short period, give them a chance to put their separate affairs in order. We can't, in all conscience, bury what we've discovered."

"Do we have any idea yet why they acted as they did?" Mordred asked.

"Not the slightest," she replied. "And I can't even begin to speculate. In many ways, that may turn out to be the most interesting aspect of the entire evening."

It was dark when they arrived at their destination. A row of Georgian terraced houses on a cul-de-sac terminated by a high park fence topped with razor wire. There was no sign indicating which dwelling was the Godolphin Club, though Ruby Parker seemed to know it. Fully-grown trees and Victorian style lampposts alternated on the pavement, the one taking away nearly all the light the other bestowed. Most of the houses didn't look lived in. All in all, this felt like one of London's gloomier, less happy-to-be-part-of-the-modern-multicultural-metropolis nooks.

They were admitted, as was common in these sorts of places, by someone whose role lay somewhere between greeter and waiter, and who, one hundred years ago – and possibly here, today, for all Mordred knew – would probably be described as a servant. About fifty, immaculately pressed black trousers, white shirt, waistcoat, bow tie, ready smile. Ruby Parker gave him their names.

"Follow me, please," he said. He turned and preceded them up a flight of stairs.

It suddenly occurred to Mordred that Ruby Parker might not hold as many cards as she thought she did. The conspirators had Phyllis, after all. How much they thought they could get in exchange for her they probably didn't know, but they might well think it was a lot. They might be right. Maybe Ruby Parker didn't think they'd stoop that low. If so, she was almost certainly wrong. If life had taught him one lesson, it was that there were no depths to which the establishment wouldn't willingly sink when it felt its existence to be under threat.

They walked across a landing with six closed doors leading off it – this place was a lot bigger than it looked from the outside: possibly, it was two houses knocked into one. They stopped before the end door. The servant knocked, turned the handle to admit them, and retired, closing them in.

The room in which they found themselves was large and furnished in typical traditional London club style. A fireplace, vertical striped wallpaper, framed antique portraits, two sofas, six or seven leather upholstered chairs, discreet standard lamps, and a variety of low-lying tables. There was a strong smell of alcoholic spirits.

They were confronted by six men and two women. One of the latter was Fenella Decristoforo-Salvaterra: she sat with a very old man in a chair, covered by a blanket, obviously her adopted father. The other five men and one woman – all smartly dressed as if for the office and in their late fifties or early sixties - were presumably the conspirators. They stood, faces turned anxiously towards the entrants. There was nothing hostile or sinister about any of them. On the contrary, they looked as if they couldn't wait for the axe to fall and end their misery.

"Thank you so much for coming over, Ruby," the man closest to them said. "Of course, we've already met on a number of occasions. Allow me to introduce myself and the rest of the room to your two colleagues. I'm Joshua Haines, the Permanent Under-secretary of State for the Ministry of Defence, and also chair of the Joint Intelligence Committee. My committee colleague, Rosie Marshall from the Foreign Office. Robin Partridge, Edward Tumwebaze and Pete Marks from GCHQ. Tom Calderhouse, who I'm now able to tell you, because he's just resigned, was the head of MI7's Blue Department. Of course, you'll already recognise Fenella Decristoforo-Salvaterra and possibly her father Peter, although his appearance has considerably altered in the last few months as a consequence of a terminal illness. Please sit down. We appreciate you probably have lots of questions."

Three seats had been reserved for them. Without asking, Haines poured three large brandies and brought them over.

"You probably know what my first question is going to be," Ruby Parker said.

"Phyllis Robinson was dropped off at Thames House ten minutes ago," Calderhouse said. "I believe Cavendish looked after her quite well, given the obvious constraints on holding a person prisoner. We've only had her for a few hours. Just long enough for her to recover from the chloroform and submit to a thorough medical check-up. She was fine once she knew who we were. As of course, she would be."

"Good. I'd also be very grateful if you could give Steven Harris his marching orders."

"That's a bit vindictive, isn't it?"

"It's common sense," she replied. "A traitorous disposition."

Calderhouse shrugged. "It's out of my hands. But point taken. I can leave it as a strong recommendation to my successor."

"I'd like to express my regret for killing one of your agents," Mordred said. "It's only just beginning to sink in. In my defence, they did open fire on us, and I honestly don't think I had much choice, given the situation."

"I don't know what you mean," Calderhouse replied. The truth seemed to suddenly dawn. "Oh, yes. I do see now. Sorry, I didn't realise it was *you* who'd made him fall. Well, you may be pleased to know that he dropped precisely fourteen feet onto a window cleaner's platform. Severely winded, bit of damage to the lower back, but he should be back at work within the week."

"Are you – serious?" Mordred said.

"With respect, what do you think happened?" Calderhouse replied. "If he'd landed in the street after falling from that height, there would have been bits of him everywhere. Even we couldn't have kept that hush-hush."

Mordred smiled. "Good. That is good." He drank his brandy.

"What do you want from us?" Ruby Parker asked.

"Want?" Haines said. "What do you think we want?"

"I take it you want to make a deal. I warn you, I can't suppress our findings, not for anything. I am, however, prepared to give you a little compassionate time to prepare your families."

"Doesn't it worry you that one or all of us may flee the country?" Tumwebaze asked.

"As I say," she replied, "it's a risk I'm prepared to take."

Haines scoffed. "Come, come, Ruby. You talk as if we're murderers."

"People *have* died as a result of this," she replied.

"We gave them the war they themselves wanted," he said. "We gave them a reason for existing. As Vernon Johns once said, 'If you haven't found a cause worth dying for, you haven't found a reason for living.'"

Alec smiled drily. "With respect, sir, that's easy for you to say."

"Do you really think we didn't expect you tonight?" Haines asked. "If so, think again. This, or something very like it – our arrest and subsequent exposure on the rack of public disgrace – was part of our intention from the beginning. In one sense, you've merely stumbled onto the stage. You're playing the walk-on roles we wrote for you long ago."

Mordred felt his hackles rise. He felt Alec's rise too.

"I'm not sure I follow," Ruby Parker said.

"I don't expect you do," Haines told her. "That's because you haven't shown the slightest curiosity about what must surely, from your point of view, be the oddest thing of all. The question of how we eight became modern-day gunpowder plotters."

She smiled. "I expected you all to deny it. I expected to have to wrangle, at best, and, at worst, fight for my reputation, perhaps even my life. I therefore put my curiosity on ice."

"As a luxury you couldn't afford to indulge," Calderhouse said.

"I take it you do *feel* curiosity," Haines asked her.

"Naturally."

"Good, because I'm going to satisfy it. I'm going to tell you, and then everyone in the world. I've been rehearsing for a long time now. This is a performance I hope I'll give again and again for the rest of my life. Welcome to its opening night."

Mordred sat back in his chair. Telling a curious story in an old-time London club. Rather like Arthur Conan Doyle.

"Somewhere in the last fifty years," Haines said. "Britain – and the world, really - went seriously wrong. It was Peter who first made me realise it, discussions we had about science. I'm sixty-two now. When I was young, we were putting men on the moon.

If you'd asked me what the future would be like, I'd have said bright. I honestly believed that by 2010, we'd have colonised Mars, eradicated world hunger, discovered a cure for cancer, and all be working two-day weeks. We all thought that, all of us. But somewhere along the way, governments everywhere stopped showing an interest in science. One by one, they were captured by finance, and one by one, that's all they began caring about. So where have we ended up? Well, as a by-product of marketing and sales, we've got the greatest social networking machinery the world's ever seen. And that's the sum of our achievement, really. Meanwhile, the best minds continue to be sucked away from urgent scientific questions and put to work on inane financial ones. In short, Ms Parker, my seven co-conspirators and I did what we did because we looked at what the world's become and decided it's not right. Obviously, we're prepared to go to prison for what we believe."

"Where does the NSA fit into this?" she asked.

"That's a matter for Washington to discover," Haines replied. "Suffice it to say, we worked together. Some of us and some of their people. It's not for us to give them up, but I doubt the CIA will have to dig deep."

"So you actually want me to call the police?" Ruby Parker said.

"We've already prepared our families," Haines told her. "When you leave here, we expect you to turn us in, yes. It goes without saying that nothing you possess can be used to incriminate Peter or Fenella. They're booked on to a private jet direct to Saint Martha's rock tomorrow morning."

"But what if the police want to question them?" Alec asked.

"We all know they're not implicated," Haines said. "What you *may* have believed about them was so much mischievous hearsay, bizarre speculation, and hardly their responsibility. Keeping them here on the grounds that the police might want to 'interview' them would be both pointless and unkind, especially in view of Peter's condition. And it could be embarrassing for you."

"Agreed," Ruby Parker said.

"In that case," Haines said, "I think that concludes our meeting. Thank you for coming to meet us."

The servant put his head round the door. Mordred wondered if he'd been listening in all along. He hadn't noticed anyone inside the room, say, pull a cord or anything.

"Could you have our coats ready, Timothy, please?" Haines asked. "Mr Mordred, I believe Peter and his daughter would like a word with you before you leave. In private."

Everyone shuffled out surreally. In fact, nothing that had happened here tonight had possessed the slightest suggestion of normality. It had been like something from a deranged Agatha Christie novel: no innocent suspects, only perpetrators and detectives, the former calling the latter to the library to explain why they did it.

Timothy closed the door on the last of the leavers. Mordred went to sit with Fenella and her father. She wore a dark brown dress and had her hair in a bun; he was covered in a blue blanket. He looked weary and emaciated, but when he spoke, his voice sounded almost healthy.

"I only wanted to say, please thank your sister for me. She gave them a good run for their money. It's not over yet, tell her. She may expect a little help from me shortly."

"I'll pass the message on," Mordred said.

"Could you come and visit us – me – on Saint Martha's Rock?" Fenella asked. "I don't think this is the end for World War O. We need to keep in touch. And I'd like to show you something I think might amuse you. You're welcome any time."

"I'm sure I can justify that on the grounds of national security. Where are Rory and Maria, by the way?"

"Downstairs, I believe," Fenella said. "Good night, Mr Mordred. Don't forget, will you?"

"I promise I'll visit as soon as I conceivably can."

When he got outside, a black taxi was waiting with its engine idling. Ruby Parker and Alec sat side by side on the back seat, talking quietly. Mordred got into the rear and sat down on the chair facing them. The car pulled away. Ruby Parker rang Phyllis and spoke to her consolingly for a long time. She told her to go home, take tomorrow morning off and report in at midday.

The car pulled up outside Thames House. Ruby Parker went inside. The two men exchanged goodnights and went their separate ways, feeling melancholy.

Chapter 29: The Best Teen Movie Never Made

The stage set and sound system arrived in the north of the island at night from France, so it was said, because the Jersey authorities refused to allow it in through official channels. Whether that was true, no one knew. The first bit was, but that might be because the authorities couldn't get it across land with all the festival-goers. Lots of roads became inaccessible, and meanwhile the Jersey States claimed they were cooperating with the organisers – Hannah and her friends – to keep the event 'safe for tourists'. No one really knew how deep that ran, or what, if anything, was going on behind the scenes that might compromise or even sabotage it. Tensions abounded. Whether the rock concert would be a success or a disaster or take place at all remained an open question almost to the last minute, and there came a point at which everyone involved wished it had never even been proposed.

In the end, money stepped in, ironically in the form of a local financier and philanthropist who agreed to provide security at his own personal expense, so that, as he put it 'everyone could finally sleep at night'.

Back in London, the Director of Public Prosecutions struggled to discover a charge under which the six conspirators could be brought to trial. On one interpretation, they had colluded to breach the Data Retention and Investigatory Powers Act 2014; but the legislation's application was anything but clear cut. Could they be brought up on the older Regulation of Investigatory Powers Act 2000? Possibly, but nothing was thought to proscribe the withholding of information by agents actually inside the institutional body responsible for gathering it. How far could allegations of professional misconduct be converted into charges of criminality? There were no precedents, hence no one knew. It might get quite a long way in court before a judge decided it couldn't stand.

The problem was complicated by the discovery that a small group of Hollywood celebrities had apparently been corralled to deflect media attention in advance of the protests. Corralled by what or whom, no one knew – the BBC called it a 'missing link' - but the idea was that the protests would help create a world in which no one need ever cross the Mediterranean in a refugee boat again.

Finally, in the absence of any clear-cut plan of action, the Prime Minister ordered a judicial review, and, in the meantime, set up a public inquiry. Since everyone knew that public inquiries nearly always went on twice as long, and cost twice as much as expected, this was supposed to demonstrate his commitment whilst deferring at least some of the accountability. Meanwhile, a small group of senior intelligence officials at Fort Meade, Maryland, USA, gave themselves up to the Federal Bureau of Investigation.

Mordred flew in to meet his patents in Saint Helier and on 30 August at 2pm, the day before the festival commenced. They tried to get over to Plemont, but there seemed no way that didn't involve a long hike across difficult terrain. Pleading concern at the probable lack of toilet facilities, his parents decided to watch events on TV at the hotel. "We'll probably see much more there," his father said. "We'll look out for you. Give us a wave if you see a camera."

Mordred made his way to Plemont alone, and spent the day watching band after band he'd never heard of and wishing he'd bought something more to drink.

The whole thing struck him as a little like the closing scenes of an American teen movie: the adventure was over, the good guys had triumphed, now it was time to rock a stadium. Twelve bands were scheduled, climaxing with Fully Magic Coal Tar Lounge at 10pm. At 11, Hannah and Soraya performed their two-song duet. Since Hannah couldn't really sing, and since she was clearly too nervous to throw herself into it, this bit was refreshingly unlike any episode of *Glee* ever filmed.

Throughout the day, volunteers collected money to help the refugees in the Mediterranean. Film stars arrived from the United States, including Jennifer Hallowell and Roger Scheffler. Once it was clear there wasn't going to be any violence, new bands, some of them quite famous, also started arriving, looking to play a set so they could tell their fans they'd been there.

After the long-awaited, now to be much-talked-about, Hannah-Soraya renditions of A Begging I Will Go and Bury Me Beneath the Willow, Hannah took the centre stage. Silence fell. Mordred's heart went into his mouth. Mind-bogglingly odd, yet true: all these people – every last one – knew who she was.

She said it had been a long journey from when they arrived in Jersey to today, but that she now realised they were fighting more than tax evasion. They were fighting the way modern business, in its biggest manifestations, worked. They were fighting for the poor against the super-rich. They were even fighting for the middle-classes – of which she was a member – against the super-rich. They were fighting against privatisation and profiteering and social injustice and environmental destruction. All those things were interlinked.

"But I also realise," she went on, "that any movement that wants to win against this sort of rapacious capitalism can't stand still. Capitalism keeps re-inventing itself – that's its greatest strength – and if we don't at the very least match it in terms of creativity, we stand no chance. These quaint Jolly Rogers – I've become so attached to them, but in a month's time, they'll be as passé as a second-hand Che T-shirt – will have to go. What am I proposing for the future? This has been a great evening, and it might feel like the end to some of you people. But it's only the beginning. Come gather round people, wherever you roam. Jersey, Guernsey, Caymans, the City of London, Delaware, Hong Kong, Singapore – remember: you heard it here first. May the first, next year: invasion two point nought. Get ready for the second round in World War O!"

She waved and left the stage. People cheered. Journalists wrote. Cameras filmed. Fireworks went off. Out at sea, ships blared their horns like animals unaware of what they were excited about, only that they had to join in. *Invasion 2.0*. Due to be the headline banner in a hundred newspapers the following day. Another band took the stage. Its lead singer asked if everyone was ready to rock. A cheer went up, and the cheesy teen movie resumed.

The bands ran out of life at 3am. Fully Magic Coal Tar Lounge played Hard Times of Old England and that was the end. The crowds thinned, the temperature seemed to drop, and the sky seemed to darken. Whatever happened now, everyone was finally going home. Until May 1 next year, possibly, but that might turn out to be pie in the sky. These things often were.

It was 6am before Mordred found his sister. She sat with Tim and the Coal Tars and Jennifer Hallowell around a camp fire. They all looked dead beat, but they were laughing and singing and apparently toasting bread. They cheered when they saw him. Hannah got up and hugged him and introduced him to the film star.

"Someone just gave us a loaf and some jam," Olly told Mordred. "Do you want some?"

"Actually, yes," Mordred said.

"Where are mum and dad?" Hannah said. "You haven't lost them, have you?"

"Back at the hotel," he replied. "Watching everything on TV. They'll be in bed now, of course. I tried to get them to come over, but I think they'd have been miserable."

"You did the right thing," she said. "What did you think of the duet?"

"It was, er, good."

"I like that. 'Er' good. About sums it up."

"Nice speech."

"Thanks."

He sat down and felt someone take his hand. He turned to see who it was. Soraya. "Hi, Jim," she said.

He laughed. "Hi."

"I'm not trying to chat you up," she said, "but could you put your arm round me? I'm freezing."

"All put our arms round Soraya!" Gaz said.

Four men bundled on top of her. She yelled and laughed. "Just Jim! That's all! Just Jim!"

He gave her his jacket and put his arm round her. There were probably better ways of keeping her warm: build the fire up, for a start. There must be quite a lot of fuel around. Litter generally burned, and if you scrunched it up really tight, you could make it last. But she didn't want to be just kept warm. She wanted a pillow to fall asleep on.

A few minutes later, Elliot suggested a dip in the sea. They all ran off. Tim and Hannah stopped about twenty yards from the fire and kissed.

"Have you ever loved someone so much it actually feels really painful?" Soraya asked miserably. "Like a burning kind of empty feeling in your chest?"

He'd assumed she was asleep. But okay.

"Once or twice," he said in an attempt to keep it vague.

She sniffed and wiped her eyes. "Yet you know you can never be loved back by that person in exactly the same way?"

He wondered who she was talking about. Then he caught her sight line.

Hannah.

Bloody hell, he'd better be careful here. Whatever the precise nature of their feelings for each other, they probably both considered the relationship priceless. Don't put your foot in it.

"'Exactly the same way' isn't the point," he said gently. "I know she loves you. It may be platonic, but at a certain level of intensity, the distinction between different 'types' of love breaks down. It's rare, but it happens. I know it does."

She chuckled. "Come on, let's go in the sea."

The next day Hannah and Tim went to meet her parents in one of the 'friendly' cafés on the east of the island. She still hadn't shown them her pregnancy, not in the flesh, and Tim still hadn't officially informed them, so they both had cause to be nervous. They took Mordred and Soraya to deflect the expected ire. Soraya dressed down to look much less glamorous, and seemed almost as nervous about the occasion as the soon-to-be parents.

"Put in a good word for me, Jim," she said, in the taxi over.

"I think Hannah's already done that a million times over," he said. "There aren't that many left."

"I must remember to call you by your real name."

"Right. It's Reginald."

"What – really?"

"No, it's just John's idea of a really hilarious joke," Hannah put in irritably from the front.

Soraya didn't smile. She looked out of the car window like she had more important things on her mind.

The café was more like a little guest-house than a simple eaterie. It stood above the tide break against a long stretch of white sand and a blue sea, with nothing but fields in the landward direction. The wind was full. The sun shone. When they went inside, they all talked as a group and ate scones and drank tea. After a while, the women stayed in the lounge with more tea and the men went to watch TV in the snooker room. A 24-hour news channel showed live proceedings of the Collingson inquiry from the House of Commons. In the dock: Sir Ashley Cavendish, looking as if someone had just reached into the back of his jacket and flicked an 'off' switch. Someone had discovered his takeover of Horvath, and the inquiry had called him in for a wide-ranging grilling.

"You say the financial and insurance sectors contributed a lot of money to the UK economy last year," Dame Hilda said. "To what extent do you think it is better to have a thriving financial and insurance sector than, say, a thriving manufacturing base, or a thriving scientific and technical sector?"

"The others couldn't exist without the first," Cavendish replied. "Obviously, you only get science and manufacturing to the extent that someone's prepared to invest in them. That requires a thriving financial sector."

"So if our financial sector is doing so well," she continued, "how do you explain our relative inadequacy in the other two areas?"

"I wasn't aware that they were inadequate."

She read him a set of facts and figures and asked, "Could it be that the 'investment' of which you speak is nearly always provided on terms overwhelmingly favourable to the financial industry itself, and rarely if ever, coincides with the public good?"

"I think that's a gross over-exaggeration," Cavendish replied, as if he didn't much care.

"Could you explain to the inquiry," Donald Wynter said, "why the Lord Mayor of London has to represent the *financial*, as opposed to some other industry?"

"Obviously, because there are a lot of such businesses in the City of London," Cavendish replied.

"But isn't that circular?" Wynter persisted. "They presumably come there because you're their international champion, or say you are. If I advertised myself as the global fish and chip shop champion, I dare say I'd end up with a lot of fish and chip shops in my constituency. It still raises the question of why I would do that in the first place."

"I *didn't* do it," Cavendish said. "I inherited it. We all did, all Lord Mayors."

"Going back to when?" Dame Hilda asked.

Mordred felt almost sorry for Cavendish now. It was obvious he wanted to swing for them. Nevertheless, he'd get through this, no problem. In a few months, he'd sink back into complete obscurity and a new Lord Mayor would take over. It was an excellent way of preserving the low-key anonymity of the office.

Frequent changes of personnel, a bit like *The Prisoner*. Who are you? I am the new Number Two. Who is Number One? You are Number Six.

His phone rang. *Ruby Parker*. He stood up. "Sorry," he told his dad and Tim. "Work. I'll take it outside."

Luckily, there was a fire exit at the far end of the room, so he wouldn't have to go through the lounge.

"Mordred," he said, when he got outside. "Is everything okay?"

"It's fine. You're due back here in two days."

"I know."

"And I understand you promised to visit Fenella Decristoforo-Salvaterra this year."

"Er, yes. How did you know about that?"

"She told me, obviously."

"You've been in contact with her then. Is she okay?"

"Very much so. I'm pleased to say, I've persuaded her to join us."

"Join us? You mean, as an agent? We're not losing anyone, are we?"

"I'm happy to report that Annabel's both staying and fully committed to her marriage. Although the latter's none of my business, I'm pleased for her sake. And Tariq's, obviously."

"What makes you think Fenella will be any good as a spy? I mean, don't get me wrong, she's a very intelligent woman - "

"Pretty soon we'll be approaching the third decade of the twenty-first century, and we've got to keep moving forward. Edna was my first step in that direction. I hired her *as* Edna Watson superstar, she may have told you why. I hired Fenella Decristoforo-Salvaterra in the same spirit. If World War O is more than a flash in the pan – and I think it is – we're going to need people who can get into the topmost echelons of high society. Edna can. And so can Fenella."

"I thought she was in mourning."

"She can't waste the next fifty years of her life being Queen Victoria. I gave her a good talking-to and persuaded her to reinvent herself. She can give you the details. She's very much looking forward to working with you. I'm only ringing to give you an option. Instead of flying back to rainy London in two days' time, you can fly direct to Saint Martha's Rock. Entirely at our expense."

"Does she actually want to see me now? Have you told her I'm coming?"

"I was last in contact with her this morning. Peter died a few days ago. Which brings me to the other reason I'm ringing."

"There's more?"

"He made a significant bequest to your sister in his will."

"He said he'd do something for her. What do you mean, 'significant'?"

"Where are you now?"

"The Carteret Café on the east of the island. Why?"

"Look around yourself. You may be interested to know she now owns whatever you can see."

"The café? She owns the café?"

"That's just the beginning."

He sat down on the step. "Carry on, then …"

"She also owns a lot of the land you can probably see from the window. She owns the farmhouse in which you took shelter during the hurricane – or what remains of it: it's being rebuilt - along with the farm itself. She owns ten properties in Saint Helier, a significant stretch of the north Jersey coast, and fourteen acres of mainly fields around Plemont. In short, she totality of Peter Decristoforo's significant possessions on the island. On condition that she doesn't sell them, and allows the existing tenants to continue living there in perpetuity."

"Bloody hell."

"Quite."

"And Fenella isn't going to contest it?"

"It was partly her idea."

"Do you know how anyone's intending to tell Hannah? I mean, in such a way that she doesn't think it's a practical joke, and she doesn't have a coronary?"

"It's customary for the family solicitor to break the news. I understand he's on his way to the island now."

"From where?"

"Heathrow."

"Well, I don't suppose there's anything I can do to prepare the ground for something like that. I just hope she isn't standing on a cliff edge when she faints. Do you think you could ring the solicitor and tell him where we are? And I'll try and keep her here?"

"I'm sure I can manage that. I now need to ask you explicitly. Are you going to Saint Martha's Rock on Wednesday, or are you coming back here?"

"The former, please."

"In that case, I'll be in touch soon with the flight details. Have a pleasant remaining few days in Jersey."

Chapter 30: The Missing Link

Mordred didn't know there was an airport on Saint Martha's rock, but it should probably have been obvious. Brian had said it was an upmarket holiday destination, and most wealthy tourists weren't going to put up with a several-hour ferry journey from the Caymans.

But why, really, was he going to see Fenella at all? It struck him for the first time when his plane left the Jersey runway. They were hardly old friends. Looked at disinterestedly - since they were members of the opposite sex and about the same age - it had all the hallmarks of a tryst, only a touch more sordid than romantic.

But it couldn't be that. As far as he'd discerned, there was nothing sleazy about her.

Yet the question wouldn't go away: why? They'd met and vaguely hit it off, but that was all. Now he was travelling thousands of miles at her invitation, to stay in her huge house. Was he walking into a trap? What could be its nature or purpose?

Maybe she was just an ingénue. Perhaps she'd spent so long out of society that she didn't know the rules any more; that inviting a single man to share her home on an unknown pretext for – that was the other thing: he didn't even know how long – might ultimately work against her. 'Scandal', nowadays, was simply whatever made people pity you in your absence. Like when you couldn't get into a proper relationship, so you had to have some penniless nonentity over. *Goodness knows what she sees in him, but so long as it makes the poor woman happy …*

But no, it couldn't be that.

The plane was squat, and furnished like the inside of a boat: lots of varnished pine, circular windows and chunky tables. Apart from the pilot, there was only one other person aboard, a young woman who spent most of her time out of sight in the front. She emerged every hour or so to ask him if he wanted anything. He ate a tagine fifty minutes after take-off, and slept for the next eight hours to elude the boredom. When he awoke, she asked him if he'd like breakfast and brought him a bowl of cornflakes. After that, he watched a pre-recorded episode of *The Dog Rescuers With Alan Davies*.

The plane touched down in Saint Martha's at 6pm local time. He looked out of the window. He hadn't seen this part of the island before, but didn't feel any the worse for having missed it. The airport was more or less just two long runways, a thin concrete control tower, and a taxi rank, all surrounded by tall grass. Nothing on the horizon except forest, and beyond that, the sea. In the other direction, of course, the volcano.

Rory was waiting in his taxi to pick him up. They exchanged pleasantries and drove straight to Fenella's house. When it came in view among the trees, he remembered how miserable he'd felt on leaving last time. In an odd and not entirely welcome way, it felt like he was returning somewhere he'd been more than once. It flew no flag at all now, and exuded hardly any gloom, despite its dark colour and ominous design.

Maria was waiting at the door for him. She showed him to a room furnished with a mix of nineteenth-century European, Caribbean and ethnic African objects. A four-poster bed was probably obligatory in a gothic mansion, but the Nigerian tribal masks that decorated the walls and the French West Indian lolling chairs gave the whole thing a museum-y effect.

"Dinner will be in about twenty minutes," she told him. "The shower is through there. Your clothes are in the two wardrobes."

"My clothes?"

"The ones we bought you."

"Oh. You didn't have to do that. Thank you. It wasn't necessary."

She smiled as if she didn't think he'd have said that if he knew what she did. Then withdrew. How did they know what sizes he took? When he tried a few items on, after coming out of the shower, they all fitted.

Twenty minutes later, he went down to dinner in the same small room they'd eaten in on his first visit. The polished walnut table, fireplace, three armchairs and sacred heart picture remained unchanged. The TV had gone. Fenella wore a beige dress with a red-flecked white scarf whose most unexpected aspect was its huge distance from any hint of mourning. They compared their separate journeys back to the island and discussed Hannah's bequest. Fenella expressed her pleasure that she hadn't rejected it, and Maria brought in two bowls of black bean soup.

"Why would she turn it down?" Mordred asked.

"It's a huge responsibility. I don't mean the day-to-day work. I mean now she's got the power to kick-start 'Invasion 2.0' on May the first. She'll be leading the whole thing again."

"You can't invade land you own. My guess is she'll start somewhere else."

"Possibly."

"Can I ask you a question?"

"Whatever you like."

"I don't mean to sound ungrateful, but why did you invite me here?"

She looked away and nodded almost imperceptibly to herself, as if in two minds whether to answer. "I was wondering when you'd ask," she said at last. "It's nice that you don't suppose I've been bowled over by your manly charms."

He smiled. "Manly charms are ten a penny nowadays."

"You do know I've been recruited by MI7? Ruby Parker came to see me very recently."

"So I've been told. It still doesn't explain - "

"Except that I won't be working for MI7. I'll be working for myself. And I want you to join me."

He pretended to be shocked. "You mean you signed up on false pretences?"

"Exactly right. And I called you here because I think we can do a deal."

He smiled. "We probably can't, but I've come all this way, and I'm eating your soup, so I might as well hear the details."

"Since we first met, I've found out nearly everything about you. I couldn't have done that without Peter, of course, but I've been very impressed by what I uncovered."

"Enough to feel confident I'll work against MI7."

"Not necessarily always, but probably sometimes."

"Go on."

Maria came in to take their bowls away. They looked conspiratorially at each other. That was something good about her: the way they could have a conversation like this without her getting riled by his apparent uncooperativeness. Five minutes later, Maria brought two plates of avocado quesadillas. She closed the doors on them.

"Okay, then," he said.

"Okay then what?" she replied. "What do you mean?"

"I'll come and work for you."

She laughed. "Oh, I see. On false pretences, like I did with MI7."

"After this, I think we should go for a walk."

She laughed as if she was astonished by his rudeness. "So that's it, is it? You simply reject my offer? Without even giving me a hearing?"

"I've just told you, I accept it."

The smile fell from her face. "I don't take kindly to being made fun of."

"You were about to make your pitch," he said calmly. "How about I tell you what you were about to say, and afterwards, I explain why I'm prepared to accept unconditionally?"

"You're … serious?"

"If you imagine I'm the sort of person who strings a conversation like this out for facetious reasons, you obviously don't know me as well as you think you do."

"Go … Go on, then."

"Firstly," he said, "you want to finish what you've begun. It was you who persuaded Peter that World War O was necessary and you, indirectly, who fired the conspiracy. And you're the 'missing link': it was you who organised the smokescreen for the protests by setting Beverly Hills celebrities to work in the Med. The idea that you're in permanent mourning has been a cover for years, and it worked. But it was never true. I realised that as soon as you turned up in your yacht at Plemont. And that you might have conceived an affection for me born of the fact that you think we can work together, which, as I've just said, I think we can. Now that Peter's no longer with us, you see yourself and your probable billions as the best effective means of continuing World War O. However, you don't think MI7 is on board with that at all, and you think you'll best be able to undermine it if you're on the inside. You're completely dedicated to your ideal."

"Brutally put, but broadly correct."

"You were about to remind me that I'm not motivated principally by love of Queen and country. I tend to follow my conscience, even in the field. Duty to me is a moral requirement, not a military or patriotic one. All of this requires that I take sides in World War O. With the weak against the strong. With you against MI7."

"I don't like the way you make me sound in all this. Quite calculating. But yes. That's the general idea."

"I don't see level-headedness as a fault," he replied. "Nor should you."

"You were going to tell me why you've decided to 'accept my offer'."

"Because you've got MI7 wrong, at least the bit I work for. Why do you think it's put up with me for all these years? Believe me, it's not because I've kept my true nature hidden under a bush. If it helps set your mind at rest, assuming you're still happy for us to work together, I'll continue to follow my conscience. Mostly, that'll mean our agendas coincide. Where they don't, it won't be because I'm blindly following anyone's orders. It'll be because my sense of what's right and fair differs from yours. But that happens in any decent partnership from time to time."

"But you've no problem with me bankrolling the resistance?"

"None whatsoever, although of course I draw the line at terrorism, and I also think that, sadly, you may be overestimating how much life World War O still has in it. The more important question from your point of view is, do you still want to be a part of MI7? If you're just joining to undermine it, you're wasting your time. There's nothing to undermine."

"My role, as I understand it, would be to play myself. I'd be obtaining access for people like you to the *haut monde*. In that case, I'd presumably be acting against the interests of powerful people with things to hide. Otherwise you wouldn't need to dupe your way in. So yes, I'm on board."

"No more nonsense about undermining MI7?"

She laughed. "No, okay then. You won't tell Ruby Parker, will you?"

"To be fair, she probably anticipated it. I'm sure that's why she was so eager to get me out here. Set you straight."

After dinner, they went for a walk on the beach. Later they played cards with Rory and Maria, and finally, Fenella suggested the internal tour. He was pretty jet-lagged, but even so, he much preferred her company to a good night's sleep.

The whole house was rather like an extension of the room he'd been given. Everywhere, the same mix of Gothic European, African tribal and Central American. The views from the towers, because it was night, were mainly of the moon and stars. As they descended, in room after room – he counted forty in the house as a whole - it was blatantly obvious she had guests over to stay on a regular basis. Beds were made up, personal effects had been left behind, overnight or long-stay necessities stood in readiness. There was clearly nothing reclusive about her at all, and she didn't mind him knowing any more. He wondered how long it had been since Jennifer Hallowell had been here. How long before Hannah and Soraya got an invite?

What kind of a person was Fenella Decristoforo-Salvaterra really? Superficially, she was plausible enough. Talkative, thoughtful, charming, the perfect hostess. But he couldn't shake the feeling that that was chiefly a long-practised act; that the real her was mainly present in the depths. Single-minded, idealistic, anti-conventional. Places no one much was welcome, although he'd been admitted on a temporary basis over dinner. Maybe she *was* in mourning; just not the conventional kind. Maybe she did really believe she was cursed. He didn't know.

"Remember when we were in London," she said, when they were back at their starting point, "and I said I wanted to show you something amusing? Would you like to see it now?"

"Seems as good a time as any."

"Prepare for the biggest surprise of your life."

He followed her along the corridor. They stopped before a heavy black door, quite unlike any other in the house. She took a key from beneath a vase and unlocked it to reveal another corridor, much lower, so that they had to stoop to enter it. She locked the door behind them. Pretty soon, they were descending what seemed like an endless series of intersecting stone spiral stairways. They passed through locked door after locked door. She switched on a seemingly infinite succession of bare-bulb lights, always fastening bolts behind them for reasons he didn't quite understand, until he could hear what sounded like the sea. The experience was living up to its promise. He was already pretty surprised. He wondered what more could be to come.

They emerged into a room carved out of the solid rock. Big enough for about twelve people to stand upright in comfortably. In front of them, a reinforced steel door with a dial lock stood closed, like the access to a Bank of England safe.

"Are you ready for the bombshell?" she asked.

"Are you sure you can find your way back?" he asked.

She laughed. "It's a long time since I've been down here, so no. Are you scared?"

"Obviously. Aren't you?"

She undid the lock and pulled the door open. They stepped through into the darkness and onto what he could just make out to be a shallow platform, wider than it was long, bounded by thick zinc railings. She flicked another set of switches. Rows and rows of arc lights came on at about a house-height above them, extending for hundreds of metres in all directions.

They were deep inside the dead volcano, an almost unimaginably huge natural vault with seawater as its floor. Halfway across stood a gargantuan scaffolding frame, supporting what looked like a series of stacked metal cylinders with a conical top. Its bottom seemed to have corroded entirely away and had a dull, ragged look. Thousands of feet below them, the ocean crashed and spluttered and roared. It seemed angry that something like this could ever have been started, and even angrier that it couldn't be completed. It took him a few moments to realise that what he was looking at was actually the remains of a herculean rocket.

"Good God," he said.

"Peter's," she said.

"Is it – what I think it is?"

She smiled. "He wouldn't talk about it when he was alive, at least not during all the time I knew him. According to what I learned from other members of the family, though, it was once a viable project. Then something about the world 'changed', I don't know what; none of them would elucidate. The whole thing was defunct long before the sea broke in. It was already ancient history when I arrived here."

Mordred couldn't take his eyes off it. She'd been right. It was the biggest surprise of his life. And she was right about it being ancient history. The sea echoed and re-echoed eerily underneath them. God help the human race, it seemed to say. All its crazy lost dreams.

If only Brian could see him now!

Acknowledgements and Afterword

The chief source of hard information for this book was undoubtedly Nicholas Shaxson's *Treasure Islands: Tax Havens and the Men Who Stole the World* (Vintage 2012), a long discussion of tax avoidance which, as the Guardian puts it, "digs far beyond its tax haven title and indicts the system that renders such crookedness not merely possible, but entirely predictable". A second important source was Richard Brooks's *The Great Tax Robbery: How Britain Became a Tax Haven For Fat Cats and Big Business* (Oneworld 2013). As a reporter for *Private Eye* – where his authorship would, as is customary in that magazine, be anonymised - I suspect Mr Brooks may have had a more important role in helping me formulate my ideas than I can exactly gauge (see below).

Part of my task, penning a story that takes place in 2015 or slightly later (the exact date is deliberately left vague, but cannot be earlier than 2015 if it is to be consistent with the other novels in the series), was to discover how much, if at all, the tax-avoiding world has moved on since Shaxson's 2012 investigation. Much of the narrative action takes place in Jersey and the City of London, and while *Treasure Islands* has significant sections devoted to both places, things, of course, may change. Sometimes they may even get better.

The Treasure Islands and Tax Justice Network websites were fully up to date and useful resources. But I also tried to get an opposing point of view. For two days, under the moniker 'Colin Jackson', I conducted a blog discussion with Peter Kelly, the author of an online article entitled, 'The Myths of the British Tax Isles'. Up until my final three attempted posts, Mr Kelly was an enthusiastic correspondent. His position – which never altered - was that Jersey is not a tax haven: it is fully transparent. I have tried to reproduce the gist of his arguments in the mouths of various characters in *World War O*, although I believe those arguments are still available to be viewed verbatim on the internet. They are essentially *a priori*, and concern FATCA (the US Foreign Account Tax Compliance Act) and Jersey's many Tax Information Exchange Agreements with other states.

Initially, Mr Kelly's position struck me as very plausible, to the point where I actually emailed Nicholas Shaxson himself, to see if he knew any more. He replied very quickly and fully, and expressed scepticism.

The turning point, from my point of view, came, as so often in these sorts of things, with *Private Eye*. Reliance on *Private Eye* in matters like this is now, sadly, unavoidable. As Shaxson points out, "Few newspaper editors now seriously consider the thorny issue of tax avoidance by multinationals - 'as intelligible to the average person as particle physics', as the *Guardian*'s editor Alan Rusbridger put it" (p276).

The 12-25 June 2015 issue of *Private Eye* contained a long article which included Jersey in a discussion of "not so pleasant tax havens" utilised by companies secretly buying up large chunks of the English countryside. Land interests in Cranborne in Wiltshire, for example, "have been transferred to Samos Investments Ltd and Mysia Investments Ltd (which also own some prime London property). Both are incorporated in Jersey but Land Registry records give an address on Avenue de l'Opera and are said to be part of 'The Jersey Settlement'. This fertile territory has yielded 4.3m euros from the EU over a dozen years." The article concluded, "These are just a few of the cases of offshore ownership where those behind the offshore company can be identified. Most can't – which is precisely the point."

At around the same time – 7 July - Channel 4 broadcast an investigative report into money lost to the Treasury through avoided tax on London Properties. Its website provided a list in two columns: (1) "Tax Haven that the Property is Registered" and (2) "Number of Properties". The second worst offender, out of 14 in that list of "tax havens" (Channel 4's words, not mine), was Jersey. 17,803 properties in England and Wales. The report concluded: "An analysis by Channel 4 News shows 73,853 commercial and residential properties in England and Wales were registered in tax havens since 2009."

The next edition of *Private Eye* (26 June- 9 July 2015) dealt with Jersey again: "A reclusive Malaysian businessman reported to have close links to the Sultan [of Brunei] has acquired 71,000 acres [of the Scottish highlands] through companies registered in the Cayman Islands with nominee directors in Jersey. Estate staff are sworn to secrecy over his identity and refer to him only by the pseudonym 'Mr Saleh'. Earlier this year another offshore company, Cluny Estates Ltd registered in Jersey, bought the 10,000-acre Cluny Estate in Inverness-shire. The Qatar Royal family, who already own property in London, are understood to be behind this company but the agents refused to confirm it … The tax authorities have been exercised by Scotland's offshore expanses for decades … While David Cameron has promised to improve transparency through a register of beneficial ownership of companies, this will be based on self-disclosure and will not apply to either trusts or offshore companies (even based in Britain's tax havens) and will thus not reveal the true ownership of much land." (p39)

I attempted to ask Peter Kelly about all this by posting three separate quotes - essentially, those above - and accompanying questions on his blog, but for some reason, this time, none of my queries ever appeared (all guest posts had to be 'approved' before actually appearing – I assume by the owner of the blog). Whether this is because Mr Kelly simply did not want to, or could not, address those issues, or because my posts did not reach him for some reason, I genuinely do not know. However, I concluded that although it was certainly possible to construct 'logical' arguments to the effect that Jersey is completely transparent, at least some of the empirical evidence suggests otherwise.

Others will perhaps say that I should have known better. As Shaxson pointed out in *Treasure Islands*, "This is another classic offshore ruse. A tax haven sets up worthy treaties that require them to exchange information with foreign jurisdictions, then they set up the structures to make sure that they never have the information to exchange in the first place. They keep their secrecy but – by pointing to their treaties – they can claim they are a transparent and cooperative jurisdiction" (p135-36).

In the end, as Hannah Lexingwood says in *World War O*, "if something's secret, you don't know it's happening. That's what the word means". What matters for a novel like this is not what *is* happening – the precise facts about any single time-slice may be very difficult to establish – but simply what people *could* be entitled to *think* is happening, given the particular history of the place in question, and that, generally speaking, history has a habit of repeating itself.

*

The internet sites John Mordred visits in Chapter 5 of *World War O* - 'Ian Evans Against Jersey Corruption And Police Brutality', 'Trevor Pitman's Blog: The Bald Truth', *The Financial Secrecy Index narrative report on Jersey 2013* and *The text of an affidavit signed by the former Deputy Chief of the States Police* are all genuine, and can all be Googled. I have Mordred express some incredulity only because that is how I think anyone with no prior information about the situation on the ground might well react. I do not intend any disrespect to any of the authors.

*

Which brings me back again to *Private Eye*, and this time to the City of London. George Osborne's July 2015 budget announced another cut in corporation tax. Down from 28 per cent to 20 per cent in 2010, it will be 19 per cent in 2017, and 18 per cent in 2020. This is supposed to at least pay for itself by attracting new businesses to the UK. But according to *Private Eye* (24 July-6 August 2015), "The Treasury's own figures contradict this. Based on what companies currently pay, the Treasury estimates that by

2019/20 the corporate tax cut will cost 2.75bn. But it adjusts this figure for the incentive the tax cut gives multinationals to 'shift profits to the UK'. Does it make money overall? Er, no. Based on what it calls 'multiple academic studies', this shift generates less than 0.3bn, leaving the change still a huge cost to the exchequer … This is classic tax haven behaviour, and something Osborne has claimed to be leading the world in stamping out."

In *Treasure Islands*, Shaxson defines a tax haven as *a state annexed by financial interests from elsewhere.* "Local politics is captured by financial services interests … and meaningful opposition to the offshore business model has been eliminated" (p10). Such apparently anti-rational behaviour as providing a tax cut to the wealthiest businesses in the UK, a cut which will leave the country facing more debt during a period of serious economic hardship for the vast majority of ordinary people, is arguably best explained on such a premise. Except that 'elsewhere', this time, is a 1.22 square mile business community in the centre of our own capital city.

JW August 2015

Books by James Ward

General Fiction
The House of Charles Swinter
The Weird Problem of Good
The Bright Fish
*Hannah and Soraya's Fully Magic Generation-Y *Snowflake* Road Trip across America*

The Original Tales of MI7
Our Woman in Jamaica
The Kramski Case
The Girl from Kandahar
The Vengeance of San Gennaro

The John Mordred Tales of MI7 books
The Eastern Ukraine Question
The Social Magus
Encounter with ISIS
World War O
The New Europeans
Libya Story
Little War in London
The Square Mile Murder
The Ultimate Londoner
Death in a Half Foreign Country
The BBC Hunters
The Seductive Scent of Empire
Humankind 2.0
Ruby Parker's Last Orders

Poetry
The Latest Noel
Metals of the Future

Short Stories
An Evening at the Beach

Philosophy
21st Century Philosophy
A New Theory of Justice and Other Essays

* 9 7 8 1 9 1 3 8 5 1 0 7 1 *